Critical Praise for SPIDER ROBINSON

"Robinson is the hottest writer to hit science fiction since Ellison, and he can match the master's frenetic energy and emotional intensity, arm-break for gut-wrench."

—Los Angeles Times

"Robinson has an extraordinary ability to create authentic human characters . . . [and] sustains the suspense right until the end."

—Library Journal

"Spider Robinson sure tells a good story . . . always colorful and sharply drawn . . . always ingenious and compelling . . . Robinson just keeps getting better and better!"

—Toronto Globe & Mail

"Like Mr. Heinlein in his prime, Mr. Robinson writes in a crisp, tightly controlled prose . . ."

—New York Times

"Robinson has a rare gift for creating characters who are instantly believable and lovable. He uses a narrative voice that is tough and flippant, and his prose is a pleasure to read."

—Quill & Quire

"Robinson's stories are by turns touching and terrifying, written with vibrant wit by a man who intimately knows writing, humans, aliens . . ."

—Redding Record

Other Books by Spider Robinson

ANTINOMY
THE BEST OF ALL POSSIBLE WORLDS
CALLAHAN'S CROSSTIME SALOON
CALLAHAN'S SECRET
MELANCHOLY ELEPHANTS
MINDKILLER
NIGHT OF POWER
STARDANCE *(with Jeanne Robinson)*
TELEMPATH
TIME TRAVELERS STRICTLY CASH

SPIDER ROBINSON

TIME PRESSURE

ACE BOOKS, NEW YORK

Time Pressure is a work of fiction. All names, characters, places and incidents are imaginary; any resemblance to actual persons, locales or events is entirely coincidental and unintended.

This Ace book contains
the complete text of the original
hardcover edition. It has been
completely reset in a typeface
designed for easy reading
and was printed from new film.

TIME PRESSURE

An Ace Book/published by arrangement with
the author

PRINTING HISTORY
Ace hardcover edition/October 1987
Ace edition/August 1988

Cover art by James Warhola.

ISBN: 0-441-80933-2

Ace Books are published by The Berkley Publishing
Group, 200 Madison Avenue, New York, New York 10016.
The name "Ace" and the "A" logo
are trademarks belonging to
Charter Communications, Inc.
PRINTED IN THE UNITED STATES OF AMERICA

10 9 8 7 6 5 4 3 2 1

For all my North Mountain friends,
hippies, locals and visitors,
and for Raoul Vezina and Steve Thomas

PROLOGUE

I guarantee that every word of this story is a lie.

ONE

IT WAS A dark and stormy night . . .

Your suspension of disbelief has probably just bust a leaf-spring: how can you believe in a story that begins that way? I know it's one of the hoariest clichés in pulp fiction; my writer friend Snaker uses the expression satirically often enough. "It was a dark and stormy night—when suddenly the shot rang out. . . ." But I don't especially want you to believe this story—I just want you to listen to it—and even if I were concerned with convincing you there wouldn't be anything I could do about it, the story begins where it begins and that's all there is to it.

And "dark" is *not* redundant. Most nights along the shore of the Bay of Fundy are not particularly dark, as nights go. There's a *lot* of sky on the Fundy Shore, as transparent as a politician's promise, and that makes for a lot of starlight even on Moonless evenings. When the

Moon's up it turns the forest into a fairyland—and even when the big clouds roll in off the water and darken the sky, there is usually the glow of Saint John, New Brunswick on the horizon, tinting the underside of clouds sixty kilometers away across the Bay, mitigating the darkness. (In those days, just after Canada went totally metric, I would have thought "forty miles" instead of sixty klicks. Habits *can* be changed.)

The day had been chilly for late April and the wind had been steady from the south, so I was not at all surprised when the snowstorm began just after sundown. (Maybe you live somewhere that doesn't have snow in April; if so, I hope you appreciate it.) It was not a full-scale mankiller blizzard, the sort where you have to crack the attic window for breathing air and dig tunnels to the woodshed and the outhouse; a bit too late in the year for that.

Nonetheless it was indisputably a dark and stormy night in 1973—when suddenly the shot rang out. . . .

Nothing less could have made me suit up and go outside on such a night. Even a chimney fire might not have done it. There is a rope strung from my back porch to my outhouse during the winter, because when the big gusts sail in off that tabletop icewater and flay the North Mountain with snow and stinging hail, a man can become hopelessly lost on his way to the shitter and freeze to death within bowshot of his house. This storm was not of that calibre, but neither was it a Christmas-cardy sort of snowing, with little white petals drifting gently and photogenically down through the stillness. Windows rattled or hummed, their inner and outer coverings of plastic insulation shuddered and crackled, the outer doors strained and snarled at their fastenings, wind whistled through weatherstripping in a dozen places, shingles complained and threatened to leave, banshees took up residence in both my stovepipes (the two stoves, inflamed, raved and roared back at them), and beneath all the local noise could be heard the omnipresent sound of the wind trying to flog the forest to death and the Bay trying to smash the stone shore to flinders. They've both been at it for centuries, and one day they'll win.

My kitchen is one of the tightest rooms in Heartbreak Hotel; on both north and south it is buffered by large insulated areas of putatively dead air (the seldom-used, sealed-up porch on the Bay side and the back hall on the south). Nevertheless the kerosene lamp on the table flickered erratically enough to make shadows leap around the room like Baryshnikov on speed. From where I sat, rocking by the kitchen stove and sipping coffee, I could see that I had left about a dozen logs of maple and birch piled up on the sawhorse outside. I was not even remotely inclined to go back out there and get them under cover.

Dinner was over, the dishes washed, the kitchen stove's watertank refilled and warming, both stoves fed and cooking nicely, chores done. I cast about for some stormy night's entertainment, but the long hard winter just ending had sharply depleted the supply. I had drunk the last of my wine and homebrew a few weeks back, had smoked up most of the previous year's dope crop, read all the books in the house and all those to be borrowed on the Mountain, played every record and reel of tape I owned more than often enough to be sick of them, and the weather was ruining reception of CBC Radio (the only tolerable station of the three available, and incidentally one of the finest on Earth). So I decided to put in some time on the dulcimer I was building, and that meant that I needed Mucus the Moose, and when I couldn't find him after a Class One Search of the house I played back memory tape and realized, with a sinking feeling, that I was going to have to go outside after all.

I might not have done it for a friend—but if Mucus was out there, I had no choice.

Mucus the Moose is one of my most cherished possessions, one of my only mementoes of a very dear dead friend. He (the moose, not the friend) is about fifteen centimeters tall, and bears a striking physical resemblance to that noblest of all meece, Bullwinkle—save that Mucus is as potbellied as the Ashley stove in my living room. He is a pale translucent brown from the tips of his rack down to wherever the Plimsoll line happens to be, and pale translucent green thereafter. Picture Bullwinkle gone to fat and extremely seasick. His full name and station—**Mucus Moose, the Mucilage Machine**—are spelled out in raised letters on his round little tummy.

If you squeeze him gently right there, green glue comes out of his nostrils. . . .

If you don't understand why I love him so dearly, just let it go. Chalk it up to eccentricity or cabin fever—congenital insanity, I won't argue—but he was irreplaceable and special to me, and he was nowhere to be found. On rewind-search of my head I found that the last place I remembered putting him was in my jacket pocket, in order to fasten down the Styrofoam padding on Number Two hole in the outhouse, and he was not in the said pocket, and the last time that jacket pocket had been far enough from vertical for Mucus to fall out had been—

—that afternoon, by the sap pot, *halfway up the frigging Mountain,* more than a mile up into the woods. . . .

I have a special personal mantra for moments like that, but I believe that even in these enlightened times it is unprintable. I chanted it aloud as I filled both stoves with wood, pulled on a second shirt and pair of pants, added a sweater, zipped up the Snowmobile boots, put on the scarf and jacket and gloves and cap and stomped into the back hall like a space-suited astronaut entering the airlock, or a hardhat diver going into the decompression chamber.

The analogies are rather apt. When I popped the hook-and-eye and shouldered the kitchen door open (its spring hinge complaining bitterly enough to be heard over the general din), I entered a room whose ambient temperature was perhaps fifteen Celsius degrees colder than that of the kitchen—and the back hall was at least that much warmer than the world outside. I sealed the kitchen door behind me with the turnbuckle, zipped my jacket all the way up to my nose, took the heavy-duty flashlight from its perch near the chainsaw, and thumbed open the latch of the outside door.

It promptly flew open, hit me sharply in the face and across the shin, and knocked the flashlight spinning. I turned away from the incoming blast of wind-driven snow, in time to see the flashlight knock over the can of chainsaw gas/oil mixture, which spilled all over the split firewood. Not the big wood intended for the living room Ashley, the small stuff for the kitchen stove. I sleep above that kitchen stove at nights, and I was going to be smelling burning oil in my sleep for the next week or so.

I started my mantra over again from the beginning, more rhythmically and at twice the volume, retrieved the flashlight, and stomped out into the dark and stormy night, to rescue fifty cents worth of flexible plastic and a quarter-liter of green glue. Love is strange.

I had been mistaken about those banshees. They hadn't been inside my stovepipes, only hollering down them. They were out here, much too big to fit down a chimney and loud enough to fill the world, manifesting as ghostly curtains of snow that were torn apart by the wind as fast as they formed. I hooked the door shut behind me, made a perfectly futile attempt to zip my jacket up higher—all the way up is as high as a zipper goes—and pushed away from the Hotel to meet them.

The woodshed grunted a dire warning as I passed. I ignored it; it had been threatening to fall over ever since I had known it, back in the days when it had been a goat-shed. As I went by the outhouse I half turned to see if the new plastic window I'd stapled up last week had torn itself to pieces yet, and as I saw that it had, a shingle left the tiny roof with the sound of a busted E-string and came spinning at my eyes like a ninja deathstar. I'm pretty quick, but the distance was short and the closing velocity high; I took most of it on my hat but a corner of it put a small slice on my forehead. I was almost glad then for the cold. It numbed my forehead, the bleeding stopped fairly quickly for a forehead wound, and what there was swiftly froze and could be easily brushed off.

When I was clear of the house and outbuildings the wind steadied and gathered strength. It snowed horizontally. The wind had boxed the compass; wind and I were traveling in the same direction and, thanks to the sail-area of my back, at roughly the same speed. For seconds at a time the snow seemed to hang almost motionless in the air around me, like a cloud of white fireflies who had all decided to come jogging with me. It was weirdly beautiful. Magic. As the land sloped uphill, the snow appeared to settle in ultraslow motion, disappearing as it hit the ground.

Once I was up into the trees the wind slacked off considerably, confounded by the narrow and twisting path. The snow resumed normal behavior and I dropped back from a trot to a walk. As I came to the garden it weirded up again. Big sheets of air spilled over the tall trees into the cleared quarter-acre bowl and then smashed themselves to pieces against the trees on the far side. It looked like the kind of snowstorm they get inside those plastic paperweights when you shake them, skirling in all directions at once.

I realized that despite having fixed it in my mind no more than three hours ago, I had forgotten to bring the chamber pot with me from the house. I certainly wasn't going back for it, not into the teeth of that wind. Instead, it shouldn't be a total loss, I worked off one glove, got my fly undone and pissed along as much of the west perimeter as I could manage, that being the direction from which the deer most often approached.

Animals don't grok fences as territorial markers because they cannot conceive of anyone *making* a fence. Fences occur; you bypass them. But borders of urine are made, by living creatures, and their message is ancient and universally understood. A big carnivore claims this manor. (The Sunrise Hill commune had tried everything else in the book, fences and limestone borders and pie-pan rattles and broken-mirror windchimes, and still lost a high percentage of their garden to critters. Vegetarian pee doesn't work.)

Past the garden the path began to slope upward steeply, and footing became important. It would be much worse in a few weeks, when the path turned into a trail of mud, oozing down the Mountain in ultraslow motion, but it was not an easy walk now. This far back up into the woods, the path was in shadow for most of the day, and long slicks of winter snow and ice remained unmelted here and there; on the other hand, there had been more than enough thawing to leave a lot of rocks yearning to change their position under my feet. My Snowmobile boots gave good traction and ankle support—and were as heavy as a couple of kilos of coffee strapped to my feet. The ground crunched beneath them, and I sympathized. I had to keep working my nose to break up the ice that formed in it, and my beard began to stiffen up from the exhalations trapped by my scarf. Mucus, I thought, I hope you appreciate the trouble I go through for you.

I thought of Frank then for a while, and a strange admixture of joy and sadness followed me up the trail. Frank was the piano-player/artist who had given me Mucus, back in Freshman year. Fragile little guy with black curls flying in all directions and a tongue of Sheffield steel. His hero was Richard Manuel of The Band. (Mine was Davy Graham then.) He only smiled in the presence of friends, and his smile always began and ended with just the lips. The corners of his mouth would curl all the way up into his cheeks as far as they could, the lips would peel back for a brief flash of good white teeth, then seal again.

The way our college worked it, there was a no-classes Study Week before the barrage of Finals Week. Frank and I were both in serious academic jeopardy, make-or-break time. We stayed awake together for the entire two weeks, studying. No high I've had before or since comes close to the heady combination of total fatigue and mortal terror. At one point in there, I've forgotten which night, we despaired completely and went off-campus to get drunk. We could not seem to manage it no matter how much alcohol we drank. After five or six hours we gave up and went back to studying. Over the next few days we transcended ourselves, reached an exhilarated plane on which we seemed to comprehend not only the individual subjects, but all of them together in synthesis. As Lord Buckley would say, we dug infinity.

By the vagaries of mass scheduling we both had all our exams on Thursday and Friday, three a day. We felt this was good luck. Maximum time to study, then one brutal final effort and it was all over. One or two exams a day would have been like Chinese water torture.

As the sun came up on Thursday morning I was a broken man, utterly whipped. Frank flailed at me with his hands, and then with that deadly tongue—Frank only used that on assholes, the kind of people who mocked you for wearing long hair—without reaching me. He and the rest of the world could go take Sociology exams: I was going to die, here, now. He left the room. In a few moments I heard him come back in. I kept my eyes shut, determined to ignore whatever he said, but he didn't say anything at all, so with an immense irritated effort I forced them open and he was holding out Mucus Moose the Mucilage Machine.

He knew I coveted the Moose. It was one of his most cherished belongings.

"I want you to have him, Sam," he said. "I've got a feeling if anything can hold you together now, it's Mucus."

I exploded laughing. That set him off, and we roared until the tears came. We were in that kind of shape. The laugh was like those pads they clap to the chests of fading cardiac patients; it shocked me reluctantly back to life.

"You son of a bitch," I said finally, wiping tears away. "Thanks." Then: "What about you?"

"What about me?"

"What's going to hold *you* together, if I take Mucus?"

His cheeks appled up, his lips peeled apart slowly, and the teeth flashed. "I'm feeling lucky. Come on, asshole."

I passed everything, in most cases by the skin of my teeth, but overall well enough to stagger through another semester of academic probation. Frank passed everything but not by enough and failed out.

If you want to really get to know someone, spend two weeks awake with them. I only saw him twice after that—he made the fatal mistake of trying to ignore an inconvenient asthma attack—but I will never forget him.

And I was not going to leave Mucus on a snowy mountainside with his only bodily fluid turned to green fudge in his belly.

As the trail made the sharp turn to the left, I saw a weasel a few meters off into the woods. He looked at me as though he had a low opinion of my intelligence. "You're out here too, jerk," I muttered into my scarf, and he vanished.

There was something electric in the air. It took me awhile to realize that this was more than a metaphor. I became aware of an ozone-y smell, like—but subtly different from—the smell of a NiCad battery charger when you crack the lid. You know the smell you get when you turn on an old tube amplifier that's been unused long enough to collect dust? If you'd sprinkled just a pinch of cinnamon and fine-ground basil on top first, it might smell like the air smelled that night, alive and tangy and sharp-edged. I knew the stimulant effect of ozone, had experienced it numerous times; this was different. Better. I knew a little about magic, more than I had before I'd moved to the North Mountain. Nova Scotia has many kinds of magic, but this was a different kind, one I didn't know.

I stopped minding the cold and the snow and the wind and the steepness of the trail. No, I kept minding them, but I became reconciled to them. Shortly a unicorn was going to step out from behind a stand of birch. Or perhaps a tornado was going to take me to Oz. Something wonderful was about to happen.

A part of my mind stood back and skeptically observed this, tried to analyze it, noted that the sensation increased as I progressed upslope (ozone was lighter than air, wasn't it?), wondered darkly if this was what it smelled like before lightning struck someplace, tried to remember what I'd read on the subject. Avoid tall trees. Avoid standing in water. Trees loomed all around me, of course, and my boots had been breaking through skins of ice into slushwater for the last half klick. (But that was silly, paranoid, you didn't get lightning with snow.) That part of my mind which thought of itself as rational urged me to turn around and go back downhill to a place of warmth and comfort, and to hell with the silly glue-dispenser and the funny smell and the electric night.

But that part of my mind had ruled me all my life. I had come here to Nova Scotia specifically to get in touch with the other part of my mind, the part that perceived and believed in magic, that tasted the crisp cold night and thrilled with anticipation, for something unknown, or perhaps forgotten. It had been a long cold winter, and a little shot of magic sounded good to me.

Besides, I was almost there. I kept on slogging uphill, breathing big deep lungfulls of sparkling air through the scarf, and in only a few hundred meters more I had reached my destination, the Place of Big Maples and the clearing where I boil sap.

That very afternoon I had hiked up here and done a boiling, one of the last of the season. Maple syrup takes a lot of hours, but it is extremely pleasant work. Starting in early Spring, you hammer little aluminum sap-taps into any maple thicker than your thigh for an acre on either side of the trail, and hang little plastic sap-trap pails from them. You take a chainsaw to about a Jesus-load and a half of alders (I'll define that measurement later) and stack them to dry in the resulting clearing. The trail is generously stocked with enough boulders to create a fireplace of any size desired. Every few days you hike up to the maple grove, collect the contents of the pails in big white plastic buckets, and dump the buckets into the big castiron sap pot. You build a fire of alder slash, pick a comfortable spot, and spend the next several hours with nothing to do but keep the fire going. . . .

You can read if you want, if the weather permits—it's hard turning pages with gloves on—and toward the end of sap season you sometimes can even bring a guitar up the Mountain with you, and sing to the forest while you watch the pot. Or you can just watch the world. From that high up the slope of the Mountain, at that time of year, you can see the Bay off through the trees, impersonal and majestic. I'm a city kid; I can sit and look at the woods around me for four or five hours and still be seeing things when it's time to go.

Sap takes a *lot* of boiling, and then some more. Raw maple sap has the look and consistency of weak sugar water, with just a hint of that maple taste. That afternoon had been a good run: I had collected enough to fill the pot, maybe fifty liters or so—then kept the fire roaring for hours, and eventually took a little more than three liters down the Mountain with me in a Mason jar. (Even that wasn't really proper maple syrup—when I had enough Mason jars I would boil them down further [and more gently] on the kitchen stove—but it was going to taste a hell of a lot better on my pancakes than the "maple" flavored fluid you buy in stores.)

At one point I had scrounged around and picked some wintergreen, dipped up some of the boiling sap in my ladle and brewed some fresh wintergreen tea with natural maple sugar flavoring, no artificial colour, no preservatives, and sipped it while I fed the fire. Nothing I could possibly have lugged uphill in a Thermos would have tasted half so good. I had not felt lonely, but only alone. It had been a good afternoon.

I remembered it now and felt even better than I had

then—good in the same way, and good in a different and indefinable and complimentary way at the same time. This afternoon the world had felt *right*. Tonight felt *right, and about to get even better*—even the savage weather was an irrelevancy, without significance.

So of course luck was with me; Mucus was just where I'd hoped to find him, half-buried in the heap of dead leaves beside the stone fireplace, where I had for a time today lain back and stared through the treetops at the sky. I didn't even have to do any digging: the flashlight picked him out almost at once. He was facing me. His features were obscured by snow, but I knew that his expression would be sleepy-lidded contentment, the Buddha after a heavy meal.

"Hey, pal," I said softly, puffing just a little, "I'm sorry."

He said nothing.

"Hey, look, I came back for you." I worked my nose to crack the ice in my nostrils. "At this point, the only thing that can hold me togther is Mucus." I giggled, and my lower eyelids began to burn. If I felt so goddam good, why did I suddenly want to burst out crying?

Did I want to burst out crying?

I wanted to do something—wanted it badly. But I didn't know what.

I picked up the silly little moose, wiped him clean of snow, probed at the hard little green ball in his guts, and poked at *his* nostrils to clear them. "Forgive me?"

But there was only the sound of wind sawing at the trees.

No. There was more.

A faint, distant sound. Omnidirectional, approaching slowly from all sides at once, and from overhead, *and* from beneath my feet, like a contracting globe with me at the center. No, slightly off-center. A high, soft, sighing, with an odd metallic edge, like some sort of electronically processed sound.

Trees began to stir and creak around me. *The wind,* I

thought, and realized that the wind was gone. The snow was gone. The air was perfectly still.

When I first moved to Nova Scotia they told me, "If you don't like the weather, sit down and have a beer. Likely the weather you was lookin' for'll be along 'fore you finish." No climatic contortion no matter how unreasonable can surprise me anymore. This was the first snowstorm I'd ever known to have an eye, like a hurricane; fine.

But what was disturbing the trees?

They were *trembling*. I could see it with the flashlight. They vibrated like plucked strings, and part of the sound I was hearing was the chord they made. Occasionally one would emit a sharp cracking sound as rhythmic accompaniment to the chorus.

Well, of course they're making cracking sounds, said the rational part of my mind, *it's a good ten degrees warmer now—*

—ten degrees warmer?

A thrill of terror ran up my spine, I'd always thought that was just an expression but it wasn't, but was it terror or exhilaration, the cinnamony smell was very strong now and the trees were humming like the Sunrise Hill Gang chanting Om, a vast, world-sized sphere of sound contracted from all sides at once with increasing speed and power and yes I *was* a little off-center, it was going to converge right over *there—*

Crack!

A globe of soft blue light did actually appear in the epicenter, like a giant robin's egg, about fifty meters east of me and two or three meters off the ground. A yellow birch which had stood in that spot for at least thirty years despite anything wind or water could do obligingly disintegrated to make room for the globe. I mean no stump or flinders: the whole tree turned in an instant into an equivalent mass of sawdust and collapsed.

The humming sound reached a crescendo, a crazy chord full of anguish and hope.

The globe of light was a softly glowing blue, actinic white around the edges, and otherwise featureless. It threw out about as much light as a sixty-watt bulb. The sawdust that fell on it vanished, and the instant the last grain had vanished, the globe disappeared.

Silence. Total, utter stillness, such as is never heard in a forest in any weather. Complete starless Stygian darkness. It might have taken me a full second to bring the flashlight to bear.

Where the globe had been, suspended in the air in a half-crouch, was a naked bald woman, hugging herself.

She did not respond to the light. She moved, slightly, aimlessly, like someone floating in a transparent fluid, her eyes empty, her features slack. Suddenly she fell out of the light, dropped the meter and a half to the forest floor and landed limply on the heap of fresh sawdust. She made a small sound as she hit, a little animal grunt of dismay that chopped off.

I stood absolutely still for ten long seconds. The moment she hit the earth, the stillness ended and all the natural sounds of the night returned, the wind and the snow and the trees sighing at the memory of the effort they had just made and a distant owl and the sound of the Bay lapping at the shore.

I held the flashlight on her inert form.

A short dark slender bald woman. No, hairless from head to toe. Not entirely naked after all: she wore a gold headband, thin and intricately worked, that rode so high on her skull I wondered why it didn't fall off. Eurasian-looking features, but her hips were Caucasian-wide and she was dark enough to be a quadroon. Smiling joyously at the Moonless sky. Sprawled on her back. Magnificent tits. Aimlessly rolling eyes, and the blank look of a congenital idiot. Arms outflung in instinctive attempt to break her fall, but relaxed now. Long, slender hands.

Well, I had wanted an evening's entertainment . . .

TWO

I GUESS THIS is as good a place as any for your suspension of disbelief to snap through like an overstressed guitar string. I don't blame you a bit, and it only gets worse from here. Con-men work by getting you to swallow the hook a little at a time; first you are led to believe a small improbability, then there are a series of increasingly improbable complications, until finally you believe something so preposterous that afterward you cannot fathom your own foolishness. My writer friend Snaker says the only difference between a writer and a con-man is the writer has better hours, works at home, and can use his real name if it suits him.

So I guess I'm not a very good con-man. Without the assistance of Gertrude the Guitar, anyway. I'm giving you a pretty improbable thing to swallow right at the start. It's okay with me if you don't believe it, all right?

But let me try to explain to you why *I* believed it.

Despite the fact that I was then a 1) long-haired 2)

bearded 3) American-born 4) guitar player and folksinger 5) college dropout 6) sometime user of powerful psychedelics and 7) bonafide non-card-carrying member of the completely unorganized network of mostly ex-American hippies and back-to-the-landers scattered up and down the Annapolis Valley—despite the fact that I could have called myself a spiritual seeker without breaking up—nonetheless and notwithstanding I did *not* believe in astrology or auras or the Maharishi or Mahara Ji or Buddha or Jesus or Mohammed or Jahweh or Allah or Wa-Kon-Ton-Ka or vegetarianism or the Bermuda Triangle or flying saucers or the power of sunrise to end all wars if we would all only take enough drugs to stay up all night together, or even (they having broken up in a welter of lawsuits three years earlier) the Beatles. I *did* believe in mathematics and the force of gravity and the laws of conservation of matter and energy and Murphy's Law. I was pretty lonely, is what I guess I'm trying to tell you: the hippies frowned on me because I didn't abandon the rational part of my mind, while the straights disowned me because I didn't abandon the irrational part. I maintained, for instance, an open if rather disinteresting mind on reincarnation and ESP and the sanity of Dr. Timothy Leary, and I was tentatively willing to give the Tarot the benefit of the doubt on the word of a science fiction writer I admired named Samuel Delany.

That's part of what I'm trying to convey. I had read science fiction since I'd been old enough to read, attracted by that sense of wonder they talk about—and read enough of it to have my sense of wonder gently abraded away over the years. People who read a lot of sf are the *least* gullible, most skeptical people on earth. A longtime reader of sf will examine the flying saucer very carefully and knowledgeably for concealed wires, hidden seams, gimmicks with mirrors: he's seen them all before. Spotting a fake is child's play for him. (A tough house for a musician is a roomful of other musicians.)

On the other hand, he'll recognize a *real* flying saucer,

and he'll waste very little time on astonishment. Rearranging his entire personal universe in the light of startlingly new data is what he does for fun. One of sf's basic axioms, first propounded by Arthur Clarke, is that "any sufficiently advanced technology is indistinguishable from magic." Confronted with a nominally supernatural occurrence, a normal person will first freeze in shock, then back away in fear. An sf reader will pause cautiously, then move closer. The normal person will hastily review a checklist of escape-hatches—"I am drunk";"I am dreaming";"I have been drugged"; and so forth—hoping to find one which applies. The sf reader will check the same list—hoping to come up empty. But meanwhile he'll already have begun analyzing this new puzzle-piece which the game of life has offered him. What is it good for? What are its limitations? Where does it pinch? The thing he will be most afraid of is appearing stupid in retrospect.

So I must strain your credulity even further. I don't know what you would have done if a naked woman had materialized in front of you on a wooded hillside at night—and neither do you; you can only guess. But what *I* did was to grin hugely, take ten steps forward, and kneel beside her. I had spent my life training for this moment—for a moment like this—without ever truly expecting it to come.

If if helps any, I *did* drop Mucus on the way, and forgot his existence until the next day.

My first thought was, *those are absolutely* perfect *tits.*

My second was, *that's odd. . . .*

The nipples on those perfect teats were erect and rigid. Nothing odd there: it was freezing out, she was naked. But the rest of her body was not behaving correspondingly. The skin was not turning blue. No sign of goosebumps. A slight shiver, but it came and went. Teeth slightly apart in an idiot's smile, no sign of chattering.

It wasn't the cold stiffening her nipples. It was excitement.

What sort of excitement do you feel while you're unconscious? I wondered.

It seemed to be equal parts of triumph, fear, and sexual arousal. A sort of *by God, I made it! Or have I?* excitement, like someone disembarking from her first roller coaster ride—and finding herself in Coney Island, one of Brooklyn's gamier neighborhoods.

My eyes and nose found other evidences of the sexual component of her excitement—

—I looked away, obscurely embarrassed, and glanced back up to the other end. Her face was vacant, but that did not seem to be its natural condition. A lifetime of intelligence had written on that face before some sort of trauma had stunned it goofy. I guessed her age at forty.

So one way to approach it is to go through a long logic-chain. This woman had materialized amid thunderclaps and bright lights. Could she be an extraterrestrial? If so, either human stock was ubiquitous through the Galaxy, or there was something to the idea of parallel evolution, or she was in fact a three-legged thing with green tentacles (or some such) sending me a telepathic projection of a fellow human to soothe my nerves.

I don't know what strains your credulity. The idea of other planets full of human beings, while admittedly possible, strained mine. How did they get there? And why didn't their evolution and ours diverge over the several million years since *we* took root *here?*

Parallel evolution—the idea that the human shape is an inevitable one for evolution to select—had always seemed to me a silly notion, designed to simplify science fiction stories. Certainly, the human morphology is a good one for a tool-user, but there are others as good or better. (Whose idea was it to put all the eyes on one side of the head? And who thought two hands were enough?)

And I had difficulty believing in aliens who'd studied us closely enough to notice the behavior of nipples, but not closely enough to know that normal skin turns blue in temperatures well below zero. If what I saw was a telepathic illusion, how come it was semicomatose? To lull me into a false sense of . . . no, the thought was too silly to finish.

And if she *was* an alien, what had happened to her flying saucer, or rather flying robin's egg? Could she be smart enough to cross countless light-years, and clever enough to escape the attention of NORAD, and dumb enough to crash-land in front of a witness?

No, she was not an E.T. (As no one but an sf reader would have phrased it in 1973.) But she was certainly not from *my* world. I knew much more than the average citizen about the current state of terrestrial technology, and no culture on earth could have staged the entrance I had just seen.

Hallucination was a hypothesis I never considered. At that time of my life, at age twenty-eight, I had experienced the effects of alcohol, pot, hash, opium, LSD, STP, MDA, DMT, mescaline (organic and synthetic), psilocybin (ditto), peyote, amanita muscaria, a few licks of crystal meth, and medically administered morphine. I knew a hallucination when I saw one.

So that left . . .

I did not go through this logic-chain, not consciously. I just knew that I was looking at a time traveler.

Which both mildly annoyed and greatly tickled me, because I had not until then really believed in time travel. There are certain conventions of sf that are, in light of what we think we know about physics, preposterous . . . but which sf readers are willing to provisionally accept. Faster-than-light travel is, so far as anyone knows, flat-out impossible—but skeptical sf readers will accept it, grudgingly, because it's damned difficult to write a story set anywhere but in this Solar System without it.

Time travel too is considered flat-out impossible (or was at that time; physics has gone through some interesting changes lately) but tolerated for its story value. It's a delightful intellectual conceit, which gives rise to dozens of lovely paradoxes. The best of them were discovered and used by Robert Heinlein: the man who met himself coming and going, the man who was both of his own parents, and so forth.

That was, of course, why I did not truly believe in time travel, for any longer than it took to finish a Keith Laumer novel: its very existence implied paradoxes that no sane universe could tolerate. A culture smart enough to develop time travel would hopefully be wise enough not to *use* it. The risk of altering the past, changing history and thereby overstressing the fabric of reality, would be too great. What motive could induce intelligent people to take such a hideous gamble?

The clincher, of course, was the question, *where were they?* If (I had always reasoned with myself) time travel were ever going to be invented, in some hypothetical future, and used to go back in time . . . then where were the time travelers? Even if they maintained very tight security, you would expect there to be at least as many Silly Season reports of encounters with time travelers as there were of encounters with flying saucers (in which I emphatically did not believe)—and there weren't.

Since I had long ago relegated time travel to the category of fantasy, it was slightly irritating to be confronted with a time traveler. . . .

But I'd have bet cash. I could see no other possibility that met the facts. I was, further, convinced that she was one of the earliest time travelers (from the historically earliest point-of-origin, I mean), if not the very first.

She certainly seemed to have screwed up her landing—

I worked off one mitten and the glove beneath, quickly placed the back of my hand against her cheek. Its temperature was *neither* stone cold, nor the raging fever-heat mine would have had if I had been naked. Her skin temperature was . . . skin temperature. The same as my hand was in the instant that I slipped off my glove, but hers remained constant. Curiouser and curiouser. It occurred to me sadly that in her time Nova Scotia might be as overpopulated as Miami, its irresistible beauty no longer protected by its shield of horrid weather.

I hastily began to cover up my hand again. The instant my skin broke contact with hers, she made the first sound she had made since she had crashed to the forest floor. In combination with the happy-baby smile on her face, it was a shocking sound: the sound an infant makes when it is still terrified or starving, but too tired to cry any more. A high-pitched drawn out *nnnnnnnnn* sound, infinitely weary and utterly forlorn, punctuated with little hiccup-like inhalations. For the first time I began to consider the possibility that she was seriously hurt rather than stunned. Perhaps some unexpected side effect of materializing in my tree had boiled her brains in their bone pot. Perhaps she had simply gone mad. Perhaps some important internal organ had failed to complete the trip with her and she was dying.

Or perhaps her body's dazzling climate-control system took so much power under these overloaded conditions that there was none to spare for trivia like reason and speech. For all I knew, she had been expecting to materialize in Lesotho or Rio de Janeiro. (She could have been a Hawaiian who only moments before had dropped money into a wishing well and prayed to be somewhere cooler.) In any case, it was time for me to stop observing and marveling and do something resourceful.

Total elapsed time since her appearance, perhaps half a minute. Trip time to house (carrying load, downhill, on ice and loose rock, in the dark, during a snowstorm which was already back up to its original, pre-miracle fury), at least half a century.

THREE

DO YOU MIND if I don't describe that trip back home? If you really want to know what it felt like, perhaps therapy could help you.

No, wait, some parts were worth remembering. A fireman's carry doesn't work when you're dressed for Nova Scotia outdoors, she kept slipping off my shoulder, so I carried her most of the way in my arms, the way you carry a bride over the threshold. I could feel the warmth of her groin against my right arm through four layers of thick clothing, and in looking down to pick my footing I spent a lot of time watching those splendid breasts jiggle. Snowflakes seemed to melt and then evaporate instantly as they struck her, soft white kisses that left no mark. Her horrid moaning had stopped. In repose her features were beautiful. Perhaps there was a little of that ozone effect left in the air. By the time I emerged from the trees and sighted my home, windows glowing invitingly, twin streamers of smoke being torn from the chimneys, I suppose that I was feeling about as good as possible for a man in extreme physical distress. Better than you might suspect . . .

I don't remember covering the last hundred meters. I don't know how I got the outer and inner doors open and sealed again without dropping her. Instinctively I headed for the living room, the warmest room on the ground floor since it held the big Ashley firebox. I vaguely recall a dopey confusion once I got there. I wanted her on the couch, but I wanted her closer to the fire than that. So it was necessary to move the couch. Hmmm, I was going to have to put her down first. Where? Say, how about on the couch? Minimize the number of trips I'd have to make back and forth. Brilliant. Very important to conserve energy. Set her down carefully. Oof. Oh well. Circle couch, tacking like a sailboat, wedge self between it and wall. Final convulsive effort: heave! Good. Circle couch again. More difficult against the wind. Oh shit, we're going to capsize, try not to hit the Ashley—

Someone whacked me across both kneecaps with padded hammers, and then someone else with a naked sledge stove in the side of my head.

Two large beasts were fighting nearby. The nearer roared and growled deep in his throat, like King Kong in his wrath, or a dragon who has been told that this is the no-smoking section. The other had a high eldritch scream that rose and fell wildly, a banshee or a berserk unicorn. It sounded like they were tearing each other to pieces, destroying the entire soundstage in their fury.

Damn, it was hot here on Kong Island. Funny smell, like toasting mildew. Swimming in perspiration. Jungle so close it fit you like—

—a coat. A big heavy furry wet overcoat, and soggy hat and scarf and gloves and many sweat-saturated layers of undergarments. The shrieking unicorn was the storm outside, and mighty Kong was my Ashley stove . . . about a meter away! I rolled away quickly, and cracked my head on the couch. But for the cushioning of hat and hair, I'd have knocked myself out again.

If things would only slow down *for a minute, maybe I could get something done! Menstruating Christ, me head's broke. . . .*

I made it to my hands and knees. The dark naked woman on the couch caught my attention. So it was *that* kind of party, eh? Then I remembered. *Oh, hell yeah, that's just the dying time traveler I found up on the Mountain. Is she done yet?*

No, she was still working at it. Taking her time, too. She was asleep or unconscious, breathing in deep slow draughts. They called my attention to the fact that her nipples had finally detumesced. Fair enough. If I couldn't stand up, why should they? I began the long but familiar crawl to the kitchen, shedding wet clothes like a snake as I went until I got down to my Stanfields.

Fortunately there was always coffee on my kitchen stove, and I had overproof Navy grog in my pantry, and whipped cream from Mona's cow Daisy in my fridge; halfway through the second mug of Sassenach Coffee I had managed to become a shadow of my former self. I set the mug on the stove to keep warm and put my attention on first aid for my houseguest.

And screeched to a mental halt. What sort of first aid is indicated for someone who doesn't mind subzero temperature? What is the quick-cure for Time Traveler's Syndrome, for *mal de temps?*

It occurred to me to wonder if I had harmed her by bringing her into a warm environment. It didn't seem likely, but nothing about her seemed likely. I had only had a glimpse of her before crawling from the room. I forced myself up onto my weary feet and headed for the living room, cursing as my socks soaked up some of the ice water I had tracked indoors.

Her metabolism seemed to mind warmth no more than it

had subarctic cold. Her pulse seemed unusually fast and unusually strong—for a human being. The skin of her wrist was soft and warm and smooth. So was her forehead. Somehow I was not surprised that it was not feverish.

The back of my hand brushed that silly golden crown perched high on her bald head—and failed to dislodge it, which did surprise me. I nudged it, found it firmly affixed. I investigated. There were three little protuberances around its circumference, barely big enough to grasp, one at each temple and one around behind. I tugged the one at her right temple experimentally and it slid outward about ten centimeters on a slender shaft. There was an increasing resistance, like spring-tension, but at its full extension it locked into place. So did the other. I cradled her head with one palm and pulled out the third, and the crown fell off onto the couch. I examined the frontal two holes, the skin around them horny as callus, and confirmed that the three locking pins had been socketed directly into her skull.

There was no apparent change in her condition. She did not seem to need the crown to survive—at least, not in this friendly environment.

It seemed to be pure gold. It weighed enough, for all its slenderness. Examined closely, it seemed to be made up of thousands of infinitely thin threads of gold, interwoven in strange complicated ways that made me think of photos I'd seen of the IC chips they were just beginning to put in pocket calculators in those days. It didn't *feel* like it was carrying any current, or hum or blink or act electronically alive in any way I recognized. (Then again, neither did a chip.) There were no visible control surfaces or connections beyond the three locking pins—which did seem conductive.

Who knew what the thing was? Perhaps it was her time machine. Perhaps it made people obey you. Or not see you. From my point of view, there was nothing to be gained, and much to be risked, by replacing it. When she regained consciousness, she could tell me what it was. Or babble in some strange tongue, in which case I might decide to gamble on the crown being a translating device. For now, it was a distraction. I hid it in the kitchen, wishing I knew whether I was being crafty or stupid.

When I got back to the living room, she had rolled over in her sleep to toast the other side. It was the first completely human thing she had done, and for the first time I felt genuine empathy with her. With it came a rush of guilt at playing Mickey Mouse games, stealing gold from an unconscious woman—

In the harsh light of the bare bulb overhead, she looked somewhat less dark than she had outside, but not much. She definitely did not have the hyperextended back and high rump of a black woman, nor the slender hips and flat fanny of an Asian. She was muscled like an athlete, and much too thin for my taste—about what the rest of North America would have considered stunningly beautiful. Her face was turned toward me, and I studied it.

Outside in the dark in a snowstorm, I had guessed her age at forty. With better light and less distraction, I decided I could not guess her age. She might have been fourteen. The hasty impression I had gotten of intelligence and character was still there, but it did not express itself in the usual way, in number and placement of wrinkles. I could not pin down where it did reside.

Thai eyes, Japanese cheeks, Italian nose, Portuguese mouth. Skin medium dark, somehow more like a Mayan or a lightskinned Negro than a heavily tanned Caucasian, though I can't explain the difference. The net effect was stunning. One thing either marred or enhanced it, I could not decide. She was *totally* hairless—she had no eyebrows, and no eyelashes. Striking feature, in a face that didn't need it.

I didn't know what to do for her. Would a couple of blankets take some strain off her odd metabolism—or put more on? I felt her forehead and cheek. Just as they had been out in the snowstorm, they were skin temperature. She did not react to my touch. I thumbed back one eyelid, did a slight double-take. The pupil beneath that Asian eyelid was a blue so startlingly vivid and pure that it would have been improbable on any face. Paul Newman's eyes weren't that blue. I actually checked the other pupil to make sure it matched.

I decided, on no basis at all, that she was asleep rather than unconscious. I could think of nothing better for whatever it was that ailed her. I lit the kerosene lamp and dimmed the overhead electric light all the way down to darkness. I went back to the kitchen, picking up my discarded outdoor clothes as I went. I hung most of them by the kitchen stove to dry, put the mittens, gloves and outer pair of socks in the warming oven over the stove, put the boots on top of the warming oven. I finished the British coffee I had left on the stovetop. I went to a shelf by the back door, found a spare pair of socks among the mittens and scarves, swapped them for the wet pair I had on and put on my house-slippers. My Stanfields were still damp with sweat, so I got a fresh set of uppers and lowers from the shelf. I emptied the kettle into a basin, added the last ladle of cold water from the bucket behind the stove (the line to the sink pump would not unfreeze for weeks yet), and took a hasty sponge bath at the sink, then toweled off and changed into the clean Stanfields. The stove's firebox was almost down to coals—bad habit to get into; I hoped time travelers weren't going to be showing up every night—so I threw in a few sticks of softwood and a chunk of white birch from the woodbox behind the stove. I made a fast trip out to the drafty back hall for more wood, wedged the Ashley as full as possible, adjusted the thermostat and damper, closed her up and hung up the poker. The plastic was peeling up at one of the living room windows, farting icy drafts, so I got out the staple gun and fixed that. (I was not worried about waking her. People who need to sleep bad enough cannot be wakened. People who *can* be wakened can answer questions. Besides, it is impossible to load an Ashley quietly. In any case, she did not wake.) I went back to the kitchen, checked that the fire was rebuilding well, added a stick of maple.

The petty chores of living in the country are so never-ending that if they don't send you gibbering back to the city they become a kind of hypnotic, a rhythmic ritual, encouraging you to adopt a meditative state of mind. I found that I was priming up the Kemac, the oil-fired burner which took over for woodfire while I slept, and that told me that I had decided what I wanted to do. So I went back to the living room.

I had two choices: carry her upstairs to the bedroom above the Kemac—the only room that would stay "warm" all night long without help—or keep feeding the Ashley at intervals of no more than three or four hours. No choice at all; I could never have gotten her to the bedroom (Heartbreak Hotel grew room by room over a hundred and twenty years, at the whims of very eccentric people; it's not an easy house to get around in). I readjusted the damper on the Ashley, got blankets from the spare bedroom, put one over her, curled up in The Chair, and watched her sleep until I was asleep too. Roughly every three hours I rebuilt the fire. I don't remember doing so even once, but we were alive in the morning—in the country you develop *habits* rather quickly.

My dreams were bad, though. My father kept trying to tell me that something or someplace was mined, and a baby kept crying without making any sound, and I couldn't seem to find my body anywhere. . . .

FOUR

I WOKE AS soon as the room began to lighten up. Dawn, through two panes of warped glass and three layers of thick plastic, gives a room a surreal misty glow, like a photograph in *Penthouse*. She certainly looked right for the part.

Externally, at least. *Penthouse* models are always either looking you square in the eye while doing something unspeakably naughty, or else looking away in a scornful indifference which you both know is faked. My time traveling nude was out cold. (Not literally cold; I checked. Even though the room and I were.) She didn't budge as I got up and exercised out the kinks, the floorboards cracking like .22 fire, and she didn't budge as I pried up the heavy stove lid and stirred up the coals, enough for a restart thank God, and she didn't budge as I split some sticks down to starting size with the hatchet, even though as usual I got the blade stuck in a chunk of birch and had to hammer it free—she didn't even budge when a flying chip struck her blanket-covered hip. I checked her over very carefully for any sign that this might be other than healthful sleep. Pupils normal. Pulse very strong but not enough to alarm. Breathing free and rhythmic as hell. I visualized myself calling old Doc Hatherly, explaining how I had come into custody of this unconscious naked bald woman. ("Well you see, Doc, I had gone out into a blizzard at night to get Mucus the Moose, when suddenly there was a ball of fire, and this time traveler—what? Why yes, I do have long hair and a beard, what has that—eh? No, I've never taken any of that . . . anyway, not since the Solstice Dance at Louis's barn—Doc? *Doc?*)

The hell with it. She would wake up when she was ready. Or perhaps she would suddenly and quietly die, from causes I would never understand. Grim logic gleaned from a thousand sf stories suggested that this was perhaps one of the best things that could happen to a time traveler. Up behind the house were about ninety-five acres of woods; I knew places where the ground might be thawed enough to dig, with some effort, near the spot where she had appeared. Meanwhile, I wanted coffee and a piss, in that order.

But of course I had to have them the other way around. Peeing was simply a matter of reaching the chamberpot. For coffee, I had to:

—fill the kitchen firebox with wood, shut off the Kemac when the wood had caught, adjust dampers—

—put back on all of last night's stove-dried clothing, including outdoor gear, all of it smelling of ancient and tedious sin—

—carry two big white plastic buckets and the splitting axe down to the stream, a trifling two or three hundred meters without the slightest cover from the wind whipping in off the Bay—

—hack through the ice with the axe, *without* cutting off my feet—

—dip up two fullish buckets and seal them with lids that

fit so snug they must be hammered, *without* wetting my gloves or other garments—

—carry both full buckets (heavy) and axe (awkward) back to the house—

—refill the kettle and assemble the Melitta rig—

—wait five or ten minutes for the kettle to boil—

—and start the coffee dripping. All of this in the zombie trance of Before Coffee. I seldom had the strength to imagine, much less undertake, a second trip, even though two buckets of water is (at best) precisely enough to carry you through to bedtime. Today I made the second trip. I had company. By the time I was back with the extra two buckets, water was ready to be poured over the coffee. (Every country home has at least a dozen spare white plastic buckets around. They coalesce out of the air, like my guest. When they're old enough, they transmute themselves into Mason jars full of unidentifiable grains and beans.)

I toasted a slab of bread on the stove and reheated some of yesterday's porridge while the coffee was dripping. It is important to be done with breakfast by the time you have finished your coffee. Another of those habits I mentioned, which come from living in the cold winter woods. Twenty seconds after I finished the coffee, I was sprinting for the outhouse. Maybe it was as much as two and a half minutes before I was back indoors again, considerably lighter and much refreshed, ready to lick my weight in, say, baby rabbits.

I had fetched along four fresh eggs from the chicken coop; like the extra water, that turned out to be a happy thought. (Thirteen chickens, four eggs: a good day. I'm told they developed a strain of chicken that would reliably lay an egg a day. One unfortunate side effect: it was *too dumb to eat*.)

The weather had, with characteristic perversity, turned rather pleasant. Snow gone. Temperature creeping up to within hailing distance of Centigrade zero (well *above* zero in the scale I had grown up with). Wind moderate, and from the north—snow wind came from the south. Sky clear except for some scudding ribbons of cloud hastening over from New Brunswick. Sunrise beautiful as always, lacking the stunning colours of the pollution-refracted sunrises of my New York youth, but with a clarity and crispness that more than compensated. I was whistling *Good Day Sunshine* as I came in with the eggs.

I checked my guest. Other than shifted position (a good sign, I felt), there was no change. My kitchen was sunny and undrafty. I sat with my chair tipped back and my boots up on the stove and thought.

If she woke, we *were* going to talk—even if it took time for us to agree on language. If we did talk there was, it seemed to me, great risk of altering the past, thereby stressing the fabric of reality, perhaps destroying it altogether. I examined my curiosity, and found that it *didn't care* if it killed the cat—or even all cats. As I said, the logical thing to do was cut her throat. Of course I had no such intention. Perhaps it's a character defect: I don't have whatever it takes to murder a pretty naked woman on the basis of logical deductions concerning something which logic said couldn't be happening in the first place.

But suppose she had no such deficiency of character? Risky interaction between us could be avoided equally as well by *my* death. This intuition had caused me to hide her golden headband—but that might not be sufficient precaution. She looked well muscled; even asleep she looked like she had a lot of quick. I didn't know even Twentieth Century karate.

I wanted leverage.

So I called Sunrise Hill.

"Hi, Malachi—is the Snaker up?"

"Ha, ha. Now I've got one for you."

"Would you wake him, man? It's kind of important."

"There's enough suffering in the cosmos, Sam—"

"Please, Malachi."

"I'll get Ruby to wake him up. Hang on."

Long pause. One advantage of commune life: there's always someone else to start the morning fires. One of the disadvantages of a spiritual commune: no coffee.

"Hazzit. Whiss?"

"Good morning, Snaker. Wake up, man, all the way up."

"S'na fucking wibbis?"

"Really, man, I got news—"

"Garf norble."

"What I tell you is true, brother. There's a time traveler in my living room."

"*—from what year?—*"

"I don't know. Unconscious since arrival."

"And you're sure it's a—" He lowered his voice drastically. "—what you said?"

"That, or an alien who arrives in a ball of fire in the woods, doesn't mind being naked in the snow, and has fabulous tits."

"Sam, you haven't by any chance—"

"Not since the dance at Louis's barn. I'm straight, Snaker."

"I've already left, but don't pour the coffee till you hear me coming over the horizon. Shit, wait—*who else knows?*"

"You, me, and God, if He's monitoring this sector at the moment."

"If He is, He's holding His breath. Damn, why does everything always have to happen in the middle of the night?"

"Snake—don't even tell Ruby, okay? Uh—" I cast about for a cover story that would account for what he'd said so far. "What you tell people there is, I've got a possible Beatles bootleg, reputed to date from 1962, and I've asked you to come over and help me decide if it's legit. Get it?"

Even half-awake, the Snaker has a quick uptake. "It's the drumming that'll tell the tale. If it's Ringo, it can't be '62."

"Good man, Snake."

"Look, it's hard to run full tilt like this and talk on the phone. See you sooner." He hung up.

The only other habitual science fiction reader on the Mountain. I had known he would come through.

I used the morning chores to calm myself down. Bank fires, replenish woodbox, feed chickens, stare at Bay. The last-named seldom fails to repair a fractured mood; I went back indoors feeling pretty good. Started to resume work on my half-finished dulcimer, and realized I had left Mucus up on the mountainside the night before. No time to get him now. I went back outside and looked at the Bay some more.

While I was wishing for the thousandth time that I shared old Bert Manchette's ability to forecast the weather by the colour of the water in the Bay, I heard the thunder of an armored column approaching. It was Blue Meanie, The Sunrise Hill Gang's ancient pickup truck, with the Snaker at the wheel. There was a mechanical roar of outrage as the Meanie went through the Haskell Hollow, a few klicks away, and minutes later the wretched thing came into view around the bend, bellowing in agony and trailing dark smoke like a squid under attack. When he shut it off at the foot of my driveway it seemed to slump.

The Snaker was well over six feet and thin as a farmer's hope. Which made him especially cold-sensitive, which made him wear so many layers of clothes he looked like a normal person. Nobody knew Yassir Arafat back then, so Snaker had the ugliest beard I'd ever seen. His brown hair was narrow gauge, neither straight nor curly, and extremely long even for a North Mountain Hippie. He was that indeterminate age that all of us were, somewhere between eighteen and thirty-five. God had seen fit to give him guitarist's fingers, without a guitarist's talent, and it drove him crazy. He had a good baritone, was named after Snaker Dave Ray, the baritone in the old Koerner-Ray-Glover ensemble. He'd sold a couple of stories to magazines in the States. I taught him licks. He lent me books. We were friends.

This morning he was as excited as I've ever seen him before noon. He leaped from the truck before it had stopped coughing, ran up to me.

"Fabulous tits, huh?"

"Well," I said in a softer voice than his, "you're awake enough to have your priorities straight."

"As good as Ruby's? Never mind, you can't compare tits. Let's see her—"

He started to move past me to the rear of the house. (Nobody keeps a door open to the wind on the Bay side of his house.) I grabbed him by the shoulder, sharply. "Hold it a second. Stand right there and don't move." I went to the living room window, got up on tiptoe and squinted in through the layers of plastic. She was still where I had left her, apparently still asleep.

The Snaker was trying to look over my shoulder. "I'll be—"

"*Shh!*" I led him back away from the window.

"Come on, man, let's go inside for a better look—"

"No."

"Why the fuck not?"

"Stand there and shut up and I'll tell you why not."

He nodded. I went inside, made two cups of coffee, put a small knock of grog in my own, stuck the golden crown dingus under my coat and went back outside. He was peering in the window again. "Dammit, come here."

I made him drink the coffee all the way down. "Tell me all," he said when he had swallowed the last gulp, "omitting no detail however slight." So I did. It took less time than I had expected.

"It comes clear," he said finally. "Your behavior begins to make sense."

"Right. When she wakes up and realizes her cover's blown, maybe she just pulls my brains out through my eyesockets to cover her tracks. It would be nice to have an ally she's never seen and can't locate, who is prepared to blow the secret skyhigh if I don't report in on time."

"Aren't you overlooking something? What if she's a telepath? Then after she does you she comes and pulls out *my* brains."

I shook my head. "If she is, we're screwed no matter what we do. Besides, I don't believe in telepathy. What I'm going to do is give you this headband gizmo to hold hostage. You take it down the line somewhere and wait 'til you hear my shotgun go off once. It could take hours, but stay alert. If the crown turns out to be some essential part of her life support or something, I want to be able to get you back here with it in a hurry. But *don't* tell me where you're going, and *don't* come back if I fire *both* barrels."

"What a nasty suspicious mind you have, my son."

"Thank you."

"Look, why didn't you just tell me all this when I first got here?"

"You couldn't have followed the logic-chain before coffee."

"Oh. True. Okay, slip me the headband. And Sam—good luck."

"Thanks, mate."

"And call me back as soon as you're sure it's safe. I'm dying to find out if you're right."

"I know what you mean." I grinned. "It's like getting a tax refund from God. I've always wanted to meet a time traveler."

"Knowing one exists would be a tax refund from God. Meeting one would be gravy. Delicious gravy, but just gravy."

"I don't follow."

"Sam, Sam! If a time traveler exists—*then the human race isn't going to annihilate itself in the near future*. Not completely, anyway."

"Huh! You're right, by Jesus."

"Of course I am. I've had coffee."

He took the golden headband, studied it and put it away.

He got back into the truck, did something that made it scream. "Have a care, son," he called over the clashing of gears. "Never trust a naked time traveler." And he was gone in a spray of gravel.

FIVE

FOR LUNCH I fried up two of the morning's eggs with some of the last earthly remains of Tricky and Dicky, the pigs I had slaughtered the previous October. I half expected the smell to wake her, but no dice. I ate in the living room, watching her. I caught myself becoming irritated at her. I hate houseguests who sleep late; I yearn so badly to sleep late myself, and a country householder *can't*. Even a time traveler ought to have enough manners to grab forty winks *before* coming to work, I heard myself think, and that sounded so stupid I grinned at myself. I dislike grinning at myself, so I started getting irritated again—

There's one thing even better than contemplation of the Bay of Fundy for calming me down, so I got out Gertrude and a handful of Ernie Ball fingerpicks. As usual, the song chose itself without conscious thought on my part; as usual I couldn't have improved on it with a week's thought.

Beloved Hoagy (still alive then) and Johnny Mercer: "Lazy Bones."

I try to do that song as close as possible to the definitive version Amos Garrett laid down on Geoff and Maria Muldaur's *Sweet Potatoes* album. I'm not fit to change Garrett's strings, I'm just barely good enough to get by professionally, but the tune is so sweet it almost plays itself. That afternoon it seemed to come out especially well. I watched her splendid chest rise and fall, and told her softly that sleeping in the sun was no way to get her day's work done. (What *was* her day's work? And what day, in what year?) For the first time in a while I attempted an instrumental chorus before the second bridge, and to my immense satisfaction it came off just fine. I grinned and finished the song, warned her that if she slept away the day, she was never going to make a dime. (Where would she have *put* a dime?) I even managed to stumble through the Beiderbecke riff (from a tune charmingly entitled "I'm Coming, Virginia") that Garrett quotes to close the song, and let the final G chord ring in the room while I admired myself.

In the last line of that song the narrator offers to wager that his listener has not heard a thing he's said, and I believed as I sang it that such a bet would be a boat-race—had she not slept through the repeated filling of a toploader stove?—so when she opened her striking blue eyes and said, "That's not true," I started so sharply my thumbpick flew off.

I left it on the floor. I had already mentally prepared some sort of welcoming speech, designed to show in as few words as possible that I was clever enough to know what she was and ethical enough to pose no danger—but it flew right out of my head. I put Gertrude carefully back in her case, to give myself time to think. "I stand corrected," is what I finally said.

She sat up, and I thought of a Persian cat I had once loved named Rainy Midnight. "That was very beautiful." Her voice was a smoky alto. It came out so flat and expressionless that it put me in mind of Mister Spock. I found it oddly attractive.

I thanked her with only a shadow of my usual wince. It *hadn't* been too bad. Her next line was very interesting.

"Do you know what I am?"

I liked that question. In the rush of the moment, I had forgotten my earlier fear that she might be a telepath, it had not been in my conscious mind. I remembered it when she asked the question—and so her question was probably genuine. Unless, of course, she could somehow read thoughts below the conscious level, or was very clever. . . .

My voice came out steady. "I know that you are a very beautiful bald lady who blew up one of my best birch trees. I believe that you are a time traveler. If so, I will do my best not to screw things up for you."

"You're very quick," she said calmly. "You understand the dangers, then?"

This was great. "I doubt it. But my guesses scare me pretty good. Changing history and so forth. What year are you from?"

"That I will not tell you."

"Okay. Why are you here?"

She hesitated slightly; I thought she was going to refuse to answer that question too. "Think of me as—"She looked quizzical, then tried comically to look up at her own forehead, where her crown-thing should have been. "Can I have my ROM? I keep some specialized vocabulary in there." She touched her bald skull. "And I'll need it to start growing hair."

I blinked. ROM meant Read-Only-Memory. The damned thing *was* an overgrown IC chip! Stored computer data! "Direct brain-computer interface—"

She smiled. It was a nice smile, but somehow it looked like something she had just learned to do. "You read science fiction!"

I had to smile myself. "They still have it in your time,

eh?" I'd always been a little afraid they'd run out of crazy ideas one day.

"You'd love it." She frowned slightly. "If you could understand it."

"I'm sorry about your ROM. It's not here now. I can get it in ten minutes' time."

She nodded. "For all you knew it was a weapon. I understand. All right, what is the current term for people who study people of the past?"

"There are several kinds. Historians study events in the relatively recent past, and try to interpret them. Archaeologists dig up evidence of the distant past, and anthropologists use the evidence, and observation of surviving primitive cultures, to make guesses about human social and cultural development throughout history. Then writers relate all that to the present."

"Think of me as a combination of all of those. The human race has come so far, its past has begun to seem unreal to it. I'm here to learn."

"How can I help you?"

"By keeping my secret, and by introducing me plausibly to your community. I promise that I will not harm anyone in any way."

"You aren't afraid of accidentally changing the past? Your past?"

"Not unless my secret becomes general knowledge."

"One other person knows. He'll keep his mouth shut," I added hastily, seeing her dismay. "He's smart enough to understand why. He's actually sold some science fiction to a magazine."

She looked dubious. "He might think it's good story material."

"Maybe—as fiction. Who'd believe a guy who's written science fiction? I'm not sure I'd believe this myself—if I hadn't seen you appear in blue fire."

"I'm sorry about your tree."

"That's okay. I'm surprised materializing where another mass already existed didn't kill you—or worse."

"So am I." I held a blink, and then stared. "That was a very bad mistake—somehow that clearing is closer to the path than the records indicate."

"Maybe I see your problem, if your fix was based on the path. The land slopes to the west just there. I wouldn't be surprised if over the next fifty years or so that section of trail just naturally migrates a few meters downhill."

"That could account for it." She shivered. "Perhaps I should not have come. That was a very dangerous error." She paused, acquired a strange expression. "I ask your pardon for having endangered you by my recklessness." She seemed to wait warily for my answer.

"Hell, that's okay. How were you to know?"

She relaxed. "Precisely my error. Thank you for pardoning it. How long was I unconscious?"

I calculated. "Maybe fourteen hours. You don't snore."

"I don't know the term."

Oh. "You sleep beautifully. And soundly."

"Thank you. I haven't had much practice."

Oh. "That must be nice."

"I have nothing to compare it to, but I suppose it is. Do you want me to put on clothes?"

"If you wish. There is a nudity taboo in this place and time, but I heed it only when others do or the weather insists. If I'd known when you were going to wake up, I'd have stripped myself to put you at ease: it's warm enough right here by the fire."

"Does it not cause you tension to be in the presence of a naked woman?" There was something odd about her voice. The subtext *don't you find me attractive?* was in there—but I sensed she had no ego involvement in the answer, was simply curious. That implied to me a cultural advance at least as startling as time travel.

"Yes it does! And the day I stop enjoying such tension will be the day they plant me. Don't dress on my account."

"Thank you."

"But if any neighbors drop by, you'd better scamper upstairs. Oh, the nudity wouldn't cause too much talk, indoors, but women bald to the eyelashes are fairly scarce on the Mountain these days. Mind your head if you do; the wall sort of leans out at you at the top of the stairs. I think the upstairs was built by a dwarf who leaned to the left at a forty-five degree angle. You'll find clothes in the bedroom to the right. Some may fit you—and of course a robe fits any size."

"Thank you."

"Are you hungry?"

"*Thank you.*" They were the most emotionally charged words she had spoken so far. "Yes. But . . . but first, can you get my ROM back? I'm uncomfortable without it: a lot of what I know about this here/now is in it."

"I can start getting it back at once; it'll arrive after breakfast. Can you walk?"

She could walk. We went to the kitchen. I warned her to expect a loud noise, stepped outside and let off a round of birdshot. Then I whipped up a scratch brunch. She said she could eat anything I could. The coffee and porridge were hot; eggs, bacon, orange juice and toast took perhaps ten minutes. I had to show her how to use a knife and fork. That was excellent bacon, I'd fed Tricky and Dicky real well; the toast was fresh whole wheat, with fresh-churned butter from Mona Bent's cow; my coffee is famous thoughout the North Mountain; the eggs were so fresh the shells still had crumbs of chickenshit clinging to them. She demolished everything, slowly. Oddly, she ate it all impassively, displaying neither relish nor distaste. She used no salt, no pepper, no tamari, no cream, no sugar. Toward the end she did think to say, "This is delicious," but I noticed she said it while she was eating a burnt piece of crust. I wondered how I would have behaved if suddenly dropped into, say, a medieval banquet. I also wondered how—and what—they ate where she came from.

I had made enough for Snaker; I expected him to arrive before the food was ready to eat, and I knew he had not broken his fast. But he didn't get there until we were done eating—and she had not left anything unconsumed. "Goddam transmission," he muttered as he came through the door, and then stopped short. He stared at her for a long moment, then became extremely polite. "Beautiful lady, good morning to you," he said, in a much deeper voice than usual, bowing deeply. Basic North Mountain Hippie bow, palms together before chest, not the punch-yourself-in-the-belly kind. She watched it, paused for an instant and then imitated it superbly, sitting down. It looked a lot better on her than it had on him. Snaker turned to me. "Oh sweet Double-Hipness," he said, quoting Lord Buckley, "straighten me . . . 'cause I'm *ready*."

"Groovy," I agreed. "Snaker O'Malley, I would like you—"

—and I skidded to a halt, feeling like a jerk, and waited—

—and waited—

—growing more embarrassed by the second. I *hate* that, starting to introduce two people whose names you should know and realizing too late that you're shy one name, and it seems to happen to me about every other time I have to make introductions. Okay, I hadn't thought to ask her name, which probably wasn't very polite—but I'd been *busy*, and anyway I hadn't *needed* a name for her, there was only the one of her—and dammit, she had demonstrated repeatedly that she was clever and quick, she had learned how to bow and extrapolated it to a sitting position at a single glance, why the hell wasn't she letting me off the hook?

After five seconds, beginning to blush and just hating it, I had to say, "I'm sorry; I didn't ask your name."

She should then have understood why I was blushing, realized she'd been leaving me hanging, and been a little embarrassed herself. When I'm in a strange place with strange customs and realize that I've embarrassed my host, *I* become embarrassed. What she said, in that cool Lady Spock voice, was, "That's all right." And then she stopped talking.

Snaker's bushy eyebrows lifted, and he gave me a glance which seemed to say, *and we thought she might be a telepath*.

So I played straightman. "What is your name?"

"Rachel."

"Snaker, this is Rachel; Rachel, Snaker; consider yourselves married in the eyes of God." It's a gag line I probably use too often, but the reaction this time was novel. She got up, went to the Snaker, wrapped him up in those big muscular arms and purely kissed the hell out of him.

I expected him to hesitate momentarily, then talk himself into it and cooperate. I guess he trusted my friendship; he skipped the preamble. Enthusiasm was displayed by both halves of the kiss. Gusto. *Joie de vivre*. For something to do I rolled a joint. When it ended, the Snaker had the grace to shoot me a quick apologetic glance before saying, "Rachel, your husband will be one *hell* of a lucky gent—but I'm afraid my pal was joking. I am already engaged to be married, and . . ." He glanced down at what was flattening the fur on his coat. ". . . and much as I might regret it, I don't regret it. If you follow me. But thank you from the bottom of my—thank you very much."

"You're welcome, Snaker. Thank you."

"Welcome to our little corner of space-time. I hope you'll like it here."

"Thank you again. I hope so too."

Dammit, I'd done all the work, and he was getting all the good lines.

She turned to me. "I don't know your name."

"Sam. Sam Meade."

"Sam, in several of the things you said earlier I found ambiguity which I took to be whimsy. May I ask you to refrain from that? I understand that you mean to put me at ease, but it will confuse rather than amuse me."

Jesus.

"In particular, reversed or multiple meanings will badly disorient me—"

Snaker and I exchanged a glance. Half the fun of being his friend is that we can both volley puns back and forth all night, an exercise which both sharpens, and displays, the wits.

Suddenly I remembered the time I had unthinkingly dropped a pun in conversation with old Lester Sabean, my nearest neighbor (perhaps a mile to the west). " 'Scuse me, Sam," he'd said mildly, chewing on his ratty pipe. "Was that one o' them plays on words there?" When I allowed that it had been, he looked me in the eye and arranged his leathery wrinkles into a forgiving smile. "Might just as well save them around me, I guess," he said. I've never punned in Lester's presence since. Flashing on that now, I lost a little of my irritation with Rachel. That kiss had been my own dumb fault—

—except that she kept on *chattering*. And she was starting to gesture, to take little steps, to glance around at things. Until now she had projected the kind of Buddhist serenity that every freak on the North Mountain was trying for. All of a sudden she was hyper, giving off sparks, spilling energy like city people when they first get here. "—inherent in the nature of humour, even though one would think the matrix itself was intrinsically—"

Well, I knew how to deal with that. I lit the joint.

She trailed off and stared at it. "This," I said from the back of my throat, holding the smoke in, "is marijuana, or reefer. It's active ingredient is delta-niner tetrahydrocannabinol. It is made of dried flowers. I grew it myself, and it will not do you any harm."

She looked dubious. "Thank you, Sam. I know that I ought to partake of all your native refreshments—"

I exhaled. "It is nonnarcotic, nonaddictive, habituating with prolonged use. It contains much more tar than processed tobacco. It is just barely illegal. It cures nausea, cramps, anxiety and sobriety. You are under no slightest obligation to accept it, and if the waste smoke bothers you we'll open the stove door and let the draft take it."

"—Thank you Sam I would prefer that please you see I am responsible to many people and drugs which cure anxiety dull alertness and that's—"

"They don't have coffee when you come from, do they?" Snaker asked.

"Beg pardon?"

Oh, hell. Of course. The half a pot she'd accepted from me had probably been the first coffee she'd ever had. I wasn't so sure I would like the future if it didn't have coffee in it. . . .

"I'm not trying to change your mind," he said. He came over by the stove and took the joint, had a toke. "But you've already ingested a mild psychedelic, and this might help counteract it. The hot black drink in your cup over here contains a stimulant called caffeine. It's legal and very common, but quite strong and fiendishly addictive. It makes you hyper, speedy—do you know those words?"

She looked dismayed. "I think I understand them."

"If you're not used to it, especially, it can make you paranoid. Anxious and uneasy. It revs you up too fast. This—" He took another hit. "—cools you out." He was trying to avoid speaking Hippie, but of course it's difficult to discuss subjective biochemical states in any other language.

"That sounds like what I am experiencing. Dammit, it's *hard* to stay stable in this environment. Cold I was prepared to deal with, but for vegetable poisons I expected more warning. And it seems so *sensible* to be this afraid. You're right, I must correct it. But I would rather do it myself, thank you." She looked at him and waited expectantly.

Snaker and I exchanged the joint and a glance.

"I'll need my ROM," she told him.

He sprayed smoke, thunderstruck. "They have Krishna in the future?"

Now she was baffled.

I lost my own toke laughing. "Spelled R-O-M, Snake."

"Read-Only-Memory-oh. *Oh*. I see." His eyes widened. "Wow." He frowned suddenly, glanced at me. "Yes, Sam?"

"Go ahead, man." I sucked more smoke in, feeling the buzz come on. I grow good reefer if I say so myself.

He shucked his coat, produced the crown/headband from a capacious inside pocket. He held it in his hands and gazed at it a minute. "Fucking fantastic. Smaller than that Altair is supposed to be, no moving parts, direct brain interface, no visible power source—how many bytes?"

"Beg pardon?"

"How much data can it hold?"

"I can't say until I access it. May I, please?" She looked like a cat that's heard the can opener working, as though she were fighting the impulse to take the crown by force.

"I'm very sorry," he said, and handed it to her at once.

"Thank you, Snaker O'Malley!"

I watched the way she put it on. The rear locking pin snapped in first, then she pulled out the other two, settled the golden ellipse down over her forehead, moved it slightly to seat the pins and let them slide home. Almost at once her face began to visibly change, in a way I found oddly difficult to grasp.

SIX

I HAD ANOTHER toke, and passed the bone to Snaker, and the light had changed and it was cooler in the room, even by the stove. "Well," I said, "as you can see, reefer not only makes you babble aimlessly, you get irresponsible: I've let my fires run down. You were wise to refuse it." I began to get up.

Snaker was already on his feet. "Sit, man. I'll get the wood, I did most of the talking." He refilled the kitchen firebox with small sticks, went out back for big wood for the Ashley.

"What were we talking about, again?"

"Whether or not I can stay here," she said seriously.

"Oh, *hell* yeah, sure you can," I said. "You don't even have to fuck me. That was a joke," I added hastily.

"I don't think so," she said. She was much more calm and serene again, now that she had her headband on.

I frowned. "Can I be completely honest with you?"

"I don't know." From another woman it might have been sarcasm, or irony. She meant that she didn't know.

"Well, I'll try, and I do better with honesty when I say it fast so pay attention: unlike Snaker I am not engaged to anybody and I would love to have sex with you at least once in the near future and maybe more but I am not in the market for any kind of romantic or even long-term sexual relationship but I *am* tremendously excited at the prospect of talking with a time traveler but you don't seem to want to *tell* me anything which is frustrating and furthermore I have some reservations about you as a roommate which are not particularly your fault but I'm a very ornery guy to live with, you have to be pretty tantric around me and unfortunately because of your cultural displacement and so forth you're not exactly the most tantric person in the world, but you wouldn't be in the way of anything and there's been a lot of cabin fever going around this winter, so for a while, hell, for as long as you want, you can stay, yeah, sure."

"Tantric? Which aspect of the Vedas—oh, you mean the sexual yogas?"

"Sorry. Hippie slang. Means, like . . ." I floundered. "Uh, intuitive. Sensitive. A tantric person can walk in and out of your bedroom without waking you up, can coexist with an angry drunk, becomes seamless with his own environment. Easy to get along with. Aware of fine nuances of others' feelings. Perceptive of small clues. Also called telepathic." Her face changed subtly. "No offense, your manners are excellent, but you lack too much cultural context to notice subtleties the way an ideal roommate ought to. For all I know, I've got more in common with a Micmac. But I like you, and even though I'm kind of a hermit I'm willing to endure the aggravation of having you around for a while in exchange for the pleasure of your company. Besides, I don't know where the hell else you'd go."

"You're right. Your help will enormously simplify my

work. Thank you for your hospitality, Sam." Her eyes were dreamy, slightly bloodshot.

"Tell me something: what the hell did you *expect* to happen?"

"How do you mean?"

"You materialize naked in the night on a cold hillside. Then what was the plan? What if I hadn't come along? How were you going to line up a place to live, a plausible identity, a set of long johns for that matter?"

"I intended to improvise."

I whistled. "You've got plenty of balls."

She blinked. "Just the one I came in."

"Sorry again. A sexist slang expression, meaning, 'you have audacity.'"

The word "sexist" puzzled her too, but she let it pass. "More like necessity. I had to come through naked if I was to come at all."

That was odd. If all she could bring back was herself, not even clothes, not even *hair*, how come the headband dingus had come along? Did that imply that it was—

—I forgot the matter. She was still talking: "That limited my options. I hoped to conceal myself in the woods and reconnoiter until I could plausibly construct an identity."

"Like I said, you've got balls. Courage."

Snaker came in with an armload, shedding bark and snow and breathing steam. I'd heard him filling up the woodbox out in the back hall while I talked with Rachel. "There's oil spilled over your kitchen wood stash out here, so I swapped it for fresh. Did you know the west roof of your woodshed's gone?" he asked cheerfully.

I rolled my eyes. "Jesus T. Murphy and His traveling flea circus. I think I'll just go back to sleep and try this day over again tomorrow." Rachel giggled—which I thought was rather out of character for her. I'd thought I was supposed to avoid whimsy.

"Bullshit," Snaker said. "We've got to build Rachel a cover story. Relax—I threw a tarp over the wood on that side. Besides, the wind hardly ever comes west this time of year. Except when it does. Make more coffee and let's get to work."

"Are you in a hurry, Snaker?" she asked drowsily.

"Eh? No. I live in a commune, none of us is ever in a hurry. Why?"

"I'd like your help in building a good persona, but first Sam and I want to have sex."

There was a silence.

"Have I been untantric again? You *did* say the near future, Sam?"

"I'll just leave you two alone and go feed the other stove for a while," Snaker said carefully.

"If you wish," she said, just as carefully. Her almond eyes were wide.

Snaker hesitated. "You don't mind if I stay?"

"Not if you want to. Three is good. Odd numbers are always good."

He smiled apologetically. "My Ruby and I are monogamous. I won't risk our relationship for anything, even for the thrill of making it with a beautiful time traveler. She's too important to me." He swallowed. "But our agreement is, we're allowed to look." He met my eyes. "You mind?"

I thought about it. "I don't believe I do." My penis certainly didn't seem to mind. "But I'm damned if I'm going to do it here. The floor's cold, and someone might drop in."

So we all adjourned to the upstairs bedroom. Snaker forgot to feed the living room fire, carried the armload of wood upstairs because he forgot he had it in his arms, and had to go back down again.

He hurried back up.

SEVEN

RACHEL HAD NO comment on my bedroom. Joel, who owned Heartbreak Hotel and let me live there, had insulated the puptent-shaped bedroom in typical North Mountain Hippie fashion: refrigerator-carton cardboard spread flat and nailed to the studs, with crumpled newspaper stuffed down behind. (You could have placed it on the standard insulation-efficiency scale, but you'd have needed three decimal places.) Then he had covered the facing surface of the cardboard with about fifty large Beardsley and Bosch prints. I have to admit I didn't spend much time up there in daylight. Also, the room's ceiling was the house's rooftree; the walls sloped sharply and a person my height could only stand erect within a four-foot-wide corridor. (Snaker couldn't manage it at all.)

But she did not seem to notice the prints, and we were not vertical for long. At some indeterminate point on the way upstairs, she had stopped being merely nude and become naked. Snaker came in and sat down as I was slipping my undershirt off; I tipped an imaginary hat, he smiled, and I turned back to Rachel. . . .

Of all that I've had to explain and describe so far, this is one of the hardest parts.

I don't suppose it's ever easy to "explain and describe" making love. Even on a purely surface, physical level, an encyclopedia could be written on what transpired during the least memorable encounter I've ever had in my life—much less this one. I remember every detail of what transpired that afternoon—and most of the parts that can be forced into words are the least important ones.

To begin with, my consciousness was fractured, asymmetrically. The largest portion was on Rachel-and-Me, which of course translates as Mostly Me. A smaller, equally self-conscious portion was on Snaker-and-Me, and that portion tried to make itself as inconspicuous as possible. Another portion was devoted to Rachel-and-Snaker, and still another to Rachel-and-Snaker-and-Me (in constantly shifting order of priority), on the thing we were building in my bedroom, and how it was changing all three of us individually.

Each of these self-nuggets was further fractured. The portion concentrating on Rachel-and-Me, for example, could not decide whether to focus on our minds or our bodies or our souls. Part of me was learning about Rachel as a person from the way she made love, and telling her of myself; part was concerned with the simple but awkward mechanics of coupling; part was distracted by the weirdly beautiful symmetry of lust spanning time itself, by the notion that the Oldest Mystery stretched both backward and forward through the centuries; yet another part of me was wondering what her people used for contraception and whether she was now using it, wondering how I would feel if she were not.

And if this were fiction—the kind the author wants you to

believe—I would tell you that all these parts were drowned out by the sheerly overwhelming physical sensations of what we were doing together, that the future folk had made unimaginable advances in Sexual Voodoo, perfected unnameable new skills and indescribable new delights, and that Rachel was one of their Olympic champions.

She was okay.

For a First Time, on a purely physical level, a little better than okay. None of the usual awkwardness. Well, some at first, all on my part, but I got over it fast; it takes two (or more) to sustain awkwardness. She knew all the things an educated woman of my time would know, and did them about as well. She didn't do anything to me that startled me (though she most pleasantly surprised me a few times). She was quite direct about asking for what she wanted, using gestures or words, and didn't ask for anything I didn't know how to do. (I believe I may have surprised her once or twice myself.) She neither hid nor inflated her enjoyment. She was perhaps less vocal than women of my time tended to be, a little less inhibited than the women I had been sleeping with lately (that is, completely uninhibited), certainly much less self-conscious than any woman I had ever known. She came quickly, but didn't make a big squealing deal of her orgasms.

And yet, while she was not self-conscious, she was to some extent self-involved, removed. My ego might have liked it better if she *had* made a bigger deal of her orgasms. If I had expected some kind of magical union, some rapture of telepathic transport, I was disappointed.

I had; I was.

I had been prepared, had been half expecting, to "lose my ego," as we were so fond of saying on the Mountain in those days, to mingle identities with her in some way, to be taken out of myself. We've spent a million years trying to learn to leave the prison of our skull through lovemaking, with the same perpetually promising results, and I had hoped that the people of the future had made some dramatic breakthrough in that direction, and that I was equipped to learn it.

No such luck. As intimately as we joined, part of us was separate, just like always. She missed subtle cues. Some of the cues *she* gave must have been too subtle for me to follow. Twice my penis slipped out of her vagina because she zigged when I zagged. I could not leave my skull, my body, my identity—partly because I could tell that she was still in hers. I could feel it in a barely perceptible tension of her skin, and see it in her eyes. I could almost see her straining against the insides of those eyes, trying to break out. They reminded me of the eyes of a wolf I had seen once, born free but long in captivity. Resignation.

In some odd way lovemaking defined the barrier between us, and so made us further apart than we had been when we started.

And at the same time I learned a great many things about her in a short period. Some were of small consequence, like the highest note that her alto voice could reach. Others were of more importance, things that would have taken much longer to learn or intuit without the lovemaking, things that she might not have known herself.

Such as the fact that underneath a very professionally manufactured calm, she was terrified, scared right down to her bones. Scared of what, I could not say, but she *needed* sex, to calm her nerves. And it wasn't helping as much as she'd hoped it would.

This was not a simple linear learning; I was simply going in too many directions at once. The age-old question I Wonder What This Is Like For Her was complicated by I Wonder What This Is Like For Him. Since he was male, I could empathize more directly with Snaker. (But Rachel was *closer*.) And since he was a friend of mine, I couldn't help wondering What This Would Be Like For Ruby when she heard about it, and What *That* Would Be Like For Him. And for me; Ruby was my friend, too. Making all thought difficult were the four restrained but quite emphatic orgasms Rachel had while I was on my way to my first, each seeming strangely to ease her fear and compound her sadness. . . .

What with six things and another, it seemed to go on for countless hours and be over before it had begun. Compared to hers, my own completion was thunderous and abrupt. The "afterglow" period of delicious brainlessness was measurable in microseconds, and then, wham, I was back inside my skull, brain buzzing, chewing on *well, that wasn't as good as I hoped nor as bad as I feared* and *Jeez I've got my back to Snaker and my legs spread, will he think I?* and *all that perfect skin-temperature control and she still sweats like crazy when it's time to be slippery* and *I wonder what in hell she's so scared of?* and *God it's good to get laid again* and so forth.

A long exhalation came from Snaker. I twisted round to see him. He was smiling hugely, a skinny stoned Buddha. He was also sweating a lot. Wood chips on his flannel shirt. Visible bulge below. Dilated pupils. Little orange bunnies woven into his outer pair of socks. Happy maniac.

"That was beautiful," he said simply.

I reached down and pulled the blankets back up over me again; even the warmth of energetic sex was only briefly equal to the cold of my bedroom in late Winter. Rachel, of course, did not need the protection and stayed uncovered; as I watched, the perspiration on her skin seemed to evaporate, or perhaps be reabsorbed.

I read about a character in a book once who could make knives appear as if by magic at need, from no apparent source; they just seemed to materialize in his hand. The Snaker does that trick with joints. They appear, lit, in his hand as he passes them to you. I accepted it from him and toked, being careful not to drip ashes on Rachel, then offered it to her. She passed. As she did so I realized I didn't want another toke myself.

"May I ask you about your feelings, Snaker?" she asked.

He glanced quickly down and to his right, then back

again at once. I'd been his friend long enough to know that little eye gesture was what he did when he wanted to reconsider, perhaps edit, the first answer that popped into his mind. But his smile never flickered. "Sure."

"Why did you not masturbate?"

Down and to the right; back up. "I'm not sure." Pause. "I want to be straight with you because I know you're an anthropologist and you learn a lot about a culture from its sex mores, but I'm really not sure myself, Rachel. I mean, I've been trying to understand *my own* sex mores for almost a quarter of a century, and I'm still confused."

"Would Ruby have considered it an act of infidelity if you had pleasured yourself while you watched us?"

Down and to the right; back up. "Again, I'm not sure. I *think* perhaps not. Maybe when I tell her about this she'll say I should have gone ahead. But I hadn't thought it through beforehand . . . and I can't rely on any judgment I make while I have a hard-on."

"Would *you* have considered it an act of infidelity?"

"Again, I'm not sure. But I think so. Especially since we haven't defined our agreement in this area yet. Uh . . . frankly, I don't think either of us ever expected the situation to come up."

"People of your time never witness the lovemaking of others?"

"Frequently, but almost always second-hand. On film, not in person."

Briefly it occurred to me to be jealous. I mean, if any woman of my own time, lying in my arms in afterglow, had initiated a complex discussion with a third party, I'd have read it a certain way. But I couldn't manage to be jealous. It just felt natural. She and Snaker hadn't touched, so they had to use words, was all.

She pressed the point. "But you said you had mutual agreement that it was okay to look."

He looked sheepish. "That was sort of a sophistry. What we meant by that was, if you see a sexy stranger go by, a temptation, it's okay to look and be aroused by it—as long as you bring the arousal home to your partner. And as long as you don't play with it, start flirting and talk yourself into a place where you might get tempted beyond your ability to control. I construed the word 'look' to cover this situation, a slippery extension—so I guess that's why I construed 'don't play with it' to mean literally don't play with it." He looked even more sheepish. "There's a chance Ruby might be angry or hurt when I tell her about this, and I guess I wanted to be able to cop a plea if I had to."

"Cop a plea?"

"Sorry. Wanted something to say in mitigation of my offense if necessary. And it might be necessary. I think if Ruby'd been here, we might well have masturbated each other while we watched you. But she isn't. I guess I've got it worked out in my head that if you don't come, you're not being unfaithful. If Ruby's as smart as I think she is, she'll accept the big charge of sexual energy that I'm going to be bringing home as a delightful gift from the gods, and we'll put it to good use together. For which I thank you. Both of you."

I smiled what was probably a pretty fatuous smile and nodded. "Our pleasure."

"You are welcome, Shaker," Rachel said. "And thank you for answering my questions. For trusting me."

"Don't thank me. I don't trust people by conscious choice. It happens, or it doesn't. Do people usually make love in public when you come from, Rachel?"

She started to answer, and then her face smoothed over.

"If I'm crowding some taboo—," Snaker began.

"No, no. It's just that your question doesn't quite translate into meaningful terms. If I take it literally, I cannot answer it, and I'd rather not get into a discussion of why not. But if I analogize its concepts, extrapolate, and translate back into your terms, the answer is, yes, we do."

"*Everyone* does?" I asked.

"Everyone," she assured me solemnly, patting my ass.

It had been a very long time since anyone had patted my ass. I liked it. "Without self-consciousness?"

She looked momentarily puzzled, then smiled. "I've warned you about those multiple-meanings, Sam. The way you mean that term, yes, without self-consciousness. Without shame or fear or guilt or anxiety."

"*When does the next bus leave?*" Maybe I was half kidding. Maybe a quarter.

She smiled again. It was a perfectly ordinary smile, physically identical to the previous one, nothing measurable changed in the placement of lips or eyes or anything I could see; your basic garden variety smile. Somehow it hauled more freight than a smile can carry unassisted. I read in it fear and regret and determination, read them so clearly that I still believed in them when they were totally absent from her voice as she said:

"Never."

Snaker looks down and to the right; I hold a blink for a few extra beats. I held a blink for a few extra beats, and said, "There's no way you can take anybody back with you?"

"Analogizing to make the question meaningful again, no, I cannot. I cannot 'go back' myself in the sense you mean."

This time I held my eyelids shut for a period measurable in seconds. When I opened them again, she still had that smile. "You're telling me that you're stuck here. That you can't go back to when you came from."

"Yes."

"Jesus," the Snaker said.

I was thunderstruck. Energy fought for expression; I wanted to jump up and pace the room. Some instinct made me hug her instead. Some impulse made me gesture to Snaker before her arms locked tight around me. He was there at once, swarmed into our embrace without disturbing it, and we hugged us.

She had come God knew how many hundreds of years—

on a one-way ticket. My opinion of her courage—already high—rose astronomically. And at the same time a little paranoia-voice made a soft *hmm* sound. This woman was in greater psychic stress than I had imagined, was doubtless in need of a great deal of emotional support, represented therefore a potential burden. . . .

Every year you live you learn a little more about yourself. It had been quite a few years since I had learned much of anything I liked.

"Rachel?" Snaker murmured in my ear, in a voice that said I've Just Had A Dreadful Thought.

"Yes, Snaker?"

"In your world—I mean, your time, when/where you came from—"

"My ficton," she said.

"What?"

"Ficton. It is the word for what you mean. I'm surprised—" She interrupted herself with a bark of laughter, and all three of us backed off a few inches.

"What's funny?" I asked.

She hesitated, then smiled. "I was about to say that I was surprised you didn't know the word, since it will be coined less than a decade from now." She gave that single small shout of laughter again, and Snaker and I both chuckled too. Let's face it: time travel makes funny problems. I remembered back to high school Latin when I had thought *I* had had *my* tenses mixed up, and laughed even harder.

A three-way laughing hug is a very nice thing to have had in your life.

But when our giggles subsided, Snaker still had his I've Had A Dreadful voice. "In your ficton, Rachel—"

See now, there again. Just the *damndest* thing. I was looking right at her from point-blank range, and not a muscle twitched in her head, and one minute it was just a smile, and the next it was that other thing that looked like one and was full of pain.

"—do people die?"

Snaker looks down and to the right; I hold a blink; Rachel does nothing at all. She did that for a few seconds. I think I stopped breathing.

"Analogously speaking, of course," Snaker added.

Suddenly, shockingly, moisture appeared in those striking eyes, welled over and spilled down her placid expression. She did not cry; she simply leaked saline water down her face.

"No," she said. "They do not."

"I didn't think they did," Snaker said softly. "But you'll die, now that you've come here, won't you?"

Her voice was nearly inaudible. "Yes, Snaker."

I held that blink a *long* time. When I finally opened my eyes, my pupils had contracted and the dim light that came through double-paned glass and three layers of plastic insulation seemed too bright.

"Rachel," I said very quietly, "let me get this straight. You were an immortal, and you gave it up? For the glorious privilege of inhabiting, for a short while, this wonderful 'ficton' of ours?"

"Yes, Sam."

Loud: "*Why?*"

"Because it needed doing. Because someone had to, and I wanted to the most."

"But—but—" I couldn't make it make sense. "*Why* did it need doing?"

"It became necessary to study this ficton—"

"Wh—"

"—for good and sufficient reasons I will not explain. You lack certain concepts; you lack even the words to form them."

"But for Christ's sake, Rachel—" I was aware that I was becoming furiously angry. I couldn't help it. "What the hell good is your research if you can't bring the data *back*?"

"I can't bring it back—but I can *send* it back."

"You can?" How? With that headband dingus?

"Certainly I can. You can send data to the future the same way, if you want. Give it to me, and I'll bury it in the same place I'm going to bury mine. When the time comes, it will be retrieved."

"Oh." Okay, so it did make sense. It was still stupid. This beautiful warm kind funny strange lady had condemned herself to death, for what seemed to be insufficient reason. Never mind that I and everyone I had ever known or heard of lived under the identical sentence of death. We hadn't chosen it!

"Do you have any idea how long you could live, here and now?" Snaker asked.

"With luck and care, about as long as you, I think. There is no way to be sure."

I rolled over on my back and closed my eyes. "Jesus Christ. That's the stupidest—literally the stupidest thing I've ever heard in my life!"

"Sam—," Snaker began.

"No, I mean it, Snake. I'll concede that anthropology is not worthless, although eighty-five percent of it bores me to my boots and no two anthropologists can agree with each other on the other fifteen. I can imagine, if I strain, someone who would want to be an anothropologist badly enough to kill for it. But have you ever heard of anybody who wanted to be an anthropologist so badly they'd *die* for it? Especially an immortal, who needn't die for *anything*? Who could have saved a great deal of effort and energy by simply consenting to live forever? It's fucking nuts is what it is, Rachel!"

My voice was loud and full of anger, but as I turned from Snaker to Rachel on the last sentence all the steam went out of me. She was scared stiff, trying not to flinch away from me. I had two realizations concurrently. The first was that if I were sojourning in the distant past, chatting with a Neanderthal, and he suddenly began to get loud and angry, I'd be scared silly. The second realization was that, in such a situation, I would certainly have fetched along a weapon for such contingencies, and would be fingering it nervously.

Maybe Rachel was as unarmed as she seemed to me. (Would the Neanderthal have recognized a pistol as a threat?) In the absence of data, it seemed like a good idea, as well as simple politeness to a guest who had just fucked me sweetly, to calm down.

Well, I don't know about you, but I had never had much luck in getting anger to go away once established, just because the rational part of me thought it ought to. Trying usually just made me madder.

And Rachel found the handle. "Why are you angry, Sam?"

Good question: the first step in dealing with anger is to peel away the artichoke layers of rationalization and get to its true root. But it was just such a perfectly North Mountain Hippie thing to say that it made me laugh.

The first four answers to her question that occurred to me I rejected as bullshit. Finally I said, "Rachel, every single thing that human beings do, from making love to looking for cancer-cures, comes from the striving for immortality, the wish to live forever. You had immortality, and threw it away, for what seem to me trivial reasons. That makes all the rest of us look like fools." I snorted and reached down to get the shirt I'd left on the floor. "Everybody wants to be rich and to be loved and to live forever. I've been rich and it wasn't all that great. I've been loved and it wasn't all that great. If living forever isn't worth it, what the hell is the point of life anyway? If you people in the future don't know, who does? I mean hell, you've got unbelievable metabolic control, you wear a computer on your head, somehow I just expected you future folk to be *smart*. And then you come up with a one-way time machine!" I looked down, realized I had put my shirt on without putting on my undershirt first. I took a deep breath and started over, beginning to shiver slightly.

"Current theory in my ficton says that two-way time travel is not possible. The device we used can recycle existing reality, 'reverse the sign' of its entropic direction—

but it cannot explore reality which doesn't exist yet, cannot *create* a future for an entire universe. Too many random elements. At any given moment, any number of futures *may* happen . . . but only one past *has*. If you use the device to send a copy of itself back in time, it arrives with the same limitation."

"But *what was your hurry?* You were fucking immortal! If it'd been me, I'd have talked myself into sitting tight for a while. Maybe in only another five hundred years or so somebody'd come up with a better theory of time travel and build a two-way machine, and *then* I'd make my trip."

"Even for an immortal, Sam, the past keeps *receding*. It took an immense amount of power and scarce resources to send me back this far. Five hundred years later the trip might not be possible at all."

"But why was the game worth the candle? Oh, I understand the value of historical research, but—"

"Every ficton needs to learn from its past. This place-and-time happens to be an especially interesting one. Here and now, on this Mountain, for a brief period, First and Second and Third Wave technology all coexist side by side."

"I don't follow."

That strange bark of laughter again. "Sorry. Again I've used terminology which hasn't quite been invented yet. First Wave technology was the club and the plow, the Agricultural Revolution, things people could make with their hands. The Second Wave you now call the Industrial Revolution, things made in factories. The Third Wave has just begun—"

"The Silicon Revolution!" Snaker said excitedly. "The information economy, solid-state technology—"

"Yes. The coexistence of all three waves is of fascinating historical significance."

I picked up my jeans. "But I don't understand why you had to come study it *in corpus*. Why weren't the usual historical channels—" I looked down and realized that I was putting on my pants before my Stanfields. My second stupid move in less than a minute, and one that was literally freezing my ass, before witnesses; my irritation started to boil over, and I drew in breath for a shouted "DAMMIT!"—

—and before I could release it, a realization came to me, and I understood one of the roots of my anger, and I let that breath go, very slowly and quietly, with a little whistling sound. I shut my eyes for a moment. "Never mind," I said. I took the jeans off, yanked on my Stanfields and both sets of socks. "I think I just figured it out." I stood up and pulled on my jeans. Now that I was nearly dressed, I felt much colder than I had naked. More clothes wouldn't help. The numbing, spreading chill was coming from *inside*. . . .

"What is it, man?" Snaker asked. "What's the matter?"

I looked at Rachel. She said nothing, poker faced as always. "You're as smart as I am, brother. Figure it out. This ought to be the *best* documented age in human history to date. We've got record-keeping even the Romans wouldn't believe. Print. Computer files. Microfilm. Photocopies. Words. Pictures. *Moving* pictures. Sound. Documentaries, surveys, polls, studies, satellite reconnaissance, censi or whatever the plural of 'census' is, newspapers, magazines, film, videotapes, novels, archives, the Library of goddam Congress—this is the best-documented age in the fucking history of the world so far, Snake, and we're living in what has to be its best-documented culture; now you tell me: *why wouldn't Rachel's people have access to all that stuff?* Why would they have to send a kamikaze back to study the place?"

The Snaker's eyes were very wide. He looked at Rachel, and she looked impassively back at him. "Full-scale global thermonuclear war would do it," he said thoughtfully. "Most of our records are stored in perishable form. If civilization fell, they'd rot with the rest of it. Survivors'd be too busy to preserve them. It might be a long time before record-keeping progressed as far as the papyrus scroll again. Trivial details, like who started the war and why, might well be . . . lost to history—" He broke off and turned to me. He touched the breast pocket which held his makings. "Sam?"

I nodded. Ordinarily I didn't allow tobacco smoking in my house. This was a special occasion. Snaker nodded back and began to roll a cigarette with frowning concentration. I watched him in silence while I finished dressing. Usually he rolled his cigarettes sloppily, like joints, but this time he put a lot of attention into pulling and smoothing at the tobacco, trying to produce a perfect cylinder. Soon he had something that looked just like a ready-made. He couldn't get it to stay lit. Rolling tobacco is finer and moister than the stuff they put in ready-mades; packed to the same consistency it won't draw right. Snaker knew that, of course.

I realized that what he was doing was putting on his jeans before he put on his Stanfields. Dithering. In his place I'd have been immensely irritated when I saw what I'd done. He just blinked at the useless cigarette, put it out and began to roll another. In the "night-table" crate on my side of the bed was a pack of Exports my friend Joanie had left behind—Joanie'd just as soon not fuck if she couldn't have a cigarette after—and I tossed it to him. "Fill your boots."

Through all this Rachel sat voiceless and expressionless and splendidly nude, that thin golden band around her head like a slipped halo. I looked at her. As long as I was rummaging in the crate anyway, I got the box of kleenex and tossed it to her.

"What is this for?"

They probably didn't get head-colds when she came from. "Wiping yourself." She still looked puzzled. "Drying your vagina; we just fucked, remember? And you're sitting on my pillow at the moment."

"Oh. Uh, it's not necessary, Sam."

I took a closer look, and she was right. Well, if her metabolism could disperse a whole body-surface worth of perspiration in a matter of seconds, five or ten *cc*s of sperm and seminal fluid probably didn't strain it any. Perhaps they *had* improved sex in the future. It sure simplified contraception.

"Rachel?" Snaker asked, puffing on his smoke. "Is Sam right?"

Her answer was slow in coming. "I . . . can neither confirm nor deny his theory."

"I know I'm right," I said bleakly. I met her eyes. "The human race has been tap dancing on the high wire over Armageddon for thirty years now, and the human race just ain't that graceful. What I want to know is: when? *How soon?*"

"Sam, I cannot—I must not—either confirm or deny what you suggest."

"*Dammit!*" I lowered my voice. "Don't you think we have a right to know?"

"No. You have already accepted the concept that there are certain things about the future I dare not tell you, for fear of causing changes in the past. Can you not see that this is one of those things? If I give you foreknowledge of the future, I risk altering history. If I alter history, even a little, all the civilizations that ever were, all of reality from the Big Bang up to my own ficton, could vanish into nothingness. Nuclear holocaust would be a trivial event by comparison.

"And even if I were *sure* that that would not happen, I would not tell you, whether you were right or wrong. I *like* you, Sam. Have you never skipped ahead to the ending of a book—and then wished you had not, because it spoiled your enjoyment of the story to know how it was going to come out?"

"Rachel's right, Sam," Snaker said. "Suzuki Roshi said you should live each day as if you're going to live forever, *and* as though your boat is about to sink. Knowing the future would make that impossible. If Rachel knew the hour and minute of my own death, I think I might kill her to keep her from telling me. I don't much want to know the hour and minute of my culture's death, either. Come to think of it, I wouldn't want to *know* the reverse, either, that we're safe from nuclear catastrophe and there's really nothing to worry about.

"Which could be true. You make a good case for your theory, Sam, but you don't convince me. There could be other reasons why Rachel's here."

I snorted. "Name two."

"There could be other reasons," he insisted.

"Name one."

"Maybe she needs to study something that can't be squeezed into historical accounts, something we don't think to keep records of. If you're trying to build a global weather model and you need data on day by day weather changes in the Middle Ages, you'll have to go back and get it, because the monks didn't think that information was worth hand-illuminating.

"Or maybe Rachel's people lost the fine distinction between fact and fiction, between history and legend—do you think you know what the Old West was *really* like? You've had a liberal education, you probably know more about the history of Rome than the average Roman citizen did—do you think you have an accurate gestalt of life in the Roman Empire? Are there records of the secret corruption that went on under Caesar's table, the true facts behind the public pronouncements? History is always written by the winning side, Sam, you know that: suppose you wanted to learn something that only the losers could have taught you?"

Rachel was still expressionless, taking in everything, putting out nothing whatsoever. I'd never seen such opacity; I made a mental note not to teach her poker.

"Fine, man," I said. "You believe what you want to believe. I know what logic tells me."

Snaker frowned slightly. "Sam . . . can you give me a reason why your theory is *logically* preferable to mine?"

I said nothing.

"I think *you're* the one who's believing what he wants to believe."

"All right, let's drop it, okay, Snake? You live as if you're going to live forever, and I'll live as if the boat is going to sink in the next ten minutes, and maybe between us we'll make up a sane human being. Meanwhile, we've got other fish to fry."

He accepted the impasse at once. "Right. Rachel needs a cover story."

"And clothes. And a wig."

Snake looked at me as if I had grown an extra nose.

"Snake, you and I like looking at her naked. So would any sensible human being. But in this weather it's bound to cause talk, no? Outdoors at least."

"Agreed. But I don't see the problem. You must have a change of clothes to your name."

He was right. She wasn't that much shorter than me, and on the North Mountain a lady in men's clothes a few sizes too large would draw no comment. Underwear other than Stanfields was optional for either sex in our social set. I had a spare pea coat that was too small for me. Enough socks and she'd fit into my boots. I went to the west end of the room, where a series of mismatched cardboard cartons and a length of rope constituted my closet, and began selecting items for her. "Right. Okay, the other two problems go together: any wig we can buy anywhere closer than Halifax will be a rug, so her cover story has to explain why even a cheap wig is better than—what are you gaping at?" I seemed to have grown a third nose. "Testing. Earth to Snaker. What'd I say?"

His voice was strange. "You pride yourself on being a pretty observant cat, don't you, Sam?"

Baffled, I turned to Rachel. She was poker faced, of course. "Do you know what this burned-out hippie is talk—," I began, and stopped. I held a blink, and then bent down and picked up the clothes I had dropped.

Some changes happen too slowly to perceive. They say there used to be Micmacs on the Mountain who could walk right up to you in broad daylight without being seen, because they could move so preternaturally slowly and smoothly that they failed to trip your motion-detector alarms. All of a sudden there they were in front of you. It's possible to raise the gain on a white-noise signal so slowly from zero that people in the room are actually raising their voices to be heard before they consciously notice the sound.

Rachel had hair.

EIGHT

NOT MUCH HAIR, yet. About two weeks' growth of beard worth, from what I dimly remembered of shaving, and all of that on her scalp. I like to think that even in my distracted condition I would have noticed groin-bristles. It looked like it would grow up to be red and curly—which didn't match her complexion. That was okay. Bad taste in hair colour was easier to explain than baldness.

I felt doubly stupid. First, for missing it at such close quarters (now that I thought back, I *could* recall stubble against my cheek; somehow the sensation had gotten tangled up with thoughts of—I dropped that line of thought hastily.) Second, for being startled when I did twig. First you cure baldness. Then you build time machines.

"Sorry, Snake. I don't know what's wrong with me today."

"I'd say the problem is in your software," he said helpfully.

I ran a hand across the territory that my hairline had surrendered over the last few years (with far too little resistance, I thought), and sighed. "Rachel, if you can teach that trick, you'll be able to buy Canada out of petty cash within a few years."

"I'm sorry, Sam. I can't. It's a stored ROM routine—and you don't have the I/O ports."

I nodded. "I figured."

"How long should I let it get, Sam? I have seen no women of this ficton. Like that?" She pointed to a nearby Beardsley of a woman whose hair would have sufficed to secure a Christmas tree to a VW bug. Snaker and I both cracked up involuntarily, and she caught on at once. "As long as yours, then?"

Mary Travers of Peter, Paul and Mary used to perform with hair shorter than mine was then. Snaker's was longer than mine. "Sure, that'd be fine. Scale your eyebrows and lashes to mine, too. How long will that take you?"

She consulted the inside of her head, or maybe that headband computer. "Another hour, if I hurry."

I poked my tongue out through my lips, bit down on it, and nodded. "I see. I guess that'll be satisfactory." Irony, like puns, was lost on her. "If anybody asks why you never take your headband off, just say it's a yoga." Snaker grinned.

"All right. What does that mean?"

"It means, there is no rational reason why."

Snaker grinned again. "About that cover story," he said.

I shrugged. "Well, given a normal head of hair, the problem becomes trivial, doesn't it? All we have to account for is nosiness and a very slight accent."

"The story must explain my unfamiliarity with local customs," Rachel added.

Snaker and I both shook our heads. "People on the North Mountain are used to newcomers being unsophisticated," I said, "not knowing how to feed a fire or feed chickens or plant a garden or do anything useful. City people are expected to be ignorant; their faux pas are politely ignored. Anything weird you do, folks'll just chalk it up to you being from civilization."

"Then we must explain why I am ignorant of the ways of the city."

"Naw. Nobody'll ask you about them. A city background is treated like a mildly embarrassing disease; folks just pretend not to notice until it's clear that you've been cured. If anybody does ask you about life where you come from, just say, 'I came here to forget about the city,' and they'll nod and mark you down as a sensible young lady. But nobody'll be really interested."

"I think you're a writer, Rachel," Snaker said. "You're doing a book on the Back-to-the-Land movement, or alternative lifestyles, or the rural experience or some such. It's innocuous enough; it'll get you into people's living rooms and get them to open up to you."

"Open up? Hell, she'll be a celebrity, Snake. Remember how popular you were until folks got it straight that you weren't going to write up their memoirs for them? If it's oral histories you want, Rachel, people around here'll talk your ear off, hippies and locals alike."

"Where's she from, Sam?" Snaker asked. "She's dark enough to be African or Far Eastern, but that accent feels more like European to me."

"I'd buy Polynesian raised and educated in Europe. Say, Switzerland. Do you know anything about contemporary Switzerland, Rachel?"

She blinked. "I have some data in ROM. Enough, I think, to deal with surface-level inquiries."

"You won't have to pass a quiz. And nobody on this Mountain knows diddly about Polynesia. Come to think, *I* don't. So you were adopted by a Swiss couple who took you home with them to live. You were going to grad school at S.U.N.Y. Stony Brook, studying . . . let me see, what discipline do we *not* have any refugees from around here? . . . studying sociology, and you dropped out to travel and write a book."

"Why the Stony Brook part?" Snaker asked.

"Well, college student explains the excellent English, the hand-me-down wardrobe, and general weirdness—and Stony Brook is good because I went there, and nobody else on this Mountain has ever been near it. Somebody back there who used to know me told Rachel that there were still a few hippies around up here in Nova Scotia; that's why she came here to research her book. The point is, Rachel, that your cover story doesn't *have* to have a great deal of definition. The vaguer you are, the more you'll ring true. *Lots* of people around here are vague about their backgrounds, for one reason and another. Far more important than where you're from is what you're like."

As I was speaking, I got one last item from a "closet" carton and noticed my old portable cassette recorder at the bottom of the box. A piece of cheese, with one of those built-in cardioid mikes, but it was adequate for spoken-word, ideal for oral history. I wondered if Rachel could use it. Come to think of it, how *did* she plan to preserve her data? What media would survive centuries of burial? Written notes on acid-free paper in sealed atmosphere? Shorthand acid-etched on steel plates? Supershielded computer tapes? Or could she simply store information in her—

—I tabled the matter. She was speaking:

"What exactly do you mean, Sam?" Rachel asked.

"Nothing that need worry you. Whether you're comfortable to be around—and you are. Whether you pull your share of the load—and I'm sure you will. Whether your word is good—and I'm certain yours is."

"Thank you, Sam," she said soberly. "Your trust warms me as much as your lovemaking." She actually blushed. "A great deal."

"Here," I said gruffly, and gave her the clothes. "Try these on for fit and then we'll go downstairs. The decor up here is deafening."

"For you too?" she asked. Here relief and surprise were evident, but I'm damned if I know where. She still had the vocal and facial expressiveness of a female Vulcan.

"Hell, yes. I don't own the place; I just live here while the owner's away. The only way I'd feel okay about revising his decor would be if I were to materially improve the house in the process—say, by properly insulating this upstairs and finishing the walls. So far, I haven't minded the decor quite that much."

She began to dress. It is always a fascinating process to watch. With her, it was riveting. I was a little surprised at how little trouble she had with twentieth-century fastenings like zippers and buttons. She picked things up quickly; she was alert all the time.

"When does the owner return?"

"For longer than a few weeks? Never. Only he hasn't figured that out yet." She raised one eyebrow, so precisely like Star Trek's Mister Spock that I had to suppress a giggle, and I saw Snaker doing the same thing. "Joel's an American hippie with rich parents. He fell in love with this place hitchhiking through, and Dad cabled him the money to buy it. He plans to move up here and 'fix it up' in a couple of years, and he lets me stay here to keep a fire in the place. What he hasn't thought through is that he has at least two drug busts on his record, plus political busts, plus time on the U.S. welfare rolls. He'll never get Landed status. The buyer actually warned him, but Joel's an optimist—"

I'd told this story to several people, I was telling it on automatic pilot—and then all of a sudden I heard the words coming out of my mouth, and froze. Snaker got it too, and looked skyward and frowned at the same time.

"What is 'Landed status'?" Rachel asked innocently.

"Thundering *shit!*" I said, smacking myself in the forehead with my palm. "*Papers!*"

"That does complicate things," Snaker agreed mournfully. "What'll we tell Whynot and Boucher?"

"What is wrong?" she asked.

"Rachel, there are three kinds of people living in Canada. Citizens, Landed Immigrants, and Visitors on temporary visas. The last two kinds need paper ID. Other than for academic purposes or special circumstances, a visitor can stay a maximum of three months, usually much less—and how much is entirely at the whim of the officer on duty at the border crossing you use. A Landed Immigrant, like Snaker and me, can live here indefinitely without relinquishing his original citizenship, and can do everything a citizen can do except vote. It's hard to get that status, gets harder every year, and because a lot of people want to live here on the Mountain without that much formality, the Department of Manpower and Immigration sends a couple of runners through here regular, looking for people who've overstayed their visa. When they find 'em, they very politely and firmly deport 'em. Considering the line of work they're in, Boucher and Whynot are nice guys, but they're very good at what they do. And we can't get you a visa or Landed status, and we can't pass you off as a citizen."

"Shit, Sam, with her color and accent she hasn't got a chance," Snaker said.

She was fully dressed now. I'd been preoccupied enough to miss some of the best parts. Damn. "Couldn't I simply avoid them?" she asked. "There are acres of forest outside. I could avoid even infrared detection methods—"

"Rachel, weird as it may sound, the country is the last place to hide effectively. It is said that if a man farts on the North Mountain, noses wrinkle across the Valley on the South Mountain. You savvy the expression, 'jungle drums'?" She nodded. "Snaker's right: with your beauty, let alone your exotic colouring, you'll be known up and down the whole damn Valley in a week. And once they know you exist, Boucher and Whynot'll find you if they have to get out bloodhounds."

"I can beat bloodhounds too—"

"It's the wrong way to go, Rachel. You can't do your work as a fugitive. That puts us under severe time pressure.

We've got to have some kind of paperwork for you by the time the Bobbsey Twins make their next circuit through the area. When was their last pass, Snake?"

"Around Thaw, if I remember right." Thaw, a brief, inexplicable week of good weather, came each year around the end of January, first week of February. "Not much action for them this time of year, but I'd look to see them again in a month or two, when things start warming up again some. Around Solstice. On the other hand, they love surprises; they could pop in later this afternoon."

"What do we *do*, Snake?" Getting somebody Landed in those days was easy, old hat: simply arrange a bogus marriage to a citizen or Landed Immigrant. It didn't even have to be a good fake; like I said, Whynot and Boucher were easygoing guys. But then citizenship papers for some country of *origin* were essential.

"We're going to need fake papers," he said. "Tricky. I'm not entirely sure how to go about it. I've got a friend in Ottawa I could call—but one thing's for sure: if we can do it at all, it'll be fucking A expensive."

I frowned and nodded. That was certainly a serious problem, all right—

"That's not a serious problem," Rachel said.

We stared at her.

"It was foreseen that it might be useful for me to have local money. My ROM includes certain useful data. Given investment capital and enough lead time, I can generate whatever funds we need."

We said nothing, continued to stare.

She looked mildly embarrassed. "I'm sorry, Sam. Of course you assumed I was destitute. I will pay for the food I eat. Do you want me to pay rent?"

"No, no! I'm not paying Joel a dime, why should you? I'm just kicking myself for being stupid, that's all. Naturally you'd have provided for a simple thing like unlimited funding. Silly of me."

"You're sure you don't want some money? Really, Sam, it'll be no extra trouble for me—"

This conversation was turning surreal. "Rachel, I have enough money to feed my bad habits; more than that is a nuisance. Thanks anyway. But even with plenty of cash, getting you forged papers isn't going to be easy."

Snaker nodded, frowning. "One of the few really backward things about Canada: its civil servants are astonishingly hard to bribe. It can be done, but you need luck and the same kind of tact it takes to negotiate with a Black Panther for his sister's maidenhead. And you said you need lead time to get a bankroll, and the Immigration boys are due in a month or two—I say we've got a time pressure problem."

To my surprise, Rachel refused to be dismayed. "Don't worry, my First Friends. From what you say, this can be dealt with. I am confident that it will not be a problem."

I didn't entirely share her confidence, but I didn't see any point in depressing her by debating the matter, and I was distracted by her honorific. "'First Friends.' I like that."

"Me too," Snaker said.

"You *are* my First Friends," she said. "Every other friend I have, I will not meet for years to come."

"Far out," Snaker said. "I'm proud to be a First Friend of yours."

I mimed clicking my heels and bowed. "And I'm honored to be First Lover. Shall we get out of this pyramid burial chamber?"

We went downstairs. Snaker and I gave Rachel her first lesson in North Mountain survival—the care and feeding of woodstoves. That killed half an hour, even though I'm quite sure she had grasped the essentials within the first few minutes. Anybody who lives with a woodstove can, and will, talk your ear off on the subject, and no two of them completely agree on technique. She listened with polite attention, and probably immense patience. Then she reached out and shut the damper on the Ashley, which I had failed to close after shutting up the stove again, and correctly adjusted the mechanical thermostat, and Snaker and I shut up.

"Can we go outside, please, Sam?" she asked.

"Oh, hell, of course. I should have expected claustrophobia from someone who's comfortable naked in a blizzard."

"It's not claustrophobia as I understand that term," she said. "It's just that I've been in your ficton for nearly a day, and all I've seen are a few seconds of nighttime forest and the inside of your home."

"I understand perfectly. But let's get you dressed for outdoors, just in case anybody happens to drive by." Spare pea coat, scarf, hat and mittens were no problem, but I had to duck back upstairs for enough socks to make my spare boots stay on her.

She watched carefully the whole airlock-like procedure of exiting through the back woodshed. Open hook-and-eye, shoulder inner door open against spring tension, step into shed, let door close, seal with wooden turnbuckle, stand clear of outer door, spin its turnbuckle open, let wind blow door open, step outside, yank door shut and secure with hook-and-eye latch.

"Sam," she said, "your home cannot be locked while you are away."

"Of course not," I said absently. "Suppose somebody came by while I was out? How would they get inside?" I was distracted, and dismayed, by the sight of my woodshed. Snaker had told me, but I had forgotten.

"It's only the one side," he said sympathetically.

Sure enough, the near side of the roof was intact. But even from here I could see that the far side was completely gone, torn free and blown clear. Four cords of drying firewood, representing endless hours of labor, were open to the next snow or rain that came along. "Snake," I said sadly, "tell me it didn't land where I think it did."

"Well, actually," he said brightly, "you got away lucky there. It only demolished the half of the shitter that you weren't using."

"God's teeth." At some point in its twisted history, Heartbreak Hotel had been what it still looked vaguely like, a little red schoolhouse, and so it had a divided four-holer outhouse, two for the boys, two for the girls. (My custom was to use one side at a time and seal up the other, rotating yearly; it kept down the aroma, and provided splendid fertilizer for the garden and the dope patch.) Snaker was right, I'd had a lucky break. Exposed firewood had to be dealt with soon, but a sheltered place to shit is a *necessity*. (Especially when company comes to stay; it's easier to share a toothbrush than a thundermug.) But I didn't *feel* lucky.

My pal sought to distract me. "I see it was a Gable roof."

I regarded him suspiciously. "I sense danger. What prompts this observation, Mr. Bones?"

He shrugged. "Gone with the wind."

I fell down laughing. So did he. We needed a good laugh. "Only to windward," I managed. "Looks fine over here on the Vivien Leigh side," and we were off again.

I realized that we must have left Rachel far behind, and looked around to apologize—and found that she had left us far behind. She was nowhere in sight; her footprints led around the house. Snaker and I sobered quickly and followed her tracks, worried about God knows what.

We found her at once—

—transfixed, banjaxed, struck dumb and frozen in her tracks—

—by the sight of the Bay of Fundy. . . .

Perhaps I felt more true *kinship* with Rachel in that moment than I had while we were making love. Until now she had been always a little off-beat, a little alien, a stranger in a strange land. But this we shared. For the first time I felt that I truly empathized with her, understood what she was feeling. I remembered my own first sight of the Bay, coming from a city background—and how much more overpopulated must her world be than mine?

The first thing that had surprised me about nature, when first I made its acquaintance, was how *big* it was. I learned this first with my eyes, and then, almost at once, with my ears, and finally with the surface of my skin. In the city, where I grew up, my visual and auditory autopilots had a scan range of a couple of hundred meters at most. Visual stimuli farther away than that tended to be filtered out, unless they met certain alarm parameters. Similarly, my ears were usually presented with such a plethora of nearby stimuli that a gunshot over on the next block might have gone unheard.

Then I came to Parsons' Cove, and stood on the shore of the Bay of Fundy. Suddenly half of my universe was sky, more sky than I had known existed. In one direction an infinite series of trees climbed up the gentle slope of the North Mountain; in the other, my eye had to leap fifty kilometers to the far shore of New Brunswick. If I stood still and listened, I could clearly hear living things kilometers away. My world expanded to encompass a larger hemisphere—all of it beautiful.

It blindsided me. I have not recovered yet. Perhaps I never will.

Snaker and I looked at each other and shared a wordless communication and smiled. The best part of that first glorious and terrifying moment when you fall in love with the Fundy Shore is that it will never really wear off. Even constant exposure doesn't build much tolerance. Remarkably sane people live along that Shore. It's really hard to generate an anger or a fear or other craziness that will survive an hour of looking at the Bay, at all that immense sky and majestic water—and *sunset* on the Bay has been known to alleviate clinical psychosis.

Suddenly I was startled to realize how soon sunset was going to be.

"Jesus, Snaker, look at the sun!" I whispered, trying not to distract Rachel.

"Well, I'll be prepped for surgery. Where the hell did the time go?" he answered as quietly.

I replayed the day in my mind, oddly disturbed. The three of us had adjourned upstairs to my bedroom just after noon; I'd noted the time. Flatter myself and assume the sex had lasted half an hour; add an hour for chatter, half an hour for Snaker and me to argue about stove lore. It should be two o'clock—three at the outside. But the sun said it was five or later.

To city folk, this may seem trivial. But if you've ever lived without electricity, you know how you get pretty good at keeping track of how much working light is left, just like you get good at keeping track of which stoves were fed how long ago. A malfunction in one of those internal clocks can be serious business. (It's ironic to recall that when I first came to the Mountain, I thought country folk were *less* time-bound than city folk because they seldom checked a wristwatch or clock before doing something.)

"I always said you grow terrific reefer," Snaker murmured.

"I guess so! The whole day's shot to shit, and we're late starting supper."

"Fuck supper, and fuck the day. Let's bring Rachel over to the Hill and introduce her around; there'll be plenty of food there."

"Vegetarian food. Thanks."

"Ruby's making chili today."

"Oh. That's different. Still, man, isn't that rushing things? Is she ready to take on your whole crazy crew? I think we ought to fill her in a bit, give her a few books to read—"

Rachel turned and interrupted us. "I'm eager to meet Snaker's family. Can you leave now?"

I blinked. "Sure. Let me get my guitar."

NINE

BLUE MEANIE HAULED the three of us east from Parsons' Cove, lurching like a drunk, engine coughing up blood and transmission shrieking, as though the aged truck knew that ahead, on the unpaved Wellington Road, axle-shattering potholes lay in wait for it, grinning.

The journey itself might have been adventure enough for anyone used to methods of travel more civilized than, say, buckboard—but Rachel had no time to appreciate it (or, more likely, be terrified by it), because Snaker and I talked nonstop the whole trip, trying to prepare her for the Sunrise Hill Gang. It would have been difficult enough to "explain" the Sunrise crowd to a normal human being of my own place and time—but Rachel didn't even know what a hippie was, let alone a die-hard hippie. She seemed barely familiar with the Viet Nam war. We needed every minute of the ten-minute drive to brief her.

"How many are in your family?" Rachel asked.

Snaker frowned and caressed the steering wheel with his thumbs. "I knew this wasn't going to be easy. Uh, at the moment there are six or seven of us around, what you might call the hard core—as soon as winter comes down, a lot of folks find pressing spiritual or other reasons to be somewhere warmer. But as to how many of us there are altogether . . . well, I'm not sure anyone's ever counted, and I'm not sure an accurate count is possible."

Rachel said nothing.

"Last summer we had as many as thirty, and I guess it averages about fifteen or so. If it helps any, there are a dozen or so names on the land deed. But half of *those* folks have gone, with no plans to come back."

"They decided to go for an actual deed, eh?" I said.

"When they saw the size of the stack of paperwork for a land trust, yeah," Snaker said.

Rachel looked politely puzzled.

"You see," Snaker tried to explain, "some of the Gang don't hold with the concept of owning land—"

Now Rachel looked baffled. Well, it baffled me too.

"—but they finally got it through their heads that if they don't own the land, somebody else will."

She dropped the matter. "Tell me about the six or seven now present."

Snaker looked relieved to be back on solid ground. "Well, there's Ruby, of course—you might want to grab a handhold here—"

All at once he *wasn't* on solid ground. We had come to the Haskell Hollow. It is an amusing little road configuration. Around a blind left curve, without any warning, the road suddenly drops almost vertically for five hundred meters, yanks sharp right, rises almost vertically for another five hundred meters, and swings hard right again. Snaker took it at his usual eighty kph.

"—and you'll really like her; she's a painter and fucking good; she has brown hair and unbelievable eyes; she thinks she's too fat but she's full of shit—"

The proper way to run the Hollow was to start accelerating *hard* about two thirds of the way down the cliff. The man who lived at the bottom made a fair dollar renting out his tractor to tourists and other virgins who chickened out and, in the hairpin turn at the bottom, lost the momentum necessary to make the upgrade. Of course, the transit was trickier on poorly ploughed snow. Blue Meanie roared in berserker fury and went for it. Rachel could have been forgiven for dampening her (my) pants at any time during the episode—but she took her cue from Snaker and me, grabbed handholds but stayed calm.

"—and she's the best cook in the place, by a damnsight. Then there's Malachi: he and Ruby used to be together once; now he lives with Sally from the Valley—"

He yanked the wheel round with both hands (the Meanie predated power steering) and popped the clutch about fifty meters from the bottom. We skidded into proper orientation for the upcoming turn-and-climb, and he had correctly solved the equation of friction and time and distance: the wheels grabbed, hard, just as we were reaching the nadir. (Snaker maintained that since that was the place where motorists tended to throw up, it should be called the Ralph Nadir.) Every component of the truck capable of making noise did so to the best of its ability; Snaker raised his voice.

"—he's big and black-haired and half-bald; carpenter and electrician; weird as a fish's underwear—he'll be the one with the eyes—"

The rear end threatened to go. Literally standing up on the throttle now, Snaker slammed his ass down on the seat and back up again, and Blue Meanie shrieked and settled down to the climb.

"—Sally's got long straight yellow hair, gray eyes; moves kinda slow and doesn't say much but she's in there; then there's Tommy, Malachi's older sister; doesn't look a bit like him, curly red hair, wiry and fiery, tiny woman but tougher'n pumpleather; she's far out. Lucas, he's sort of the resident spiritual masochist, salivates at the mention of the word 'discipline'; but he's one of the *decentest* people I ever met; brown hair and reddish beard; real handsome."

We'd begun the climb at perhaps 120 kph. We covered the last fifty meters to the summit at a speed that the speedometer claimed was zero, slowing even further for the curve. Then we were back on level road, entering the fishing village of Smithton.

"Then of course there's the Nazz. One of the craziest and most delightful cats I ever met in my life, a man who has clearly taken too much acid and is the better for it; a stone madman; you never know what he'll do next except that he'll be smiling while he does it and you'll be smiling when he's done. Curly black hair and beard, both completely out of control. He's named after an old Lord Buckley rap about Jesus—the *Nazz*-arene, dig it?—and it suits him."

That is how long it took us to completely traverse Smithton. At the posted speed limit of 30 kph. Then Snaker accelerated sharply and took the right onto the Mountain Road in a spray of gravel. The slope is nowhere near as sharp as the back leg of the Haskell Hollow, but it goes on forever, and in snow season better vehicles than the Meanie have had to give up halfway, slide back down backwards and take a second run at it. Snaker went for it.

"Rachel," I asked, "is any of this getting through?"

"Some. Most of it, I think."

"I'm surprised. He's been speaking Hippie."

"Somehow when Snaker uses idiom or colloquialism, I take his meaning more often than not."

"Far out," he said apologetically. "Sorry, Rachel, I wasn't thinking." He grinned. "When I first moved in with Ruby, my first day at the Hill, Malachi dropped by in the afternoon just after we'd finished making love, to talk something over with her. Damned if I know what it was. A few minutes before I'd been certain that Ruby and I were, like, totally telepathic for life—and then she and Malachi started talking, and I did not understand a single thing they said. They were using what sounded like English words, but

I couldn't even grasp the general shape of the conversation, much less follow it. And remember, I was already fluent in Hippie . . . city Hippie, anyway. Uh, I'll ask people to try and stick to Standard English—shit—" He had lost the battle to keep the Meanie out of first gear.

"No, Snaker. Immersion is the best way to master a dialect. If I need an explanation, I'll ask for one."

"Don't be afraid to ask for one with others around," I said. "As an exchange student, you won't be expected to speak Hippie."

She nodded. "Can you give me a primer?"

So we did our best to outfit her with basic vocabulary. Dig, into, trip, groove, cool, out of sight, righteous, stoned, spaced out, holding a stash, copping, manifesting, agreement, yoga, freak out, and of course, the ubiquitous far out (an acceptable comment in any situation whatsoever). Since all of these terms had multiple (often contradictory) meanings, depending on context, tone of voice, and the daily Dow-Jones average, I could not be certain we were accomplishing anything, but she kept nodding. Blue Meanie kept swapping up hill momentum for engine noise, which didn't make it any easier.

Two thirds of the way up the north slope of the Mountain, we came to the Wellington Road. Snaker took the turn from half-plowed uphill pavement to level but unplowed dirt road with gusto, throwing Rachel hard against me. As Blue Meanie began to roar in triumph and gather speed, he coaxed the wretched thing into second gear and accelerated sharply; the wheels bit just in time to keep us out of the substantial drainage ditch on my side of the road. "As for the physical plant," he said mildly in the sudden comparative quiet, "we've got three and a half houses on either end of a big parcel of land, about a hundred acres altogether." He took it up to 70 klicks (about 45 mph) and held it there. He raised his voice again. "We'll come to the Holler first, stop and see if anybody wants a ride to dinner. Then we'll go on to Sunrise Hill, to the Big House, and you can meet Ruby."

"I look forward to meeting her," Rachel called back.

The engine noise was less now, but the unpaved road was a washboard rollercoaster and the truck a giant maraca. The net effect was noisier than the desperate uphill run had been, except for the relatively calm intervals when we were on an ice-slick and flying free. Every so often a pothole the size of a desk tried to shatter the driveshaft and axles, or failing that, our spines. "Sorry if this makes you nervous, Rachel," Snaker said, "but you can't drive this road slow in winter, or you get stuck."

"That would be bad," she agreed, straight-faced. "Is there anything else I should know, to be a proper guest? Local customs or manners?"

I was impressed by her control and courage. This kind of transportation had to be a nightmare for her, and all her attention seemed to be on the coming social challenge.

Snaker looked at me. "Sam, what do you think the Gang would consider excessively weird behavior in a guest?"

I thought about some of the people I'd seen come and go at the Hill. "Gunfire. Personal violence. Arson."

"There you go. Rachel, we're all pretty weird ourselves, by contemporary standards. It's made us kind of tolerant."

"Of outsiders," I added.

He nodded reluctantly. "Yeah. Among ourselves we sometimes get kind of conservative. But visitors are welcome to do pretty much as they please. As long as they respect our right to be weird, we'll respect theirs."

I couldn't let that pass. "Aw, come on, Snake. Tolerate, yes, but respect?"

Snaker started to answer, then closed his mouth. Rachel looked back and forth at the two of us, settled on me.

So I said, "The Sunrise Hill Gang have this thing about honesty and truth, Rachel. As defined by them. To be fair, they don't lay it on strangers too much—but what it comes down to is, the longer you hang around them, the friendlier you get with them, the more they feel that they have the right to . . . well, to get into your thing." I paused. How to explain that concept? To anyone, much less a time traveler? "To ask you extremely personal questions, and criticize your answers. To question your behaviour and beliefs. Sometimes they can get pretty aggressive about it." I looked over at Snaker again, met his eyes. "I'll concede that their intentions are good—but I find them hard to take sometimes. Malachi in particular has a gift for figuring out just what topics of conversation will make you most uncomfortable, and then dwelling on them, in the friendliest, most infuriating manner imaginable. He so obviously genuinely sincerely wants to help you—whether you want help or not—that you can't even manage to dislike him for it. And that makes me want to punch him. Especially when the rest of the group gets the scent of blood and joins in."

I glanced to Snaker to see if he wanted to rebut. He frowned. "I've seen him straighten a lot of people, Sam. I'm not saying I find him easy to take, myself. There's a lot of stash between us because of Ruby. But I have to admit he's good with hangups. He's got the instinct of a good shrink. Uh, sorry, Rachel, a good psychiatrist. You savvy 'psychiatrist'?"

"Oh, yes."

"But he doesn't have the *training* of a good psychiatrist," I insisted, "or any kind of license to lead group-therapy practice on non-volunteers. Why I'm bringing this up, Rachel, is to warn you to be careful around Malachi. You've got a lot to hide, and evasive answers make his ears grow points. The man has industrial-strength intuition."

Snaker frowned even deeper. "I can't disagree. Malachi demands a pretty high truth level around him. If he gives you trouble, Rachel, I'll handle him."

"Does it bother *you* to conceal truth from your family, Snaker?" she asked.

"No," he answered at once. "I place high value on truth myself—but there are higher goods that can take precedence sometimes. That's where I part company with most of the rest of the Gang."

"What takes precedence over the truth?" she asked.

"Duty, sometimes. And compassion always wins if there's a tie. Also preservation of self or loved ones, I guess. I'd lie to save Ruby if I had to."

She touched his near arm. "Does it bother you to lie to Ruby?"

He began to answer, then exhaled through his nose and started again. "Yes. But I can handle it. I really do understand the stakes, Rachel: the continued existence of reality. Like I said, I'd lie to save Ruby—even lie to Ruby herself."

It was beginning to dawn on me that I had screwed up. "I'm sorry, Snake."

"For what, man?"

"I've put you in a difficult position by sharing Rachel's secret with you. And it turns out it wasn't even necessary."

"So how could you know that? You were protecting yourself the best way you knew how against a reasonable presumption of danger. I'd have done the same in your shoes. Besides, can you imagine how stupid I'd feel if there was a time traveler on the Mountain and *I didn't know it?* Don't answer, I know that doesn't make sense." He grinned. "But I'm glad you told me."

What could I do but grin back?

"Yonder comes the Holler," he told Rachel, down-shifting.

I glanced at her, realized how beautiful she was . . . and a sudden thought occurred to me. "Whistling Jesus—I nearly forgot. Rachel: stop growing your hair!" I don't know if she'd forgotten; she just nodded. Her hair, an uncombed sprawl of chestnut curls, was now short for a Hippie, but long for a straight person; it covered all of her golden headband except the span across her forehead. Brows and lashes were appropriate.

The road ahead sloped down gradually, ran over a

culvert, and swung left to disappear behind the trees. Just past the culvert and before the curve, Snaker snapped the wheel to the left and locked the brakes. The Meanie spun off the road to the left, rotating as it went, and came to rest, nose out, precisely in the truck-sized carpark that had been shoveled out for it, its rear wheels nestled right up against the log barrier. He put the engine out of its misery and we got out. I watched, and Rachel's legs were steady. Perhaps her time had even more hair-raising modes of transit. But I felt she had simply decided to trust Snaker before getting into the truck, and then thought no more about it.

"It's very peaceful here," she said, looking around her. There was nothing much to see except a mailbox with no name on it and a lot of snowcapped maple and birch trees and a rough path winding away downhill among them.

"It's very peaceful anywhere that truck is not running," I said.

She shook her head. "I mean more than ambient soundlevel," she said. "It is *peaceful* here."

Snaker smiled broadly. "I know what you mean," he said. "It got to me too, my first time here. Tranquility. Wait'll you see the Tree House."

And at that there was a loud explosion as Blue Meanie's left front tire blew up, followed by a diminishing cascade of metallic groans as the noble old truck went down on one knee.

No, Rachel's bravery was neither ignorance nor faith in Snaker. He and I both jumped a foot in the air, and he certainly went white as a ghost and I probably did likewise as the implications sank in . . . and then we saw each other's expressions, and fell down laughing in the snow. But I was watching her when the tire let go, and here is what I saw. The instant the report sounded behind her she was in motion—but almost as the motion registered on my eyes it changed. One microsecond, she was crouching and spinning with unbelievable speed; the next, she had aborted the crouch and was simply turning toward the sound at normal human speed. The change came, I was sure, before she had turned far enough to have the truck in her visual field. She had to have deduced what the bang must be, and then come down off Red Alert, in a shaved instant. In her place, I'd probably have panicked; it seemed to me that someone who had grown up expecting to live centuries barring accidents would be *very* afraid of sudden loud noises.

But I didn't think much about this at the time. I was busy rolling in the snow and howling with laughter. It did not occur to me to wonder *how* she had deduced the source of the noise.

"'Tranquility,'" Snaker whooped. "Oh, my stars!"

"'Such peace,'" I agreed, flinging handfuls of snow in his direction.

An inquiring hoot came distantly up through the woods. Still giggling, Snaker and I helped each other to our feet and brushed snow from ourselves, and Snaker hooted back reassuringly.

The North Mountain Hoot is a rising falsetto *"Wuh!"* that carries a kilometer or two in the woods, and you can pack a surprising amount of information into its intonation and pitch. The hail meant "Hello," and "Are you all right?" and "Do you need help?", and Snaker's answer meant "Everything's cool," and "I'll be right there," and "I'm bringing company."

He went to Rachel and took her hands. "So long as you're with Snaker O'Malley," he said in a fake Irish brogue, "no harm can come to you."

"But it'll sure God bark outside your door a bit," I said, still grinning. "Well, what do you say, Snake? Fix the tire now, or come back with help?"

He looked sheepish. "Well, see, it doesn't even matter that we don't have a jack—"

"God's teeth." I could guess what was coming.

"—on account of we don't have a spare either."

"Shitfire." I thought it over. "Rachel, our options have

narrowed. We either walk a few miles in the snow tonight, or we crash here. Pardon me: 'crash' meaning 'sleep' in Hippie, not the literal meaning. Do you have a preference?"

"Not yet."

"Let me know if you decide you need to split."

An odd thing happened. This was not the first time I had absently used a Hippie term she could not be expected to know—but it was the first time she seemed to get angry about it. Her eyes flashed. Then, in an instant, she cut loose of it. "'Split' means 'to leave'?"

"Sorry. Yeah. If you want to split, slip me a wink when no one's looking and I'll extricate us. You savvy 'wink'?"

She winked. I fought the impulse to grin. Can you imagine Mister Spock tipping you a wink? "Good."

We set off downhill along the twisting path. It was not shoveled, of course, but there were enough prior footprints to let us negotiate it with minimal difficulty. Before long we came to the Gingerbread House. I was not surprised that it wrung an actual smile from Rachel.

Picture the Gingerbread House that Hansel and Gretel found. Now alter it slightly to reflect the fact that it is constructed—brilliantly if eccentrically—out of the remnants of a hundred-year-old chicken coop plus whatever came to hand. Malachi ceremonially destroyed his T-square and plumb bob before beginning construction. There isn't a right angle in the structure. Every single board had to be measured and handcut. There are nutball cupolas and diamond-shaped windows and a round door. No two shingles are the same size and shape. The first time I saw the G.H. I thought of Bilbo Baggins.

But no one was inside at the moment, so we kept following the path downhill and took the first left. Now the path was *really* downhill. Rachel, in unfamiliar boots, kept her footing expertly despite the large roots that lurked beneath the snow. It didn't seem likely that the skills of woodscraft could still exist in her ficton; I decided she was just naturally graceful.

We came to the bottom, to the stream. It's not a big stream. At full run, as now, you could have crossed it in three long strides and got wet to the knees; in summer it sometimes disappeared for days at a time, leaving small dwindling pools full of frantic fish. But it had pervasive magic about it. Its murmuring chuckle permeated everything, pleasing the ear in some subconscious way, conveying a kind of low-level ozone high.

A footbridge spanned the stream and the path continued downstream to our right. But we stopped on the nearside and faced left, to give Rachel—and ourselves—a chance to dig the waterfall. Snaker lit a pre-rolled cigarette, and smoked it like it was a sacrament, blowing smoke to the four winds Indian-style.

It was not a Niagara-type straight-drop waterfall, but a gradual cascade. A stepped escarpment of shattered rock turned the stream into a hundred little waterfalls by which it dropped maybe twenty meters in the space of five. White water for three mice in a boat. At the bottom it regrouped and rushed off downstream to the sea. It wasn't really much noisier than the rest of the stream, just more treble-y. It was prettier than hell, primevally delightful.

Like the Fundy Shore, that waterfall was the kind of place that could ground you spiritually, lend perspective, bring your rushing thoughts to a temporary halt and allow you to take stock. I breathed deeply through my nose, absently walking in place to keep my feet warm, and reflected that my friend the science-fiction-writing hippie and I were bringing a time traveler to Sunrise Hill for dinner. The three of us were sitting on what might very well be the deadliest secret that had ever existed, and we were about to introduce her, after fifteen minutes' briefing, to the *nosiest* customers to be found anywhere in the Annapolis Valley. I had not thought this through.

It would be irony even beneath God's usual standards if it turned out that all of reality, every last human hope and aspiration, were to be destroyed by the passion of a bunch of die-hard hippies for truth.

Fuck it. *If that is the final punchline,* I told myself, *then let's get to it.* "Let's go. It's getting late."

Snaker looked around and nodded. Back up in the real world the sun had not yet quite set, but down here in the Holler it was already getting dark. "Right on," he agreed.

And we tried to explain to Rachel what "right on" meant as we walked downstream to the Tree House.

TEN

I DESPAIR OF describing the Tree House. You have nothing to compare it to. The Gingerbread House was an eccentric enough structure, but the Tree House made it look like a Levitt tract home.

It was never designed; it simply occurred. Over a period of three years or so, five or ten talented and twisted minds had, with no plan and little consultation, simply done whatever stoned them, as materials or tools or willing labour became available, or as their individual spirits moved them. If a contribution by one of them foiled another's plan, he looked upon it as a *bonsai* challenge and rethought his concept. Three of these minds belonged to expert carpenters, one of them world class. Another co-creator couldn't have driven a nail if it had automatic transmission. The taste of all of them differed widely but not sharply. As near as I can see, the only thing they all had in common was that each carefully considered the effect his efforts would have on the tree.

A man Snaker's height could have just managed to walk underneath the house upright with a top hat on his head, though there were substantial areas where he could have safely used a trampoline. (Of *course* the main floor was not level. What fun would that have been to build?) Above the more-or-less first floor the house bisected. Two asymmetrical structures wound up into different parts of the mighty rock maple tree: a substantial section of two additional stories, and a slimmer but taller one that had a tiny fourth-floor meditation chamber. One could travel between the two third-floors by stepping up onto a window ledge and swinging across on a rope. There was strategically placed hand- and footholds on the intervening tree trunk in case of screwups, and the drop of the roof below was not severe.

The tree itself was magnificent. It continued on up another fifteen or twenty meters above the highest point of the House, its two mighty arms in the attitude of a man caught yawning. There was not another tree that size in the Holler, and I'll never understand why the loggers passed it over decades ago. Just possibly they had a sense of poetry in them somewhere.

A tree has always seemed to me a sensible place to keep a house. You don't think so? Consider: in the winter you have plenty of sunshine, in summer plenty of shade. You have partial protection from rain and snow. There is never any standing water in the basement. When it's summer and the windows are open, birds wander in and out, cleaning the kitchen floor. In winter, it takes one holy *hell* of a snowdrift to block your door. And you can haul up the gangplank if you want . . .

I watched Rachel as we approached the Tree House. It's always interesting to catch people's first reactions to it. She had not commented on the Gingerbread House; perhaps "odd" and "quaint" and "funky" were not concepts that traveled well across the centuries. But I was willing to bet that any denizen of any human culture would find the Tree House striking.

I was not disappointed. Her jaw did not actually drop, of course. She stopped walking and her nostrils flared. She raised first her right eyebrow, then her left, and stared at the place for a long twenty seconds. Snaker and I left her alone with it. Finally she smiled. It was the broadest, happiest smile I had seen yet on her face.

She turned to us, her eyes shining. "Thank you, my First Friends. This is a good place."

We smiled at her, and then at each other, and then at her again. Snaker took a last puff on his smoke and put it out. We moved on.

When we were close, Tommy's voice rose faintly above the rushing streamsound. She was singing that John Prine song about blowing up your TV. As we passed between pilings and under the House, it emitted a man. Well, part of one. The cellar door dropped open suddenly and I was looking right into the merry eyes of the Nazz, no less unmistakable for being upside down, from a distance of perhaps twenty centimeters. He was grinning hugely. (In future, unless I say otherwise, assume Nazz is *always* grinning hugely.)

"Visual interface," he told me joyously.

I couldn't argue.

"Excuse me," he said. One arm emerged from the house, carrying a long peavey. He reached down with it and opened the hatch of the root cellar by our feet. Then most of his torso emerged from the House; he made a long stretch and came up with a bag of turnips on the end of the peavey. He removed half a dozen or so, tossing them back over his head, up and into the house. "Gotta soak overnight." He dropped the sack back down into the root cellar, tipped the lid shut, sealed the anticritter latch, and hauled himself partway back up so that he was at eye level with me again. "Pictorial, really. Evolved versus learned, right? Self-evident. Groks itself! Completely new operating system."

The house reabsorbed him, with a sound exactly like the one Farfel the dog used to make at the end of the word "cha-a-w—clate" in the Nestlé's commercials.

Snaker and I looked at Rachel. She looked at us. We resumed walking. The Nazz reappeared briefly behind us, said, "Hello, pretty lady," and was gone again before we could turn.

There are several ways into the Tree House, but we took the elevator. It's a simple open-air affair. You haul yourself up on a good block-and-tackle. We got on, I put my hands to the rope, and feeling faintly silly as always, joined Snaker in the ritual shout that politeness demanded.

"Umgawa!"

And we hauled away, as the shout echoed through the Holler.

Okay, it's dopey. When in Rome, you shoot off Roman candles. To an inhabitant of the Tree House, that shout means, "A fellow hippie is here." Rachel made no comment.

We stepped off onto the porch, whacked snow from our pants, scraped and kicked it from our boots, untied our laces and entered through the keyhole-shaped door. Snaker and I each took an armload of wood in with us from the stack on the porch, and Rachel followed our example. Just inside the door we stepped out of our boots. There was welcome warmth, good smells of maple syrup and woodsmoke and reefer, the sound of crackling fires.

From the cheaply carpeted living room I could see Tommy working in the kitchen. She was cleaning the sap taps. There are eight set into the living wood of the kitchen wall, hoses running in parallel to a boiling pot on the stove. At the end of a day's run it's a good idea to wash out the hoses.

She turned and saw us through the kitchen doorway. "Howdy," she called. "Far out—good to see you, Sam. Be right there."

We added our firewood to the box by the living room

stove, standing a few of the more snow-soaked sticks on end of the front of the battered old Franklin to dry. Rachel examined the room. It was furnished in Rural Hippie. Kerosene lamps. Candles. Psychedelic posters. Several mandalas. Macramé. Plants. An enormous and functional brass narghile with four mouthpieces. Cushions. Cable-drum tables. A superb old rocking chair painted paisley. Zen epigrams printed on the walls here and there. An arresting painting of Ruby's, a portrait of Malachi. A wrinkled print of Stephen Gaskin leading Monday Night Class at the Family Dog. A hand-sewn sampler depicting a field of daisies and bluebells surmounted by the legend: **flowers eat shit.** Along one wall a shelf was lined with paperbacks that all concerned cosmic consciousness and how to achieve or sustain it.

Tommy came in, wiping her hands on her shirt. "Hi," she said to Snaker and me, and then a separate, friendly "Hi," to Rachel. "What's happening, guys?" she went on. "Was that one of them damn hunters again? We thought maybe y'all got shot for a moose."

(The Sunrise Hill Gang don't seem to have the custom of introductions. A newcomer is welcome to introduce herself, or not, as suits her. If she chooses to wait a bit, perhaps pick a name that's not being used already, that's her business.)

"Naw," Snaker said. "It was Blue Meanie throwing a shoe."

"Far out," she said, grimacing sympathetically. "Looks like it was a good landing; you walked away. Is it in the ditch?"

"Happened just as we were slamming the doors, thank you Buddha."

"Wow. That's *far out.*" Her eyes sparkled. "What a trip."

"Tire's a total, no spare, so I guess we hike to dinner."

She shrugged, a gesture that thrust her chin out and flounced her red curls. "Far out. I don't know if I'm into dinner—"

"Ruby's making chili."

"Hey, Nazz! Quit doodlin' and get your coat. Ruby's making chili tonight!"

The Nazz's bushy head appeared around the kitchen doorway. "Out of state," he called. "Just a third." When Nazz uses clichés they come out all wrong. He doesn't do it to be cute, it's just a mental short circuit.

Tommy was already half-dressed for outdoors. "Did you bring your guitar, Sam?"

"Left her in the truck."

"I'll help you carry it if Snaker'll take my flute. You look real cute with your hair short like that, hon—I think I might try that myself."

When two women meet, they size each other up. It's not necessarily a competitive thing. They just take each other's measure. Men do it too, but they do it differently, and I'm not sure how it's different. Women seem to take a little longer. They don't rely as much on sight, but I don't know what they use in its place.

"It will look very good on you," Rachel said, and I knew they were going to be friends.

Which was nice, because Tommy weirded out a lot of women, particularly ones as emphatically feminine as Rachel. Even with her long and curly red hair, Tommy could easily have passed for a teenaged boy; her flat-chested hipless body, her manner right in with a construction crew. She was by no means a lesbian. She was the only true neuter human I've ever known. She had absolutely no sex drive whatsoever, and by that point in her life, her mid-thirties, she had long since given up pretending—or minding. She told me about it the night I made my pass. No physiological dysfunction, no horrid childhood trauma—she simply wasn't interested. She was quite capable of orgasm—an experience she likened to a sneeze, both in intensity and desirability. She was baffled and amused by the importance everyone placed on it, convinced that it was enormously overpriced at best.

This placed a certain basic gulf between her and many other women—not to mention many men. City-folk in particular, sex-charged to the point of frenzy by media hype, frequently resented her. But Rachel seemed to take to her instantly, and Tommy, once she was sure it was genuine, responded.

(I was slowly getting it through my head that Rachel was not what I thought of as "city-people," that in spite of the logic of a million science fiction stories, the future was not necessarily going to urbanize to the point of inhumanity. Whatever it was like when she came from, they were still flexible and tolerant—which city folk, in my experience, were not. Including myself when I first came up here.)

The Nazz came bustling into the room, beaming and brandishing computer paper. Lord Buckley once said of his namesake, the carpenter-kitty from Bethlehem:

Nazz had them pretty eyes. He wanted everybody to see out his eyes so they could see how pretty it was.

and it suited this Nazz as well. He sweetened the climate where he was at. He waved two sheets of computer paper at us. "It just now came to me," he said. "Check 'em out." He handed me one. "Find a letter that was sent to Hewlett-Packard on February 18."

I looked at the sheet. It was a printed list of about fifty computer files, displaying title, type of file, date of creation, lost modification and size in bytes, arranged alphabetically by title. I ran my eye down the list: there were ten files with "Hewlett-Packard" or "HP" in their title, six of those were letters, the second from the bottom was dated "18 Feb."

"Right here," I said, pointing.

"Four point nine seconds," Nazz announced happily, looking up from a stopwatch. "Gravy. Here. Find it again." He handed me the second sheet.

I blinked at it. It was hand-drawn. The same approximate

number of files were represented—by arrays of little pictures in groups, with meticulously printed labels beneath each. Little three-ring binders indicated reports; little tear-sheets were article extracts; the little envelopes were obviously letters. My eye went to them at once. Beneath the pictures were names; "HP 18F" leaped up at me. "There," I said.

"One point eight. Sixty-three percent faster. Far fuckin' up."

"Visual interface," Snaker said wonderingly. "Pictorial, really."

"Hard on," Nazz agreed. "See, the ability of the brain to interpret *text* is learned behavior, no older than the pyramids. But the brain has been interpreting *pictures* from *in front*. Much older circuitry, much faster traffic-flow, much more information-density. It's why movies kill books. Your face and breasts are extremely beautiful."

This last, obviously, was to Rachel. She was not at all taken aback. "Your hands and mind are extremely beautiful," she said.

They smiled at each other. Two more friends.

"Let's go eat," I said. I was starving.

"Remind me to call Palo Alto when we get to the Hill," Nazz said. "Couple of guys I want to mention this to. Less intimidating than a bunch of text in the damn ugly computer font; it's *friendlier*. Need a whole new language, though, and one of those new eight-bit chips—"

"Christ, i'nt he something?" Tommy said admiringly. "Gets such a kick out of little pictures."

"They're going to change the world," he assured her.

"For sure. So is Ruby's chili. Come on!"

We filled up the Franklin while Nazz found his poncho, and all left together.

The sun was below the trees on our left, throwing long shadows across the Wellington Road to the trees on the other side. We walked in the ruts that trucks and cars had made in the snow. Usually there were just the two, right down the center of the road, but infrequently there was a place where two vehicles had met and managed to pass each other.

The trip from the Holler to Sunrise Hill can be done in five minutes, if you don't mind falling on your face on arrival. It took us nearer twenty. It was beginning to get cold out, making the footing slippery. Gertrude the Guitar slowed me down. And the Nazz lit a joint, an enormous spliff which he said he had been saving for a special occasion. He always says that. Always means it, too. To pass a doobie on slippery surface, you have to stop, so everyone else has to stop to wait for you, and eventually it seems sensible to just form a circle. So we did. Rachel joined it, but politely refused the joint. "Perhaps later," she murmured, and the Nazz beamed at her. The rest of us shared it in silence.

The forest on either side of me began to sparkle. The random dance of shadows on branches suddenly became a pattern, that teetered on the edge of recognition. I was suddenly aware of my position, clinging to the face of a vast spinning planet, whirling through the universe. I heard the stream behind me, every leaf that fluttered for a hundred meters in any direction, the sounds of birds and a deer to the north. My friends became Robin Hood's Merry Men. And I was very hungry.

"Good shit, brother," I said to Nazz. My voice came from a hundred miles away through a filter that removed all the treble.

He beamed. "Xerox PARC."

Snaker broke up. "*Xerox Park?* Like, where people go to reproduce?"

We all cracked up. "No, man," Nazz said, "Xerox pee eh are *see*. On the Coast, man, Palo Alto. Dude that gave me this weed works there. Synchronicity, man—he'll freak when I tell him about my flash. All I need now is a way to *point* to stuff on the screen. . . ."

None of us had the slightest idea what he was talking about. But you don't have to understand joy to share it. We congratulated him, and finished the joint, and resumed walking.

The Wellington Road was a fairy wonderland, a winter carnival. Magic was surely in the air. And soon enough, we came upon some.

Mona and Truman's place came up on the right. Mona and Truman Bent were locals in their mid-forties, products of a century of inbreeding and poverty, and some of the nicest people I knew. (If you are going to giggle about the name Bent, would you please do so now and get it over with? It is an extremely common and highly respected name in Nova Scotia, as are Butt and Rafuse and Whynot.) Their home was a small showpiece of rural industry, ingenuity and courage, inside and out. It sat close to the road, with a little bit of a lawn and a swing-set out front. A driveway led past it to the big tired-looking barn in back. Truman's immense one-ton truck was pulled halfway into the barn so he could work on the engine out of the weather. As with many properties on the North Mountain, the area around the barn was littered with almost a dozen wrecked vehicles and their guts—but the garden beyond the barn and the area around the house itself were neat as a pin. Mona is a fuss-budget, and tough as cast iron.

And a sweetheart. When we were close enough to recognize what was lying in the center of her driveway, right by the road, we stopped in our tracks.

"Oh *wow,* man," Tommy said.

"Is that far out or what?" Snaker agreed.

Nazz shivered with glee. "Rat own, Mona!"

The Bents kept a pair of old tires on either side of the driveway, with flowerboxes set into the hubs. In summer they brightened the driveway considerable. In winter they were usually buried under snow. Mona had evidently had Truman dig one up, remove the empty flowerbox, and leave the tire in the middle of the drive.

"I don't understand," Rachel said.

"They heard our tire blow," I explained. "That one's for us."

"How do you know?"

I shook my head. "I just do. Come on, I'll show you."

Sure enough, there was a note stuffed into the hub:

This ai'nt mutch but it wil get
you to the gas station I gess

"See, there she is in the window," Tommy said. We all waved our thanks to Mona. She gave a single wave back. Snaker pantomimed that we would pick the tire up on our way back from dinner, and she waved again, then closed her curtains.

"Wow," Snaker said. "We gotta do something nice for those people."

"Right field," Nazz agreed. "Let's get the whole family thinking on it."

We trudged on. "Mona and Truman are amazing people," I told Rachel. "They can't have kids, so they foster parent. Constantly. There's always five or six kids around the place. She's strict as hell with them, and they always worship her. She'll take retarded kids, kids that are dying, kids that are crippled, whatever the agency sends. There are a couple of social workers that would die for her."

"And as you can see," Snaker called back over his shoulder, "she's adopted the whole goddamn Sunrise Hill Gang."

"I look forward to meeting her," Rachel said.

"She's a trip," Nazz called. "You'll love her."

"I already do," Rachel said, so softly that only I heard.

It was only another half a klick before the forest on the left side of the road ended and we were come to Sunrise Hill.

We all came to a halt again, because the sun was just setting over the Bay. Rachel took my hand and Snaker's.

After a time we roused ourselves, trudged past an acre of snow-covered garden, and came to Sunrise itself, also called The Big House.

It was a simple wood-frame two story perhaps fifty years old, a much more conventional structure than either the Gingerbread or Tree Houses, and larger than both of them put together. Unlike them it stood right by the roadside, in the middle of five or six more or less cleared acres. The only external signs of hippie esthetic were the small sprouting-greenhouse built onto the house in front and a solar shower in back. Fifty meters back from the house, and about the same distance apart, stood a small cedar-shake toolshed and a smaller outhouse. Between them was an ancient Massey-Ferguson tractor covered by an orange tarp, and next to that an even more ancient one-lung make-and-break engine under a black tarp.

We entered through the usual woodshed airlock, which also contained a wheezing old freezer and huge sacks of grains and beans. Inside, the Big House looked much more like a hippie dwelling. The downstairs was a single enormous room, with a giant front-loader woodstove at either end. The bare wood floor was completely covered with a once brightly colored painting, now faded, involving rainbows, dragons, and an immense myopic eyeball that stared biliously at the ceiling. The parts that Ruby had done looked great. On the left, a J-shaped counter and a small cookstove defined the kitchen. On the immediate right, a stupendous table which had begun life as the west wall of a boatshed defined the dining room and conference area. On its surface was painted a large vivid sunrise. Assorted wretched chairs lined one side of it; on the other was a single homemade bench three meters long. Beyond that an open staircase took two zigs and a zag to reach the upstairs. Past the staircase was open area. Beanbag chairs, ratty cushions, cable-drum tables, shelves of hippie books, milk crates full of this and that, drying herbs hanging in bundles from the overhead rafters, a bunch of Ruby's canvases arrayed by the east window, a small shrine to the Buddha in the far right corner.

The kitchen window was the only one on the north or Bay side. It let in enough of the glory of sunset to make the enameled sunrise on the table even more vibrant, but it was getting time to fire up the kerosene lamps. Both fires were roaring away, with a lot of birch in the mix, and the whole building was suffused with the overwhelming fragrance of simmering chili.

Ruby turned as we entered, left off pumping water and made a beeline for Snaker, drying her hands on her apron as she came. I liked to watch those two meet. Their joining was like slapping together two chunks of uranium: the energy levels of both went through the ceiling. I envied them.

When they were done hugging and kissing and making small sounds of contentment, Ruby backed away. She looked Rachel up and down, smiled and opened her arms again. Rachel took the cue. "Hi, I'm Ruby," Ruby said over Rachel's shoulder. "Hi, I'm Rachel," Rachel said over hers. They disengaged in stages, first pulling back to hold each other by the upper arms, then backing away further until their hands joined, then separating altogether, a spontaneous and oddly graceful movement.

"Welcome to Sunrise Hill," Ruby added. "That's a beautiful headband." Rachel thanked her gravely. "Hi, guys," she said to the rest of us. "You're just in time; dinner's nearly ready. Somebody set the table, a dishtowel for everybody, somebody else pump water and get the cider, somebody give a hoot out back for the others. Rachel, you sit, you're a guest. Sam, I could dig some music; would you mind pickin' a little?"

"Not if the Snaker can join me."

"Well," she said, glancing at him, "I had some other uses in mind for his hands. But that's a choice I'll never confront him with. Go ahead, babe. Oh, yeah, *was* it the Beatles?"

Snaker pulled a blank. So did I. And it was up to Rachel to save the situation. "I think we are agreed it is not. The drumming is too good to be either Pete Best or Ringo, and the accents are wrong. But it's an excellent fake."

Ruby nodded, said, "Too bad," and went back to the kitchen area. Snaker and I exchanged a glance and mimed sighs; we had forgotten the excuse we'd originally used to get Snaker over to my place. "Well," I said, unpacking my guitar, "there's the old philosophical question as to why a near-perfect forgery isn't as good as the real thing."

And we jawed about that while Snaker and I got tuned together and warmed up with instrumental blues in E. Ruby scatted along with us. As Tommy came in with her younger brother Malachi and Sally and Lucas, we were just starting that Jonathan Edwards song about laying around the shanty and getting a good buzz on, and everybody joined in on that one. When it was done, the table was set, Ruby was in the final stages of her magic-making, and there was barely time for a verse of Leon Russell's "Soul Food" before supper was on the table. As the lid came off and the smell reached us, Snaker and I stopped in the middle of a bar and put away our axes.

There were four loaves of fresh bread, two whole wheat and two rye, baked Tassajara-style. There were about fifteen litres of cider in one of the ubiquitous white buckets, with a dipper. There was an equal amount of well water in another bucket. There was a bowl big enough to be the hubcap off a 747, overflowing with lettuce-based salad; another full of carrot flake and raisin salad. Four homemade dressings. There were great bulk-purchase slabs of margarine (the Sunrise Gang were strict vegetarians). There were tamari and brewer's yeast and tofu and peanuts and sprouts and tahini and a little bit of soybean curry from the day before. To accommodate all this there were plates and bowls and mugs and silverware (no items matching). And in the center of the table, in a pot large enough to boil a missionary, were about thirty litres of Ruby's Chili.

When we dug in, the table was groaning and we each had a dishtowel of our own. A while later the dishtowels were all saturated with sweat and we were doing the groaning. And grinning.

"Is there a recipe written down for this, hon?" Snaker asked his lady, gulping cider.

"Sure," she said.

"Better destroy it. It's evidence of premeditation." She threw a piece of bread at him.

Between the happy cries of the scorched and the clatter of utensils and the roar of eight conversations going on at once and the growling hiss of the stoves and the thunderous volley of farts that attends any gathering of vegetarians, we made the rafters of the old house ring. Nonetheless most of my sense-memories of the occasion are oral. Ruby made *good* chili, so good I actually didn't miss the meat. I never did get to observe Rachel meeting Malachi, Lucas or Sally; it must have occurred at some point when my eyes were watering and the wax was running out of my ears. (I did notice that while Rachel shoveled in chili as rapidly as the rest of us, she didn't begin screwing up her face in Good Chili Spasm until all of us had been doing so for a while, and didn't begin to sweat until a few minutes after that. By the end of the meal she had it down.)

We drank the cider and water buckets dry, and another bucket and a half of water. We ate everything on the table, save for perhaps five litres of chili, which tomorrow would be folded into chapatis for lunch. And then the conversations all trailed off into heartfelt compliments to Ruby, and there was a moment or two of silent respectful appreciation, a contemplation of contentment and a sharing of that awareness. Shadows danced by kerosene lamplight, the simmering of dishwater on the stove became the loudest sound in the house. . . .

Lucas broke the silence, with a diaphragm-deep "AAA-OOOOOOOOOOOOOOOMM—" Malachi and Snaker picked it up at once, an octave higher, Malachi on the tonic, Snaker on the dominant. The rest joined in raggedly in whatever octave was easiest for them, and the sound swelled and rose and steadied as we all sat up straighter and got our breathing behind it.

Have you ever done an Om with a large group of people? Large enough that the drone chant takes on a life of its own, and doesn't ever seem to change as individual chanters drop out to inhale? If you have not, put this book down and go find ten or fifteen people who aren't too hip to learn something, and give it a try. So many things happen on so many levels that I'm not sure I can explain it to you.

On a musical level alone, the experience is edifying. The harmonics are fantastic, and they actually get a little *better* if one or two folks can't carry a tune so good and the note "hunts" a little.

On a physiological level, there is a surprisingly strong tranquilizing effect. The AAAAAOOOOOOOOOOOO-OOOOOOOOOOMMMM syllable is the oldest breath-regulating chant on the planet, basic and irreducible and autohypnotic.

On an emotional level, it's together-bringing and happy-making. It's proverbially impossible to get any three people to agree on what time it is; to get ten or fifteen together on even something as simple as a single pure sound is exhilarating. If you Om with people you don't know, you'll be friends when you're done. If you do it with friends . . .

On a spiritual level—well, if you're alive in the Eighties you probably don't believe there is such a thing, so I won't discuss it. Just try an "Om" sometime before you die. Come to it as cynically as you like.

Sunrise Oms were just a trifle frustrating for me, though, at that point in history. When the group had first spontaneously formed, a few years before, the Oms were the best I've ever been in, before or since. Partly because we had more participants, nearly thirty that summer, but mostly because the Oms were freeform improv, an unrestricted outpouring of the heart. Those who were not musicians—the majority, of course—held onto the tonic or dominant to keep us all centered, and those with musical talent jammed around the basic drone, sometimes adding harmonies to make chords, then spontaneously mutating them in weird shifting ways; sometimes throwing in deliberate and subtle dissonances, then resolving them creatively; sometimes doing raga scales, or Ray Charles gospel riffs, or whatever came out of our heads and hearts and mutual interaction. The results were always interesting and frequently breath-taking.

But of late the Sunrise Gang had, typically, gotten a little too spiritually conservative (read: "tight-assed") and had decided that having people chant all over the place offered too much encouragement to Ego (a word which had for them roughly the same emotional connotation that "Commie" held for their parents). Surely Ego was out of place in a spiritual event. So the current Agreement was to limit the Om to the tonic and dominant notes. That was more democratic. More pure. More basic and simple.

Also more boring—and as a guest, I was of course required by politeness to conform, and listen to my own solos only in my head. It itched me a little—and I knew it itched Snaker too, because we'd discussed it. Still, any Om is better than no Om, and I was simply too well-fed to sustain irritation. So I settled into contemplation of the sound we were making—

—Rachel began to improvise—

—brilliantly, from the very first riff, I hadn't been fully aware until then that she was participating in the Om but Jesus you couldn't miss her warm-honey alto when she started to blow, it was something like the sudden appearance of a darting trout in a pellucid pool, and a shared thought-chain flashed around the table in an instant, *what the—? Oh, it's cool, she's a stranger, doesn't know any better; Jesus, listen to her* do *it,* as she wove a strange liquid melody line around her drone, and after a very slight staggered hesitation the Om steadied and came back in strong behind her.

Well. The ice having been broken by the guest, I wrestled with the part of me that Malachi insisted was my ego . . . and went into the tank. When my current breath ended, I sucked in a joyous deep new one, paused an instant, and took off after her. Her eyes met mine, and we both thought of our lovemaking that afternoon, and wrapped our voices around each other. We did a modal thing, started it simple, cluttered it a bit, brought it home again—measuring each other, feeling each other out, alto and my baritone seeking harmony—

—and I caught Snaker's eye and lifted my brows, and he took a deep breath and jumped in an octave above me, duplicating my line to show that he understood what was happening—

—Ruby hesitated a few seconds and then began to parallel Rachel's line—

—and we all looked to Rachel, and at her signal we banked sharply and cut in the afterburners, riding that magic carpet of drone like the Blue Angels, heading for the clouds in perfect wordless communication—

∞

—and a long happy indescribable time later it was over, the statement was made, it hung in the air and in our minds' ear like a skywritten mandala, hung and spread and drifted and dissipated as the last breath of the last voice—Tommy's—ran out.

We all smiled in silence together for a long time, too happy to speak. It was clear to us that God had been here and gone, but that was okay: He'd be falling by again sometime.

"Wow, that was far out," Malachi said at last, and from

the tone of his voice I knew we were in for a session. Well, Rachel had to meet him sometime or other.

"It sure was," Ruby said, ignoring the subtext of his tone with the long practice of an ex-lover. She was smiling dreamily at Snaker. He was going to be very glad he had been a good boy at my place earlier.

"Right *up*," Nazz agreed, also oblivious.

Malachi pounced. "It's far out how something can happen spontaneously like that and it's a stone, that one time, because it's like perfect for the moment, you know?" Malachi had the mad burning eyes of a born saint or poet or revolutionary, though he was none of these, deep-set eyes smouldering under shelves of forehead like banked coals at the back of deep caves. He could disappear into the woodwork when he wanted, but when he put on his guru voice, he drew attention effortlessly. "Rachel didn't know our custom about not hamming up the Oms but that's *far out*, because she brought good vibes to the party and that's what counts. Even if we wouldn't want to Om that way all the time."

"I'd like to Om like that all the time," Snaker said with just a little edge.

"I think we have Agreement on that," Malachi said softly.

To my surprise, Lucas spoke up. "Maybe we should examine the Agreement." He was staring at Rachel.

Malachi rolled with it. "Far out, maybe we should."

Lucas was wearing weights strapped to his wrists and ankles, for three reasons. Because it was good physical exercise, because it was good spiritual discipline, and because it hurt. Any of the three would have sufficed. "I could dig some more Oms like that. Once in a while, anyway." He looked away from Rachel suddenly. "I think I'd give my right arm if I could make my voice do that stuff."

"Uh huh. Isn't that kind of why we made the Agreement?" Malachi asked, and one or two people began to nod.

"What exactly do you mean by 'agreement'?" Rachel asked.

Malachi turned those eyes on her. When she didn't flinch, he seemed to smile slightly. "See, we're a spiritual community, so we have to make some basic Agreements to live together, and then stick to them. Like, it's our agreement to be strict vegetarian, and you can rap for days about whether that's far out or misguided—and we have, still do—but meanwhile it's our agreement to do that thing, so we do. And if that's a drag for some of us—" Snaker squirmed. "—well, hopefully the spiritual solidarity from the Agreement is worth the drag. The way you were Om-ing—please don't think I'm laying blame, it was beautiful and you didn't know—but we used to Om that way here, and we found that it was easy for it to turn into a kind of exclusive thing, almost an elitist trip. Like it divided us up into the talented and the drones, if you dig. It brought us apart instead of together, and we wanted an Om that was more symbolic that we were all doing the same thing here, so we made that Agreement. You see?"

I'd been subconsciously expecting something like this for hours. I'd always found Malachi infuriatingly difficult to argue with—as they say around the Mountain, he's slick as a cup of custard—and I just knew that Rachel was a match for him, that she was going to lay him out, stop his clock with some splendid zen epigram. And she sideswiped me.

"I think that is a wise decision for you," she said. "I will make that Agreement with you all."

Snaker's jaw dropped too. Ruby gave Rachel a Closer Look. Malachi blinked.

Irritated at how often and easily Malachi could make me irritated, I spoke up. "Look, I have no Agreements at all with you guys except the ones that come under being a good neighbor, but I'll tell you this: while that Om was happening I was part of God and totally stoned—"

"Me, too," Snaker said.

"—and that seems like a silly thing for a spiritual community to turn away from."

"That's the trip, Sam," Malachi said with exasperating compassion. "*You* were totally stoned. Not everybody was. We want to *all* be part of God."

I could see myself responding, *but we* were *all stoned,* and then going around the table, *you were stoned, weren't you?* only by that time half of them would be wondering if they *had* in fact been stoned, Malachi had that effect on them, and I had climbed these stairs before. So had Snaker; he shot me a look that said, *thanks for trying, brother.*

"Far out," I conceded reluctantly.

"Clean-up crew," Ruby said loudly and clearly.

People began scraping plates, and stacking them. I caught Rachel's eye and stood up. She took her cue and followed me to the sink. She was supposed to be from the city, so it was okay for me to lecture her on the art of dishwashing without running water. I don't think she'd ever washed a dish under any circumstances, but she was a very quick study. At one point she should have burned her wrist on the hot water kettle, but the skin declined to burn. Malachi was nearby, scraping leftovers into the compost bucket, but he didn't seem to notice. She and I traded off washing and drying while others cleared and washed the table and put away the dried dishes and stoked the fires and adjusted the lamps, and Ruby watched in regal contentment. (One of the commune's more sensible rules is that whoever cooks dinner gets to fuck off the rest of the night.) (Except that Ruby wasn't fucking off; she was, ninety-five percent certainly, thinking about her next painting.)

Though she was concentrating on the dishes, Rachel managed to take in the whole scene. One of her rare smiles lit her face. "This is beautiful," she murmured to me.

I looked around to see what she meant. I got it at once. Many people working in concert, with no wasted words, moving at high speed but never bumping into each other, a marvelous improvised choreography. Calmness in activity, a perfect Zen dance. It was what attracted me to Sunrise Hill, this quality; if the place had been like that all the time, perhaps I'd have moved in. My irritation with Malachi leaked from me, and I began to enjoy myself again almost as much as I had during the Om. And then a strange and terrible thing happened—

ELEVEN

I WAS WASHING; Rachel was drying. I had pointed out to her where a particular bowl belonged, and turned away, then realized I'd misinformed her; I turned back to give a correction. Tommy was at the counter next to Rachel, whacking a stainless steel bowl against the underside of the cupboard to dislodge some sticky food into the compost bucket beneath it. Rachel was looking toward her, away from me. On top of that rickety cupboard were many large mason jars containing grains and beans. Tommy's energetic whanging of the heavy bowl was causing one of the big jars to dance forward on its ledge. I saw it—and saw that Rachel saw it too. I remembered her phenomenal reaction time when the tire had blown, knew she would react faster than I could—which was good because I was off-balance, leaning the wrong way.

And she did. It was over in an instant, but I saw what she did with terrible clarity, as if in slow motion. Her eyes widened slightly as she measured trajectory, realized the falling weight was going to catch Tommy leaning forward and slam her face down against the counter. Rachel's lips tightened as she computed the mass of the load: about three kilos of mung beans and a half-kilo of glass. She clearly understood that the impact could very well be fatal. Her mouth opened and her face began to contort for a shout and her whole body gathered itself to spring—

—and she relaxed. Her features smoothed over and her mouth closed.

She did not know that I could see. I wasted nearly a whole second gaping in disbelief, did not get off my own shout until the jar had actually overbalanced beyond recovery.

"Tommy, *duck!*"

The woman had a lot of quick; she nearly managed it. She did manage to duck her head enough so that the jar struck her a glancing blow at a favorable angle: her forehead *just* missed the counter. The jar did not, and broken glass and mung beans flew from hell to breakfast. Tommy straightened at once. In a loud, clear voice she said, "For my next magical trick—" Then her knees let go and she started to go down.

Rachel caught her under the arms.

It was twice as horrible because I understood it at once. I don't think there was an instant in which I blamed Rachel. In the moment that she did what she did—nothing—I realized exactly why she was doing it. I saw clearly that she hated doing it, and felt she had no choice; most horrible of all, I agreed with her. And all this transpired in the space of a second, yet it wrenched all the events of the last twenty-four hours out of my memory banks, and jammed them back into my head at a slightly different angle.

By traveling through time, Rachel had accepted the terrible risk of altering the past. But as an ehtical time traveler, she must have a horror of altering the past *too much*. Reality was stretching to accommodate her existence in my timeline. If she overstressed it, it might tear.

But how much was *too much?* A good rule of thumb might be to avoid major changes . . . such as altering the birth or death dates of any person. If someone would have died without your presence in that ficton, then die she must—

—but Rachel *cared* for Tommy, I knew that despite her poker face. They had made eye-contact, they'd touched, they'd joined hands in the Om, it had been clear that they were friends-in-the-making.

—but she'd done it. Done what she had to do, which was (as far as she knew) to watch her new friend Tommy get her brains broken by a jug of mung beans. I totally understood the moral imperative behind this before I even got my own warning shout halfway up my throat . . . but I felt different about Rachel because she had been capable of it. Not blaming, certainly, I told myself. Just different.

It changes your perception of a house-guest, bed-partner, someone you've begun to think of as a friend, to learn that under no circumstances would they do anything to prevent your scheduled death—even at no cost to themselves. Even if you understand and approve the logic, it changes things.

I did not know just how, though, because the entire incident struck much too close to something I never ever ever thought about, some*one* I never ever thought about, and the inner conflict was so painful that I needed the thirty seconds of total confusion which followed Tommy's narrow escape to recover my own equilibrium unnoticed. I wished desperately that I could take Snaker outside or upstairs, alone somewhere, and talk to him, tell him what had happened and ask him how I felt about it. Or Snaker and Ruby would be even better, this tasted like the kind of hurt she was good at mending . . . except that Snaker and I had promised not to tell her Rachel's secret.

I had felt uniquely blessed to be the man on the scene

when the time traveler came—now I was realizing that history is made by the unlucky.

Before I was ready for it, Tommy was thanking me. I heard myself answer automatically. "Hell, Tommy, anybody would have done the same." And heard internal echoes: *anybody who* could *would have done the same*, and: *who are you to criticize, pal?*

Those echoes must have shown on my face; I saw Tommy frown. Alarm bells went off; the Sunrise Gang all had incredibly sensitive detectors for guilt, conflict and deception. They all firmly believed that when a hassle or a hangup was observed, the thing to do was haul it out on the table and get it straight before anything else was done. Neither politeness nor tact nor respect for personal privacy was allowed to stand in the way. The only things that made this practice forgivable were the remarkable compassion they displayed in rummaging around inside you psyche, the absolute tolerance they had for any honestly held opinion however startling, and their damnably impressive success-rate. A person suffering from internal conflict tended to shrink from them the way a man with a stiff neck will avoid the company of a chiropractor. If he learns of your affliction, he will insist on hurting you—and most annoying, when he is done, you will feel better. You will thank him.

By approaching it as a spiritual conditioning exercise, I had learned to appreciate the custom—and as it made me stronger, I had come to enjoy it.

But I had a secret now. Truth was a contraindicated medicine. I didn't have the right to take it, for it might kill my friends. Everyone's friends.

Which awareness I kept from my face as I set about lying to my friend Tommy. "Whew," I said, shaking my head briefly but violently. "That shook me up. I saw you dead for a second there."

At once she was understanding. "Wow, yeah. Pretty heavy. Your death thing again."

"Yeah. 'Scuse me—I've got to go visit the shitter."

My "death thing" was an old, counterfeit hangup which had long since been taken as far as it would go. If Tommy insisted, I was willing to haul it out again, as a diversion. But she grinned and cut loose. "You've got to get more beans in your diet, Sam. Here, take a lantern."

I avoided Rachel's eyes on the way out. Maybe she avoided mine.

The Sunrise shitter was more than fifty meters down a sloping, well-trodden path from the Big House, both to keep it downhill of the well, and to make it as handy to the fields as to the house. Instead of following the path to it, I veered left as I exited the house and took an equally well-trod path through the snow to The Chapel. The Chapel is nothing but a ledge, where the land drops abruptly away perhaps fifteen or twenty meters. It is a chapel because from there you have an unobstructed view of the Bay in the distance. It is the origin of the name Sunrise Hill, and it is a good place to be at sunrise.

It was a good place to be at night, too. Saint John glowed on the horizon. The Moon was up. The sky was spattered with stars, vast and glorious. What wind there was came from the north, from the Bay into my face: no snow tomorrow.

The assumption Rachel was working under was very close to the hippie-borrowed concept of kharma. Kharma is subtly different from predestination—it says that you make your own predestination—but it has that same unpleasant taste of inexorability, implacable fate. You will pay for every sin, sooner or later; you will have to earn every lucky break; each new disaster is only what you deserve. Combined with the doctrine of reincarnation, it *becomes* predestination, for the bad choices you make in this life are a result of bad kharma earned in an earlier life. It's sort of the spiritual equivalent of There Ain't No Such Thing As A Free Lunch, eternity as a zero-sum game.

But what does it do to your kharma to watch a friend die?

That was a question to which I badly wanted an answer myself . . . so badly that I could not remember why. . . .

If it had been a movie scenario, and the same choice set up, the screenwriter would have *had* to have Rachel opt to save Tommy, and to hell with the fate of all reality, or else the audience would have hated the picture. The choice she made was artistically unsatisfying. Unpalatable. Did that make it wrong? Her logic was remorseless. There's a classic sf story called "The Cold Equations". . .

I was out there for a long time.

When I heard approaching footcrunch I guessed Rachel. But it was Snaker who came to me out there in The Chapel, and silently stood and shared it with me for a few minutes.

"What a night," he said at last.

Whatever he meant, I agreed with it.

"I got Ruby aside and talked with her privately."

"You didn't—"

"Naw. She wouldn't *want* me to have told her about Rachel's secret if I did. If I had. If you follow. But I had to tell her about watching you guys ball."

"Oh. Yeah. Uh . . . how did it go?"

"Amazingly well. I found an extraordinary woman, Sam. Get this: *she didn't interrupt*. She let me tell her how it was, and she didn't say a word until I was done. Then she ran it through intellectually and decided she had no reason to be jealous, looked me in the eye and decided *emotionally* she had no need to be jealous, and cut loose of jealousy: I could see it happen. She asked me what it'd been like, and I told her. Her pupils dilated. Finally, she validated my judgment, that what I'd done, and not done, was within the spirit of our Agreement, and she said she admired Rachel's courage. I think we're going to fuck our brains out later tonight."

"You lucked out, brother."

"Seem-so. But that was just for openers. Once we'd dispensed with the trivial distraction *I'd* brought up, Ruby dropped her own bomb."

I closed my eyes briefly. "Yeah?"

"The test results came back from Halifax. She's pregnant."

"No *shit*? Wow, that's *great*! Congratulations, man, that's the best news I've heard all winter. It couldn't have happened to two nicer people, really."

I was saying all the right things, and I did feel joy for my friend. But I was sort of sorry he had told me *then*. A large part of me was numb. Too much had happened to me in the last while, and I had no room left in my brain. Snaker and Ruby were pregnant; neat. Love was great. For those who could believe in it. Or were capable of it.

"It's a real stoner," he agreed happily. "Anyway, the long and short of it is, I am virtually *certain* we are going to spend tonight fucking our brains out. Which leads gracefully to why I am suddenly in a hurry to put Mona's old tire on the Meanie and get you two back to the Red Palace. You grok?"

"Oh." I thought about it. "Listen, Snake: a long walk rolling a tire through the snow, changing it, a half-hour round trip on bad roads in the dark with an undependable vehicle, and all the while your woman is cooling off back at home . . . fuggit. We can crash here."

"Uh—" Snaker began, and hesitated.

"Really, man, I'd just as soon let my stoves go out; I've been meaning to shovel out the ashes and—"

"Think it through, man. If you crash here, where do you crash?"

"Ah." Either in the same upstairs with Snaker and Ruby, or on bedrolls on the floor immediately underneath their room. The huge vent in their floor, designed to let warm air come up, would easily pass sound. In either direction. Lucas slept in the Big House, but he didn't count: his room was the only airtight, relatively soundproof one in the structure; he liked it that way because it was colder. The point was that if we stayed, Snaker and Ruby would have no privacy to celebrate their happy news.

"I think Ruby finds the *idea* of someone watching while she's making love stimulating. But I'm sure she's not ready to deal with the actuality just now. Some shit like that went down around the time she and Malachi were breaking up, before I got here. I gather it was pretty intense for her." I could well imagine. Malachi had put her and Sally through a horrid long time when he could not decide which he wanted to live with, and so lived with both to see if that would shed any light on the matter. It eventually did, but with the light came much waste heat, and Ruby was badly burned. Snaker had come to the Mountain just as I was nerving myself up to move her into my place, on an emergency first-aid basis.

"Snake, I'll try to say this just right. I like you and Ruby. I would be honored to be present sometime while you two made love, as observer or . . . whatever. But you don't owe me anything, okay? You two have something special and private to celebrate. Just because I showed you mine doesn't mean you have to show me hers."

"Or my own. I hear you, Sam. Thanks. For myself, I'd be happy to reciprocate if Ruby were willing. Maybe it'll happen some day. Meanwhile, I know I'll be thinking of you and Rachel at several points this evening."

"'If it's a good lick, use it,' as Buckley used to say."

"Pun intended, of course."

We went back indoors, collected Rachel, said our good-byes and set off on the journey back home. As the three of us walked along the Wellington Road, he told Rachel his and Ruby's happy news. She congratulated him gravely, breaking out one of her rare smiles for the occasion. I searched her features in vain for any sign of the kind of inner turmoil that was chewing me up. But how much could be accurately read from that stone face by moonlight?

I wondered why I had passed up the opportunity to

discuss my own emotional turmoil with Snaker. He had missed Rachel's failure to prevent Tommy's accident, and I couldn't bring it up then, with Rachel walking along beside us. Slowly I realized I was never going to bring it up. Maybe it was like the secret he hadn't told Ruby: he wouldn't have wanted me to have told him, if I had. Still, I thought briefly, I ought to warn him, not to think of Rachel as someone he could depend on to get him out of a bad fix. But I did not.

In retrospect, I think I did not bring my problem to Snaker for the same reason I did not bring it before the whole rest of the Sunrise Hill Gang. Like them, he would have solved it—that is, have seen to the heart of it, forced *me* to solve it. And I was not willing to give it up, would have died to keep it. . . .

The tire-change went smoothly. There was some idle chatter on the drive home, praise for Ruby's chili, anecdotes about some of the people Rachel had met and some of the more spectacularly tangled chains of relationships. She asked good questions. She had seen some of Ruby's paintings, and praised them intelligently. When we got to Heartbreak Hotel, Rachel asked Snaker if he would come in for a while. He grinned and gunned the engine. "Darlin'," he said, "it's too complicated to explain, but if I get *right* back home tonight, I'll wake a happy man, and if I'm two minutes late I'll have to cut my throat. It's a pleasure to know you, and I'll see you sometime again." I got out of the cab—

—and she leaned over and kissed him for a full minute, while I stood there as discreetly as I could—

—and she sprang from the cab and slammed the door, and "There goes my margin," Snaker said dizzily and was gone in a shower of slush and gravel. Blue Meanie dwindled in the dark, roaring at both ends, like a flatulent lion.

The Ashley was still going; I packed it full and damped it down for the night. The kitchen fire was dead; I lit the

Kemac oil-jet in the back of the firebox, filled the firebox with softwood for a quick blast of heat to warm the bedroom above, and refilled the hot-water well. At my direction, Rachel replenished both stacks of wood from the shed. I came upon her in the living room, looking over the books and records. I wondered if any of the names could mean anything to her. I offered to show her how to use the stereo, and she politely declined. (I suppose if you dropped me back into Edison's home, even politeness and great respect could not make me sit through more than one or two of those damned scratchy cylinders.) I said that I was very tired.

She nodded. "Do you want me to sleep with you?"

I remembered she had once implied that she did not make a habit of sleeping. Or did she mean—?

I did not know what she meant, what she wanted. So I had to fall back on what *I* wanted. What I wanted was for her to decide. "Suit yourself," I said, and gave her a hug.

She pulled back far enough to look at me. "Sam? You have brought me much joy today. I have many new friends, I have learned so much."

"My pleasure."

She kissed me, more thoroughly than she had Snaker since we were not squeezed into a truck seat, and then let me go. I went upstairs and the last thing I remember is walking through the bedroom doorway. My mind must have fallen asleep before my body did.

TWELVE

SYMMETRICALLY ENOUGH, MY body woke up before my mind.

Have you ever awakened to find that you are making love? And have been for some indeterminate time, under the impression that you were dreaming? An indescribable, blessed experience.

My mind's awakening was a slow, sequential process, a series of cumulative steps. I am fucking. I live. No enemies near. I am a mammal. I'm home. This is nice. I'm a male human being. My head hurts. I don't care. This is good fucking I'm getting. Oh, I remember who I am—

—like that. If one must wake up, that is the way to do it. It was a sweet slow lazy time, a healing and a nourishing. I became aware of Rachel's existence almost in the instant I became aware of my own, and the distance that had been between us when I fell asleep was melted before I was awake enough to recall it.

And when I did recall it, she knew it, by the minute hesitation in my rhythm, and murmured in my ear, "Please forgive me, Sam."

I chuckled. "I forgave you in my sleep. My subconscious sentries passed you through sometime in the night, so you must belong here. Forgive me for sitting in judgment on you?"

Okay, it was a silly question. Her answer was nonverbal but quite emphatic. So I asked a few nonverbal questions, and the dialogue became spirited.

At some point in there we began singing together, literally singing in great rhythmic cadences, in weird harmonies that diverged and converged again—like the lovemaking itself, it had been going on for some time before I noticed it. Briefly she quoted a riff she had sung in last night's Om, and mockingly I answered it with the featureless drone Malachi preferred, and she pinched me. And then we let our voices go free as our bodies, and raised up both in song, and it was good, oh good. . . .

Did she really say, in the warm afterflow, "I knew you would understand"? Or did I imagine it?

Over breakfast she raised the subject of our Agreement, and we killed several hours refining it. She planned to spend her days traveling around the Mountain, interviewing people for her imaginary book, storing data and impressions in her headband in some fashion I didn't understand. In the mornings and evenings she was willing to lend a hand with chores. She did not know how to cook but was willing to learn, and would take a crack at anything else. She would follow my customs while under my roof. I would not ask her anything about her ficton or near-future events in my own—more accurately, I could ask, but I agreed in advance not to so much as frown if I got a circumscribed answer or none at all. She stated that within a few weeks she would supply me with ten thousand bona fide Canadian dollars, with which I agreed to try and arrange legal residence in Nova Scotia for her. I did not ask where her money was coming from. She offered to pay cash rent in addition to labour, but I refused it. As I was searching for a tantric way to raise the remaining aspects of our Agreement, she charged right in.

"These are all what you call 'material-plane' matters, Sam. Now we must make our emotional, spiritual and sexual Agreements."

I blinked, then grinned. "I've spent my life yearning for a woman who didn't bullshit around. The reality is a little unnerving. Okay, I'll take a hack at it. Would you know what I meant if I said, 'I love you'? I'm *not* saying it—I'm asking how good a language course you got before you left home."

She looked wary. "Good enough to treat that phrase like an armed bomb. According to my dictionary, it has dozens of mutually exclusive meanings, and guessing the one or ones intended is terribly important."

"That's one reason why I never use the word."

"It can mean, 'I will meet your price for sex,' or 'I am fond of you,' or 'Your happiness is essential to my own,' or 'I claim ownership of you,' or 'I feel that I am or could be your other half.' Are any of these close, Sam?"

I blinked. "Uh—yes to one and two. Emphatic no to three, four and five. I'll have sex with you whenever we both want to. I don't mind if you have sex with others as long as you keep the noise down when I'm trying to sleep. I may have sex with others myself from time to time, although I don't expect it to cause any great traffic problem. I care about you a lot. I don't think *anybody's* happiness is essential to my own. I don't keep slaves. I don't think half of me is missing. I will be your friend. I'll keep your secrets. I'll teach you anything you need to know about this ficton. I'll keep you from harm if I can, and I know and understand and accept that you can't make the same promises. And I'll help you with your work, even if that means leaving you alone with it and dying of curiosity. Your turn."

She didn't answer right away. Maybe she was thinking over everything I'd said. Maybe she was just looking at me. Whichever, it was nice. Usually I can take it or leave it alone. Being looked at, I mean. When Rachel looked at you she left eyetracks on you. "Part of my mission is to study sexual mores and customs at this pivotal juncture in history. I am surprised and pleased by your non-exclusivity clause."

"Careful! I'm unconventional for this ficton. So, at least in theory, are some of the other Hippies—but almost none of the Locals. As a rule of thumb, I'd suggest you use great discretion in offering sex to any man without both long hair and a beard, or any woman wearing a brassiere. Oh, there are a few sexually conservative Hippies—the Sunrise Gang in particular are strong on monogamy these days, and the Ashram crew down in the Valley are into celibacy—but they're all used to people who feel different, they won't be offended if you ask."

"Thank you, Sam. As for the rest of what you say, I echo most of it and agree to all of it. I care about you a great deal too. I will be the best friend I can be to you. I thank you for your generosity to an uninvited guest. Will you want me to sleep with you?"

"Huh? Oh—" I don't know about you, but when I'm talking with someone, half the time I'm not really listening, I'm thinking of what to say next or where I'd rather be or something. I was getting it through my head that you couldn't do that with Rachel. "Pardon me, the question has never come up before. At least not in this sense. Let's see. It certainly isn't reasonable to expect you to waste a third of your day lying still." Suddenly I felt almost guilty that I would be leaving her to her own devices for such long intervals. "Uh . . . times we make love at night, would you stay with me until I'm asleep, try to leave without waking me? And perhaps curl up with me from time to time when you weren't doing anything else anyway?"

"With great pleasure. And the house will be warmer at night if there is someone to keep the fires fed."

I smiled. "I think we have Agreement."

She smiled. "Shall we seal the bargain?"

I frowned. "The chickens are hungry."

She kept smiling, rose from her chair and stood before me. "Then we must hurry."

"Yes, we must."

That night she called me from Sunrise Hill, to say that she would not be home, as she was going to be having sex with Snaker and Ruby. I wished her joy, and banked my fires and went to bed.

And woke, by God, the same way I had the day before. . . .

I am fucking. I live. No enemies near. I am a mammal. I'm home, on my back. This is nice. I'm a male human being. My head hurts. I don't care. This is good fucking I'm getting. Oh, I remember who I am—

Jesus Christ, I'm fucking *Ruby*!

—she's even better than I thought she'd be—

Jesus Christ, Snaker's lying right beside me!

—Rachel rides him, as Ruby rides me—

Jesus Christ, this is dangerous!

—not necessarily—

Jesus Christ—

I was wide awake. At least three friendships and a marriage were at stake, and the point of no return was near, if not here and gone—quick, Sam, run it through!

An even number, that was good. Genders balanced, that was good. All friends, all reasonably sane, stable types, all grownups, all discreet, all clean. Neither female at risk: one protected, one pregnant. I cared about all three people. . . .

In the soft glow of dawn through layers of plastic, my eyes traveled up Ruby's splendid nude body, and she was wearing the smile of the canary who has swallowed the cat.

"Good morning, Sam," she said, moving lazily up and down on me. "I've fantasized about this."

"Uh, me too. Good morning. Morning, Snake, Rachel."

"—mornin', brother—"

"—good morning, Sam—"

"And congratulations, Ruby—Snaker told me the happy news the other night."

She smiled even wider. "Thanks, Sam." We stared together at her naked belly, thinking of the life that lurked inside. Spontaneously we began to rock together.

I giggled suddenly. "Now do you see why folks around here don't lock their doors, Rachel?"

Rachel smiled. She reached over and stroked Ruby's shoulder, undid a snarl in her hair. Ruby turned to her and kissed her. They put an arm around each other. We all synchronized rhythm while they held the kiss. I watched them forever, hypnotized and profoundly aroused. *Why* are there so few Lesbians? I'll never understand it.

The obvious corollary probably struck me at the same instant that it did Snaker.

We must have looked comical. I turned my head quickly—to find his face a few inches away from mine. His mouth was open too. Both our mouths were open. Almost touching. Our shoulders *were* touching, our arms. Our hands.

His hand touched my belly, moved to the place where his lady and I were joined. I gasped. I reached blindly, touched his chest. It felt strange, weird, hairy and flat, warm, alive, interesting. My fingers came to a nipple, like a miniature of a woman's nipple. I experimented; he sipped air. A working miniature.

We both glanced up briefly to see Ruby and Rachel caressing as they rode us, and then our eyes met again and we kissed.

I had had two other sexual experiences with males, years before, brief, furtive, unsatisfactory. I had never kissed a man. It was even weirder than I had thought it must be, rough and prickly and *peculiar.* We did not kiss with our tongues—I had morning breath, he was a smoker—but we did not kiss tentatively or fraternally, and when I decided that it did not hurt, was not intrinsically disgusting, did not seem to leave a stain, and actually kind of felt nice, not only did the skies not fall, but I found myself even harder in Ruby's pelvic clutch. Or was she clutching me tighter? Someone's fingers were in my hair. We all seemed to be heading into the home stretch. Ruby and Rachel were humming, harmonizing; suddenly Snaker and I were too, humming into each other's mouths; we were making a drone, then a harmony; with the women we made a chord, a splendid four-note diminished chord, a chord of transition that rose and fell as we rose and fell, that sought resolution as we did, that rose, rose, swelled until it was no longer song but shout; Snaker and I broke our kiss and pulled our women down to us and roared against their throats as the world blew up—

"Thank you, darling," Ruby said next to my ear awhile later.

"Whuffo?" Snaker asked. (How did he know—how did *I* know—that he was the darling addressed?)

"For holding off on your cigarette. I appreciate."

"Huh! Never thought of it, love."

The two most awkward moments at an orgy are just before undressing and just after the orgasms. "Uh . . . good morning to you guys, too," I said.

Ruby kissed me. "Sam, how come you and I never got around to this before?"

I thought about it. "Silly reasons at first, and for a while. And then Snaker came and you guys got engaged and decided to be monogamous."

She nodded. "We still are. It's just . . . well, Snaker says there is very little difference between you and him."

"Under the circumstances, I will not contest the slander

at this time," I said. "Uh . . . how shall I put this? . . . to what do I owe this pleasure?"

Ruby grinned. "What the hell are we doing here, you mean? Good question." She reached across me and poked her husband in the ribs. "How *did* this happen, honey?"

On the far side of him, Rachel raised up on one elbow. Snaker is right: you can't compare tits. "It was the effortless unfolding of the universe," she murmured.

"It was like hell effortless," Snaker said, breathing like a smoker. "But they're right, Sam: it wasn't so much planned as discovered. Ruby and I got to talking about me watching you and Rachel ball, and talking about it got us horny, and then we got to talking about that with Rachel, and we learned that Rachel enjoyed watching too, and then we learned that Ruby thought she'd like being watched, and shortly after that we learned Ruby liked *watching* too, and so when the three of us had been researching the whole phenomenon long enough that I couldn't seem to get another hard-on, Ruby pointed out that you had constituted an entire third of the original Broadway cast and might have interesting data to share—"

"You're telling me that you three screwed all night long and then, in the cold rosy dawn, came over here to get laid?"

"That's about the size of it," Snaker agreed.

"Perhaps there is a God. Uh, can I cook you folks breakfast?"

Ruby chuckled, a purring sound. "Rachel and I brought plenty to eat. And I don't know about her, but mine's getting cold while you guys are talking."

I began to roll up onto one elbow, with a view toward walking a few fingers down her belly toward the area under discussion—but she pushed me back down flat on the bed, flung a leg over me and quickly sat astride my chest. I got the palms of my hands on her buttocks and coaxed her forward. "Magnificent," I said with great sincerity as the sweet knurled pinkness came into view.

Ruby had terrific lips, and this pair were the best. If the genetic cards had been cut the other way and she'd been born male, she'd have been hung like a horse. If—as I did then—you were to reach around her thighs and take each of those lips between thumb and forefinger and tug them gently up and out, opening the orchid, you would understand—as I did then—what that symbol truly is which we call a heart, although a heart looks nothing like that; understand what it is we admire in the butterfly. Like butterfly wings I tugged them down toward me, pursed my own mouth and blew a stream of cool air up and down the channel they formed, heard Ruby's hiss of pleasure. I heard Rachel murmur something too soft to hear, and Snaker agree. The bouquet was rare, the sauce piquant, the meaty petals delicious, separately and together: I feasted. Ruby's fingers explored my hair, met behind my head and guided me. . . .

When I felt a mouth on me, on my belly and then on my penis, I wondered vaguely whose it was. But my vision was blocked in that direction, and it didn't seem important. There were *two* mouths on me, kissing each other around me, for several minutes before I noticed. Ruby's clitoris, proportioned to match those labia, was like a miniature penis under my tongue. I experimented; she gulped air. A working miniature. Her thighs clamped my ears, I tasted a trace of my own semen, a gentle finger opened me and I was neither male nor female nor gay nor straight nor even bi but only human—

Breakfast for four is four times easier than breakfast for one. Four pairs of hands— One of the few things I've ever really envied the Sunrise Gang, one of the few good points of communal living to my way of thinking, is the division of labcur, and the ability to renegotiate that division. If you'll go chop us some water, and he'll take care of the chores and critters, and she'll get the house warm, I will happily rustle up the eggs and flapjacks and crack open the last jar of peach preserves, and breakfast will be a thing of joy instead of the first false step in an infinite cycle of frustrations alternating with disappointments. Perhaps tomorrow I'll be the one who least minds suiting up and going outside to get the water, and you'll be in the mood to turn out some johnny-cake or porridge while others feed the stoves and chickens.

In the country, it is so much easier to live with almost anybody than it is to live alone, that a person who does live alone must be very fussy, or very timid, or very undesirable, or just plain stupid. I wondered, that morning, which applied to me. Had I not lived alone too long?

Wood heat, for instance, is remorseless and implacable, worse than bondage to cocaine or tobacco or even one's own belly and bowels. Every forty-five minutes you must throw a stick of wood on one fire or the other. Think about it. Every forty-five minutes. You must. You can stretch it to an hour, to an hour and a half or more, but you will do so as seldom as possible, because when you do, you catch cold, and sniffle a lot.

So the presence of even one housemate means that you can with some confidence undertake an activity, or a thought train, of as long as an hour's duration, *without* having to literally pay through the nose. Luxury! *Three* companions is wealth.

Never mind three talented sex partners—

"Why don't you two move in here?" I asked as we sat down to breakfast.

Snaker opened and closed his mouth, Ruby did the same, he looked at her to see why she wasn't answering, she did the same, he made an "after you" gesture just as she did the same, and the three of us broke into giggles. Rachel watched all this with grave interest.

"Because we're committed to Sunrise," Ruby said finally. Snaker said nothing.

"Yeah, but you'd have more *fun* here."

"There's more to life than having fun."

"*Is* there? What?"

"See what I mean, Sam? You're never serious."

"I've never been more serious. If there is a higher purpose in life than enjoying myself, it has yet to be demonstrated to me."

"Sam, please. We've had this rap. You want to live alone, fine. Snaker and I want to learn how to live with others, without ego or competition or hierarchy. We're trying to find out if people *have* to always be strangers, or if it's just easier. We're trying to get telepathic, to find out if brotherhood is more than just a word. It's important to us."

"And how are you doing?"

"Huh?"

"I say that what happened upstairs awhile ago was the most telepathic, sharing, ego-transcending thing that ever happened to me. How about you? Has anything that telepathic happened at Sunrise lately?"

That generated enough silence for me to get half my breakfast down.

"That last Om," Snaker said finally.

"And look how it turned out," I said, and ate the other half of my breakfast.

"Sam," Ruby said after a while, "why don't *you* move in with *us?*"

The notion startled me; I laughed in self-defense. "I'd sooner have an orchidectomy. Groups aren't my thing."

Snaker spoke up. "I wish you would, Sam. The community could use you. *I* could use you. It'd be nice not being the House Materialist for a change, you know? It'd be comforting to have one other person around who believed in rationality and logic and arithmetic and capitalism and that shit."

I had a sudden flash of insight. "No, it wouldn't."

"Why not?"

"Don't you see, Snake? They tolerate you *because* you're the House Materialist, the sole voice of and for reason. If there were two of you, they'd have to throw you out." I had another flash. "Sooner or later they will anyway."

"You're wrong!" Ruby said.

"Maybe so," I said obligingly. Why make Ruby feel bad when it cost nothing to lie?

But Snaker said nothing. So did Rachel.

As I was thinking about getting up and leaving the shitter, to try again another time, Snaker came in and took the adjacent hole. I grunted a greeting, and he mumbled a reply. Snaker and I had shared an outhouse before, shared a chamber pot—hell, we'd shat in the woods together and wiped our asses with leaves. This time we were uncomfortable. For a while the only sound was Styrofoam creaking under out butts as we shifted our weight.

"Good time, wasn't it?" he asked at last.

"It sure was. It sure was. Uh . . . I'd just as soon not repeat it real soon, if you know what I mean."

Relief was evident in his voice. "I know what you mean. As a regular thing, it'd . . ." He trailed off.

"Yeah." I wondered what he meant, what I meant. "That's one reason why I'll never move into Sunrise with you guys."

He looked surprised. "You mean, you think if we were around each other all the time . . . hell, Sam, that's just backwards. What happened last night would never have happened at all at Sunrise. The community is monogamous, you know that."

"Now that Malachi's satisfied with his partner, yeah. But you don't understand what I mean. I'm not talking about sex, I'm talking about intimacy."

"How do you mean?" he asked.

"Look, you and I had our conversation about bisexuality a year and more ago."

"Yeah. We both felt that if their heads weren't all full of mahooha, everybody'd be bisexual—which is why aggressive cultures make it their business to fill everybody's heads with mahooha."

"And you told me about your couple of experiences—"

"—and you told me about yours, and we agreed that intellectually it all made sense, but emotionally, having been raised in this culture, the best it'd ever been for either of us was Not Totally Awful. That we were both . . . how did you put it?"

"'Bisexual in theory, monosexual in practice.'"

Snaker suddenly grinned. "Jesus Christ, I was hinting like crazy, wasn't I?" He glanced down and to the right, then back up. "*Flirting* is the fucking word for it, I was flirting." Down and to the right, back up, still grinning. "Wasn't I? And you, bless your heart, you played dumb."

"Yeah, man, I was scared. I hadn't had a friend as good as you in a long while. I didn't want to fuck it up. Besides, by then it was shaping up to be you-and-Ruby, and I didn't want to complicate her life either. Or mine, for that matter—but Ruby'd definitely had all the heartache she needed just then."

"Huh! You know, maybe that's why I was flirting with you. I was sensing how heavy it was going to get with Rube—and the part of me that liked being a swinging bachelor started looking around for an escape hatch. What do you know about that?" He had the mild frown of a man for whom many things have suddenly fallen into place.

"Right there," I said, "is why I'll never join your group."

"Huh?"

"It took you a year to be ready to have that insight. But you wouldn't have been allowed to *take* that long if the Gang had known about it. The Sunrise Gang believe in flushing every hang-up a person has out of its hiding place and stomping it to death, right now, right away, no excuses or delays, and that is *not only* intolerable, but wrong." He looked like he wanted to argue, but he said nothing. "Everybody there insists on messing in your thing, getting into your private hang-ups, knowing all your secrets—" A few things fell into place in my own head. "You remember back when Rachel first arrived, before she woke up? How scared I was of her at first?"

"That business with the shotgun signals and all? Yeah, I guess I thought you were being a little paranoid—"

"And you an sf reader. What I was afraid of—so afraid I damned near cut her throat instead of calling you—was that Rachel might be a telepath. *That's* why I wouldn't join Sunrise Hill in a hundred years. You people are deliberately trying to become telepathic: you say so out loud. To the extent that you succeed you are terrifying and dangerous to me. To the extent that you try you seem insane. Snake, *human beings aren't supposed to be telepathic*. There are reasons why our minds are sealed in bone boxes. Look at Malachi. He *is* telepathic, a little bit—and what does he do with it? Snoops and probes and pries and chivvies and powertrips people, finds your weak-spots and lets you know he knows them, finds your blind-spots and stores the knowledge . . . Ask anybody, who's the leader of Sunrise Hill? Oh, we don't have a leader. But when was the last time the big bald son of a bitch lost an argument he really wanted to win? And *he* isn't even really telepathic—that's just hippie jargon for what he is, which is observant and empathic and clever and insightful and glib. The only reason he's tolerable is that there is no evil in him. And he can be fooled by someone as clever as himself.

"But a *real* telepath? Someone who knew your innermost thoughts and feelings and dreams and secrets? If I thought there was one near me, I'd try my best to kill him—and maybe the worst part is that I'd never succeed."

Snaker was frowning. He was busy. "Kill him why?" he grunted between waves.

"Two reasons, either one sufficient. First, plain old intelligent paranoia. A telepath *owns* you. You live at his sufferance. If he chooses to kill you, you can't stop him: he will *always* be one move ahead of you. Unforgivable.

Intolerable. Even if his intentions are utterly benign . . . they could change. Get outside his effective range *fast,* whatever it is, and lob grenades at him. It's your only sensible option. Noboby should be able to see through the bone box. It's too much power for any human to have.

"And the second reason has to do with, like, intimacy, dignity, privacy, the right to be free from unreasonable search and seizure inside your own head. A telepath would be the ultimate Peeping Tom. The ultravoyeur. The eavesdropper and the diary-reader and the unethical hypnotherapist rolled into one and cubed. Invasion of privacy on that big a scale calls for the death penalty; I think so, anyway. I don't know about you, but I have secrets in *my* head that *I'd* kill to protect. Even from you, old buddy. Not even things that could be used against me, necessarily. Just private. Personal."

Snaker was looking thoughtful.

"It keeps coming back to what I was talking about before. Intimacy. When I moved up here from the States I hadn't been intimate with anyone or anything in . . . anyway a long time. Typical uptight city kid.

"Then I come up here. Wham! One by one my walls started tumbling, boundaries crumbling. People up here share a chamber pot and don't think anything of it. Men don't turn their backs to the road when they feel like taking a piss, ladies squat with you standing right there. A new kind of intimacy. Nobody locks their doors, or cars, or bedroom doors: another kind of nakedness. People swim and bathe literally naked together, for that matter, and work too, sometimes, I've seen the Sunrise women topless in the garden on a hot day just like the men. The hippies and the locals each have their own jungledrum networks, so interwoven they might as well be left and right hemispheres of the same brain, so efficient that as we sit here there are people down on the South Mountain, back up in the piney woods, who are already working out what they're going to say to the Chinee Book Writer Lady when she gets around to interviewing *them*. To live here in the Annapolis Valley is to be naked to everyone else in it.

"So I have—dubiously, reluctantly, suspiciously—taken off several layers of armor that I carried around with me for years. And on the whole it has been good for me. It's pretty safe around here without armor.

"But enough is enough. I have reached my limit. What happened between us last night is the most intimate I ever want to get with anyone, and I don't want to do *that* very often."

I reached up and touched Snaker's face, touched his left cheek above the beardline with three fingers of my right hand. He backed away. "You see? You flinch. So do I. Whether it's instinct or learned behavior, what's the difference? Even friends or lovers need at least a little bit of distance. There's a use for layers of formality, restraint, inhibition, that *prevent* telepathic exchange, that bottle up the moment-by-moment unpleasantnesses and uglinesses of consciousness and give us time to edit ourselves into tolerability." I stood up and adjusted my clothing, ladled a couple of scoops of stove ashes and lime into the hole, and handed the ladle to Snaker.

"I need you for a friend, Sam," he said, finishing his own ablutions.

"And I need you for a friend. If we lived together maybe we'd become more than that, and I don't know that I need that. If *you* do, you have Ruby for it. Everything doesn't always progress naturally toward blissful unity, Snake. Your problem is, you want to marry *everybody*. If you could get all your best friends and loved ones and soul mates in one room, and give us some new drug that made us all be telepathic together . . . we'd probably go for each others' throats."

Snaker was frowning and nodding, zipping up his overalls. "If my thought-dreams could be seen . . . Yeah, I read that Poul Anderson story, too, man. '. . . *Get out! I hate your bloody guts!*' said the only two telepaths in the world to each other. Is it really that disgusting inside a human head?"

"Isn't it?"

He hung the ladle, put the wooden lid down over number two hole and straightened up. I popped the hook-and-eye, the door flew open, and we stepped out into the cold wind. By tacit mutual agreement we walked past the house and halfway down the driveway to where he had a good view of the Bay and the sky. We shared it in silence for a few minutes. He had some ready-mades, Players, and smoked one. Being around smokers bothers me. It seems to comfort them so, the times it isn't just a reflex. I resent a crutch that I can't use, to the extent that it works. It's only fair that it should kill them.

"Yeah, I guess it is," he said softly at last.

He fieldstripped the butt and pocketed the filter. I watched the sun dance on the water.

"There's a hole in your logic, Sam. I can smell it." He sighed. "But I can't find it."

"You're a romantic, man. You want life to be perfectible. It ain't."

"What's the harm in trying? You know that old chestnut about the two frogs that fell into the bucket of cream."

"The Persistent Frog survived only because it was cream in that bucket. A bucket of shit, for instance, gets *softer* when you churn it. And the smell becomes more offensive. The thing about blind optimism, man, it's *blind*."

"Your pessimism is just as blind, brother."

"Granted. But I know which way to bet. It'd be nice if the human race could *all* get telepathic and all love one another one day—but it ain't gonna happen. If, God forbid, some dedicated researcher does stumble across true telepathy, the race will be extinct in a generation. The handful who survive the Total War won't dare get close enough to anyone else to reproduce."

"Jesus!" He took out another ready-made. Eight matches

later it was lit. "That's a hell of a story idea, you know. Creepy, but interesting."

"It's yours. If you sell it, buy me a flat of beer."

He looked thoughtful—then frowned. "No. It'd be a good story: I mean, it'd sell. But it's not the kind of story I want to write. Listen, Ruby and I have to get back—there's a meeting today, to start planning the garden."

I grinned. "Not a moment too soon."

Does it seem odd that the Sunrise Gang were planning their garden in late March, when nothing goes in the ground in Nova Scotia before the first of June? Then I haven't conveyed the Spirit of Sunrise: hot air. The Gang were perfectly capable of spending several weeks debating Whether It Was Far Out To Wear *Imitation* Leather Since That *Too* Bought Into The Kharma Of Slaughtering Animals. Something as genuinely involving as The Next Year's Food—not to mention Three Months Of Backbreaking Labour—could easily take them over two months of constant discussion to thrash out. If D-Day had been as overplanned as a Sunrise Hill garden . . . it would probably have turned out just as chaotically, I suppose.

One thing I must admit: they seemed to have learned the secret of arguing without fighting, of wrangling without getting angry. In cabin-fever season, that is one *hell* of an impressive achievement, when you think about it.

"Yeah, we're thinking about adding a third acre. Soybeans."

"You're crazy. Soybeans won't grow here."

"Well . . . Nazz and Lucas have a theory. And we won't really be self-sufficient until we grow our own soybeans."

"It's your back, pal. Good luck. Listen, you mind if Rachel and I bum a ride a ways? I want to introduce her to Mona and Truman. She's been bugging me about it since Mona laid that tire on you the other day."

"Sure. She can sit . . . huh! I started to say, Rachel

could be the one who gets to sit in the back, since she doesn't mind cold. But we'd never explain that to Ruby."

"We'll both ride in back, let you two lovebirds have the cab to yourselves."

"Begin redrawing the lines, Sam? Start puttin' the fences back up?"

"Isn't it time?"

Sigh. "Yeah. Yeah, it is."

He started to head back indoors. I stopped him, turned him, hesitated a split second and hugged him, hesitated an intact second and kissed him. He hugged me back and kissed me back without any hesitation.

It really is hard to manage two beards. Do you suppose that's why they invented shaving?

"It was fun," Snaker said finally, breaking the hug. "Ten years from now we'll do it again."

"Talk about extended foreplay. It's a deal. Uh . . . for what it's worth, you give good head."

"Yeah," he agreed. "Yeah, I do. I always thought I would, if it was somebody I cared about. So do you." He grinned. "But Ruby's better."

"You're a lucky man, Snaker."

"I know. I know."

THIRTEEN

LET ME TELL you about the last time I mistook Rachel for a city person.

Living in Nova Scotia had encouraged me to divide the human race into city people and country people, and since Rachel came from the future, and it was axiomatic to me that future meant huge population, higher and higher tech, progressive hyperurbanization, I thought of her as a city person. I assumed, for instance, her ignorance of woodstoves and outhouses and gardening, woodscraft and carpentry and such things. In my own time, they seemed already nearly obsolete.

I *think* I was often right. But not always. It turned out, for instance, that she knew more about gardening than I'll ever know.

But the day I took her to meet the Bents, I finally shook the City Mouse stereotype out of my subconscious.

On the way over, huddled under a blanket in Blue

Meanie's truckbed with her, I tried to brief her about Mona and Truman Bent. I've learned to see, a little bit, since I got here, and I can now see that Mona is very beautiful. But when I first arrived, a city person, my notion of beauty was not mature enough to stretch to encompass Mona's missing teeth, or her fireplug figure. Similarly, it took me some time to realize that her strident voice could seem mellifluous to some ears. It took me longest of all to understand why the herd of ragamuffin kids she tyrannized so ruthlessly loved her so unreservedly. To be sure, she handed out hugs and kisses and treats liberally to those who earned them, and her weirdly beautiful smiles were not too expensive for a child to earn. But she also enforced a stern and unyielding discipline by lashing them with her harsh voice, once in a while by cracking them across the mouth with a horny hand—and once I saw her kick a little mongoloid boy square in the ass.

It was that particular episode that triggered understanding at last, brought me to realize that orphaned inbred diseased retarded rejected foster children who had been shuffled around for months and years by bad luck and bureaucracy before landing at the Bents' might require a special kind of loving, and that unsophisticated uneducated Mona might just know more about it than I did. Seeing her kick that kid had reminded me of something.

When I was a teenager I did a couple of weekends of volunteer work. They sent three of us to an orphanage in Far Rockaway; we were supposed to take groups of orphans on outings, to see the Hayden Planetarium and the Statue of Liberty and so forth. Boys, aged seven to twelve, from the mean streets—the toughest little sons of bitches I've ever met in my life. Orphaned by murder or overdose or suicide or the electric chair or Castro's revolution, they were the kind of inner-city gutter rats you patted down for shanks before leaving the grounds. We were dumbass future-liberals from Long Island. The first day, a nine-year-old with his leg in a cast to the hip, a kid with the kind of sweet, almost effeminate features that make grandmothers swoon, asked my friend Petey for a cigarette. Petey told him he was too young to smoke. The adorable little kid hauled off and broke Petey's shin with his cast. The other kids fell down laughing.

While the staff liaison was taking Petey off to the Infirmary, my only remaining partner Mike approached the kid with the cast. The boy put a hand into his pocket and left it there. Mike smiled at him, held up his hands in a conciliatory gesture, and with no windup at all kicked the kid in the balls so hard his cast banged back down on the floor. Mike took the kid's knife, turned to me and smiled and said, "The first step in training a mule is to get the mule's attention," and we had an uneventful visit to the Empire State Building that day. . . .

So when, years later, I saw Mona kick slack-jawed, almond-eyed Joey because he had deliberately hurt a smaller child, I swallowed my liberal instincts and watched to see how Joey took it. Like that sweet-faced thug with the cast, he reacted not with anger or fear, but with something like respect, something oddly like satisfaction, relief, as though the essential order and correctness of the universe had been reaffirmed.

I tried to tell Rachel all of this and more, on her way to meet Mona and Truman for the first time, to prepare her, because I was thinking of Rachel as a city person and city people sometimes disapproved of Mona on first meeting. (It was usually three or four visits before people got enough sense of Truman to know whether they liked him or not.)

Rachel cut me off. "Sam, I must not allow your opinions to colour my observations. I know you mean well, but please, let me form my own impressions." Exasperated, I agreed, and spent the rest of the trip worrying.

And of course, within ten seconds of the introduction, Mona and Rachel had established a rapport deeper and wider than I had managed in three years.

• • •

It wasn't anything they said. If I quoted you their dialogue it would bore you to tears. What happened was simply this: that in the moment their eyes met for the first time they knew each other. Recognition signals were exchanged, mutual respect was acknowledged, in some way I could dimly perceive but not even dimly understand. They forgot to pretend I was there.

I went out back and tried talking with Truman, which of course didn't work. Truman was a very pleasant man. He looked like Raymond Massey with three teeth missing. He never had any more or less than two days' growth of beard, and the beard was white even though his hair was brown. Truman didn't talk much. He hadn't learned how until he was fifteen. Mona had just plain bullied him into it. He never would learn to read, he simply wasn't equipped, but she wouldn't stop trying to teach him until one of them died. He was probably the *nicest*, most loving man I knew. Certainly the strongest: I once saw him carry a rock the size of a beer-fridge ten meters, his boots sinking ankle-deep in unturned soil. Like the kids, he worshipped Mona.

I found him splitting firewood. I got his spare axe and joined him, spent twenty minutes in "conversation" with him across the chopping block. As always I wondered if he appreciated the courtesy or dreaded the ordeal. Most of his vocabulary was "Guess so," and "I don't s'pose, naw."

If you are City-Folk, you may have the idea that Truman was stupid. Once I came upon him in the midst of a disassembled combine. It is so complicated a machine I despair of describing it; its very complexity stuns the eye. He was *wearing* it, slick with grease and sweat. It looked as though some hideous insect lifeform had him half swallowed. "Figure you can get that thing back together again, Truman?" I asked.

He blinked at me and thought about it. "A man made it," he said, and went back to work. And had it running before nightfall.

You may suffer from the delusion that you know what intelligence is. I don't. Illiterate Truman owned his own home, owned (and maintained) the one-ton truck with which he earned enough to feed and clothe and warm a whole brood of raggedy kids, owned a great deal of land and other shrewd investments. I had a liberal arts education, sophisticated musical skills and a glib tongue—and I owned a guitar and some books and records. Talking with him always made *me* feel like a moron.

In the background I could hear Mona and Rachel talking a mile a minute, two kindred souls.

I left after half an hour and they never noticed. Rachel was standing behind Mona, kneading her shoulders; they were deep in conversation, thick as thieves. I wandered up the road to Sunrise and ate soyburger and got into the argument about their garden, a waste of time if there ever was one.

In the end, my stock with Mona went up because I was the one who had introduced her to Rachel.

"Sam," Rachel said to me after we got home that night, "you are exasperated about something. What is it?"

I'd been thinking about that very thing. "I think I'm jealous."

She looked surprised. For her. "Really?"

"Yeah. Of you and Mona. You and Sunrise Hill, for that matter."

Now she looked surprised even for a human being. "I don't understand, Sam."

"I'm not sure I do either. I'm working this out as I speak." We were in the living room, sharing the warmth of the fire before I went upstairs to sleep. It really was turning out to be nice, having someone to keep the fire going all night long, sometimes, waking up to a warm house. Well, a less cold one. "It's just that . . . that . . . dammit, I'm a science fiction reader, all my *life* I've been training to meet a time-traveler, here you are, I meet you . . . and people who've never read *anything* seem to know you better than I do, in ways that I can see, but will never understand. It just isn't right. If anyone on this goddam *Mountain* ought to know you, ought to have rapport with you, it's me. Snaker's the only other sf fan for a hundred miles, except maybe Nazz. And there is something between you and Mona for Chrissake Bent that is deeper and stronger than anything I've managed to build with her in three years' acquaintance. Sometimes I think you have more in common with the superstitious anti-tech clowns at Sunrise Hill than you do with me. You spend as much time over there as you do here, and whenever they start running down science and reason and I argue with them, like tonight when you came in on the Garden Meeting, *goddammit, you won't fucking back me up!*" I was pacing around the living room now, gesturing with the cast-iron poker. "I thought we'd have something special in common and we don't really seem to; you and Mona shouldn't have *anything* in common, but you do anyway. And I don't even understand what it is. Why did you hit it off so quickly with her?"

Sprawled gracefully in my recliner chair, Rachel watched me pace and gesticulate with grave interest. "What I love in Mona is her need to love."

"What do you mean?"

"We talked about you a lot, Sam. She thinks you badly need someone to love. Do you think she is right?"

The question came from left field; I answered automatically and honestly. "I have never been in love. I have successfully faked it eight times since I was sixteen years old—half those times in order to secure a steady sex partner, and the other half because I felt a need to convince myself that I was capable of loving. I gave it up doing it for either reason. Not soon enough. Not when I realized how much pain I was causing to innocent ladies; considerably after that. Considerably. To my certain knowledge, I have not loved anyone since my mother. I have been sexually fixated for brief periods. I've been jealous of a mate, like, stingy with a possession. But I've never felt that thunderbolt they talk of, that dizzy compulsion to be with someone else constantly and make them happy and tear down all the walls between us. There has never been anyone in my life that I would die for.

"If love is what Robert Heinlein said, the condition in which the welfare and happiness of another are essential to your own, then I have never loved. The welfare and happiness of another have often been relevant to my own . . . but never really essential. I'm still undecided whether I'm a monster, or everyone else is kidding themselves."

(Jesus, the last time I had spoken thoughts like this aloud to anyone had been . . . Finals Week, to Frank. Which reminded me of something, but I couldn't pin it down.)

I opened up the Ashley and made elaborate unnecessary adjustments to the logs inside, banging and clanking and swearing under my breath as much as possible. Rachel watched in silence until I had closed it up and reset the damper. The only place I had ever seen faces *that* expressionless, not even a wrinkle to show that an expression had ever been there, was in a—

"Sam? When was the last time you pretended to be in love?"

I waited, honestly curious to know whether or not I would tell her; heard my voice decide: "No. That I won't talk about."

"That bad?"

"Look." My face was warm. "Look. You have things you won't talk about, right? Questions *I* have that aren't just idle curiosity or being polite, questions that really matter to me that you won't answer, right? Well, this is one of those for me."

"I'm not being polite, Sam—"

"—damn right you're not—"

"—or idly curious. Are the cases parallel? Do you say

that reality itself might crumble if you answered my question?"

"No. I mean I don't want to talk about it, and I won't."

Very softly she said, "You'll have to talk about Barbara *some* day to *some*one—"

"How do you know her name?" I roared, the hair standing up on the back of my neck.

"Because what your conscious mind refuses to touch, your unconscious cannot leave alone. You cry out her name at night sometimes. Sometimes you talk to her."

I did like hell talk in my sleep! And if I did, it wouldn't be to Barbara. I started to say so—

—and paused. How did I know? How long had it been since anyone but Rachel had stayed the night? Could she possibly be right?

But Barbara was dead. Asleep or awake, I didn't believe in ghosts, and calling out someone's name in my sleep was just too corny. I could not believe it of myself.

But how else would Rachel have known her name?

I thought of a way, and it wasn't just the back of my neck now, my whole scalp was crawling. Either I wasn't nearly as tightly wrapped as I thought—

—or Rachel was a telepath after all. . . .

"What do I say to her in my sleep?"

"I can't say. You mumble. Uh, you apologize to her a lot."

"What for?"

"I don't know."

I searched and searched that unreadable face of hers. How much did I trust Rachel, after all? I had never caught her in a lie.

It came to me that if she *were* a telepath, I never would . . .

—which suggested the thought that if she *were* a telepath, I was thinking thoughts that could get me killed. . . .

—which suggested that since I was still breathing, she was not a telepath . . .

—or she was a very clever one . . .

My head began to hurt. I looked away from her almond eyes and opened the Ashley's damper a quarter turn to inspire the fire. "Let's change the subject."

"All right. Why did you come to Nova Scotia?"

The damper spun in three complete circles, sending smoke puffing out from under the lid of the stove, and the heavy iron poker dropped to the floor with a crash. I used the time it took me to pick it up to think hard.

Suppose that Rachel *was* a telepath. Surely, then, she knew that the moment I became convinced of that, there would be a death struggle between us. Was she now trying to provoke it?

Suppose she was *not* a telepath. How, then, in the *hell* did she know that "Who is Barbara?" and "Why did you come to Nova Scotia?" were the same question? I refused to believe that I could have talked enough in my sleep for that.

Or could it be total coincidence, one of those improbable synchronistic ironies that happen to everyone at times? At various times I had heard her ask the same question of Ruby, Tommy, Nazz, Malachi and others. It was a logical question for a cultural anthropologist to ask an immigrant; only a matter of time until she'd gotten around to me.

It was just the timing that was so hard to swallow. It could easily be read as a refusal to change the subject. Malachi did that sometimes; he would "drop a subject" by approaching it from another direction. It was just the sort of thing Malachi would be doing now if he had a hint that I had a hangup called Barbara, if he ever suspected that my avowed reason for being here was a lie.

So there were only two ways to go. Make a break for the shotgun that hung over the back door, two rooms distant—and if I were right, die on the way. Or assume that Rachel was *not* privy to my secret thoughts, that her question was innocent, and give my avowed reason for being here.

It wasn't much of a choice.

"It wasn't much of a choice. I could go to a hot place

where everyone shot at me, or a federal prison, or a cold place where everyone was friendly and decent. The day my draft board classified me 1-A, I crossed the border." I sat sideways on the couch facing her, head cradled on my forearm.

"You did not support the Viet Nam war."

"I never addressed the question. If people wanted to do that, they were welcome to. I just figured that if there was no person I loved enough to die for, then I certainly wasn't going to risk it for an abstraction. My father being a military man of rank, it became necessary to go somewhere far away. Here I am."

"You are a pacifist?"

"No, no, no. I am a *coward*. Cowards can't be pacifists. Pacifism involves a moral commitment, a willingness to die rather than use force. I'm not certain any such people exist. I am certain I'm not one of them."

"You could kill in self-defense?"

"And for no other reason I can think of."

"Would you kill for Snaker?"

I hesitated. "Maybe. If it was the only way to save his life, yeah, maybe. Ruby too, I guess. Hard to imagine."

"Would you die for them?"

"No. I'd like to think I would, but I wouldn't. Friends are nice, but I can live without them. I can't live without me." I changed position, lay with my feet toward Rachel, looking up at the ceiling beams.

"Do you think Snaker would die for you?"

That one took me by surprise. I had to think a minute. "Yeah," I said finally. "As his lights went out he'd be regretting it, calling himself a jerk—but if he didn't have too much time to think about it, he probably would. There's a lot of people and things he'd probably die for. Snaker can love, or can kid himself that he does, which comes down to the same thing."

"Do you wish that you could?"

"Look what it gets him and Ruby. He loves her, and she

loves him and the commune. One day soon she's going to have to choose between them—and he's scared to death."

"But you envy him."

"Sometimes. I used to more than I do these days. I'm pretty used to who I am by now. Simple intelligent self-interest seems to be enough to make me a decent neighbour. That'll do.

"But you, Rachel, what you've done I will never understand. Coming all this way, exiling yourself to a drastically shortened lifetime among strangers in a primitive time—to go through so much in pursuit of abstract knowledge—what drives you? I just don't get it. Is it love, duty, fear, need, what? Is this a sacred kamikaze mission for you, or is it your punishment for horrid crimes? Or is it just that immortals stop fearing death?"

"Some of all of those," she said. "It's like your Barbara. I won't talk about it."

Which left me no comeback. The subject was dropped.

It kept going like that, as Rachel worked her way across the North Mountain, "interviewing people for her book": the people I had expected her to have the most trouble relating to were usually the ones with whom she established immediate empathy and mutual respect. Locals, as we hippies called native Nova Scotians, did not, as a rule, "take to" strangers quickly. Oh, they'd be friendly, more than polite—but they held back something, they didn't really fully accept you into the community until you'd survived your third winter without quitting and moving south, been around a few years and shown some stuff, demonstrated that your word was good and your skull occupied.

But Rachel was the rare newcomer who was taken nearly at once to the collective bosom of the locals. She shared something with them that my hippie friends and I did not, and I could not for the life of me pin down just what it was. The phenomenon was not always as strong and noticeable as it had been with Mona Bent, but it was pretty nearly universal. It was as though they looked deeply *once* into her eyes and saw all they needed to see; within minutes they would be allowing her to rub their necks, and chattering happily about The Old Days. And telling her the real inside story, too, as near as I could tell.

There were exceptions, like old Wendell Rafuse, of course.

How can I explain Wendell? East of Heartbreak Hotel lies the home of Phylippa Brown, whose husband inconsiderately died a decade ago and left her with two girls, Pris and Cam, and damn little else. When Phyl's oil furnace died a couple of winters ago, the next morning two true cords of cut split stacked firewood had magically appeared by her front door, *without waking her or the girls*. That same winter, Wendell Rafuse's furnace failed too, and he was a frail sixty-two—but Wendell was known to have cheated his brother out of a valuable piece of land, by misusing a power of attorney while the brother was in hospital. No wood appeared outside Wendell's door. He could afford a new furnace . . . but he burned up a lot of furniture in the three days it took to get it delivered and installed.

People like Wendell tended to decline to be interviewed by some kind of Chinese nigger woman who paid no fee.

But even some of that type accepted Rachel, perhaps because her cover identity offered the hope of seeing themselves in print some day, perhaps simply because they were lonely.

Most of the local people let her into their homes, gave her tea and cakes, answered her questions, talked about their lives, many of them accepted her offer of a massage—a great many as the word began to spread about how good she was at it. She did not ever repeat anything she had been told in confidence, however juicy; somehow the word spread about that too. Blakey Sabean said of her once approvingly that, "She don't smile just to dry her teeth."

It surprised me how quickly and easily the local folk,

both Mountain and Valley (and good books have been written on the subtle but important differences between the two kinds of people) took Rachel into their homes and their hearts. What surprised me even more was how easily the hippies took her into their beds.

Not the fact itself. Rachel was an attractive female, with dark exotic good looks, and early Summer was the traditional time for the hippie folk to play Musical Beds if they were going to. What surprised me almost to the point of awe was how gracefully and painlessly she managed it.

Her experience with Snaker and Ruby and me seemed to be typical. She had the mystic ability to enter a home, have sex with everyone in it, open them to new ways of loving, and then exit painlessly, leaving behind relationships *stronger* than before.

We had had sexual superstars pass through in previous years, attempting to seduce anything that wore clothes and often succeeding. But usually when such carnal comets blazed over the Mountain, they burned what they touched. This one left no trail of wreckage, no clap, no crabs, no regrets. Most extraordinary. This was the woman I had thought untantric.

Part of it must have been her very straightforwardness. Anyone could see that there was no evil in Rachel, no guile. When she gave of herself it was not to rack up a score, not for reasons of power or manipulativeness or bargaining or mischief, but just for the joy of it. She was a noncombatant in the battle of the sexes, and she was *temporary*, as perhaps a more textured personality could not have been.

Here is the closest I can come to explaining it:

One winter I was on a Greyhound bus, returning to college after Christmas vacation. A blizzard descended; the bus driver was forced to leave the Thruway. We were stranded for a week, totally snowed in, miles from civilization, nearly five dozen of us in a single large room.

A bar. All expenses paid by Greyhound. . . .

All the passengers were students, returning to assorted

midstate colleges and universities. The male-female ratio approached parity. We had four guitars, a sax, a flute, and eight people who could play the house piano. We had unlimited food and booze, and adequate drugs. I guess you could call what developed an orgy. It was a vacation from reality. All the rules were suspended. You could create a new self, without necessarily having to live up to it. Everyone slept with everyone, without jealousy or pain. There were *no* fights, not so much as an argument. Amazing music was played. When the big plows finally came by we all found our clothes and boarded the bus and went back to our lives, and I do not believe any of us so much as wrote to one another. We had not exchanged names let alone addresses.

Can you imagine that head-space, the dreamy accepting state of mind in which you have the vague conviction that *this doesn't count*, that you are comped and covered and exempt and it's safe to go on instinct?

Rachel was that condition on two legs. And they spread easily.

But not wantonly. Her judgment was fine. She did not, for instance, make a pass at Tommy, nor at the monks-in-training down at the Ashram, nor at any of the handful of other voluntary celibates among the hippies. She side-stepped around Malachi and Sally when they were having struggle in their relationship, presumably out of a sense that it would be a destabilizing intrusion—and yet she made it with Zack and Jill while they were squabbling, and they came out of it stronger. She got it on with bachelors of both sexes, and with couples married and unmarried, and with the three-marriage over on the South Mountain and the six-marriage over in Mount Hanley and the two gay men who lived together but weren't lovers down in Port Lorne (when she left they were lovers). She did it with George and Annie from Outram a week before Annie gave birth—and was there for the birth, cut the cord I'm told. Maybe they had planned to name the kid Rachel anyway.

Whether she had sex with any of the locals, I could not say for sure. Their grapevine worked differently from ours; they were more reticent about such things. But I'm inclined to think that she did not . . . or that she did so rarely and quite selectively. Most of the locals lived by a different moral code, which precluded "fooling around." Extreme sexual openness tended to open hippie doors, but it would have closed most local ones. There were, of course, exceptions and borderline cases, especially among some of the younger locals. All I can say for certain is that the scandal I constantly half expected never materialized. No one shot or cut anyone—or even punched anyone—over Rachel.

If none of this is ringing true for you, if your stereotype of country folk is that they are conservative, intolerant, stiffnecked and deeply suspicious of anyone or anything strange . . . well, you haven't been to the North Mountain, that's all.

Rachel was extremely good at drawing them out, scribbling copious notes in an impressive impenetrable shorthand which she admitted privately was fake. Folks didn't all bond with her as solidly as Mona had, there was something special about that relationship. But they all brought out their best china for her, if that conveys anything to you. I went along with her on her first half-dozen calls, realized by the third that I was superfluous, realized by the sixth that I was a hindrance and stopped coming along. She was launched.

She used Heartbreak Hotel as a home base. Two or three days a week she would be there to help me with whatever work I was doing. Two or three nights a week she was there for me to have sex with, and held me until I fell asleep. In between she popped in for unexpected and always pleasant intervals, then disappeared again. She would tell me where she was going if I asked. Other than that I kept in contact with her mostly by grapevine. Fairly close contact, that is to say. I always had the sense that I was her Special Friend.

But I never had encouragement or opportunity to be more than that, to come to depend on her in any sense.

A few months went by.

Those months were the ones that connect Winter to Summer in Nova Scotia. (We don't get Spring.) That made them the most achingly beautiful time of the year—in a province which is never less than stunning—and the second busiest. (The busiest time is when Winter is coming on fast and you still don't have your firewood cut or your house banked.)

With the approach of Summer, people who've spent months marking time, caning chairs, battling cabin fever, all suddenly step outdoors, blink at the absence of snow, tear off their Stanfields and become whirlwinds of activity as they realize that they will have a maximum of four months' grace to lay up enough nuts to last through the *next* Winter. To compensate them for this, the world turns warm and fecund and friendly; almost overnight the North Mountain turns into the Big Rock Candy Mountain, and people's faces start to hurt from smiling so much.

Fair-weather friends began to drift back to Sunrise Hill from all around the planet to help get the crops into the ground, repair the ravages of the winter past and initiate new construction. That year's crop of Hippie transients began passing through, backpacked and headbanded and Earthshoed and fluted. Summer-resident property owners made their annual reappearance from Halifax or the States, to take their Mountain homesteads down off the blocks and jumpstart them again. The stinking goddamned snowmobiles were silenced, and the equally grating but somehow more tolerable sounds of chainsaws and rototillers and tractors were heard in the land. Deer and rabbits and weasels and crows were somehow synthesized out of the defrosting bedrock of the Mountain and began to scamper around the landscape, which turned several hundred colours, nearly all of them called "green" in our poor grunting language. The Bay suddenly filled with vessels of every kind and type, small fishing and lobstering boats close-in (one popular model looked very much like a phonebooth in a bathtub), and big tankers and freighters farther out. Those people who earned their living by milking tourists began sacrificing to the gods in hopes of a good harvest, and calculating how badly they dared burn Americans on the exchange rate. Farmers and seeds began making intricate conditional promises to one another, both sides with fingers crossed behind their backs. A busy, happy time, full of square-dances and house-raisings, shared work and shared pleasure, new lovers and old friends, fresh food and fresh dope, fresh faces and fresh hope.

Some of this I shared with Rachel—but as the weeks went by and Winter wore itself out, she spent less and less time at Heartbreak Hotel, and more and more time at her work, talking to the people of the Annapolis Valley, resident and transient, hippie and local, asking them about their lives and the way they lived them, about the choices they had made and the choices they wished they had, what it was like here when they were children and how it had changed, the things they were most proud of and the things they regretted. And massaging them as they talked.

On the morning of the day before the big Summer Solstice Celebration, I saw her for the first time in over a week. She'd gone to the South Mountain for a while, an area so upcountry and backwoods that it makes the North Mountain seem like suburbia. (I met someone there once who claimed she had never in her life actually seen an electric light up close. I believed her.) We had breakfast together.

I remember the last time I saw Rachel in this life. I stood on the hard rock shore of the Bay of Fundy at low tide, spray at my back, rich shore smell in my nostrils, watching her walk toward me from my doorstep a hundred meters away, watching her cross the road, clamber down the four-meter hill, stride across fifty meters of scrubby marshland, pick her way with easy grace through the treacherous jumble of bleached driftwood that lines the shore, navigate the ankle-breaking rock of the shore itself without hesitation or awkwardness, walk right into my arms and into a kiss without ever having removed her eyes from mine from the moment she'd left the Hotel. "I have to go now, Sam," she said. "I promised Ted and Jayne and David I'd help them get the rest of their garden in the ground before it's too late."

"Sure, hon," I said, "Give them my best."

"I will. I'll come back tomorrow and help you carry things over to Louis's barn for the Solstice Feast."

"Thanks, Rachel. That'd be a help."

She let go of me, turned and retraced her steps to the road. The process was as beautiful to watch from behind as it had been from in front. "Sweet night," I called after her, and she nodded without turning. She turned right when she reached the road and started walking toward Parsons' Cove, in no hurry at all. When she was out of sight around the bend I turned back to the sea and returned to my thoughts.

And that was the day I had the thought that killed me.

FOURTEEN

THE SUMMER SOLSTICE party was sort of Woodstock Nation's Last Gasp, the sort of jamboree that, cynical travelers assured us, could no longer occur within the borders of the United States of America. There was nothing particularly structured, certainly nothing remotely commercial or professional about it. No organizers, no steering committee, no Board of Directors. No tickets; no steenkin bodges. It just seemed to happen every year: the annual Gathering of the Nova Scotia Hippies.

Primarily, of course, it was a gathering of Annapolis Valley Hippies, for that was where the province's hippie-density was highest. But New Age people came from as far away as Yarmouth, over a hundred kilometers west; from Barrington Passage, a hundred and fifty klicks south; from Amherst, nearly three hundred klicks' drive away up around the Minas Basin; and from Glace Bay four hundred and fifty klicks to the east, out where Cape Breton Island thrusts its jaw truculently out into the cold North Atlantic. For that matter, random travelers came from all over the planet—but the above parameters roughly defined the boundaries of the Hippie Grapevine, and incorporated most of the people who could expect to be recognized, by reputation if nothing else, when they arrived.

I remember an early Solstice with no more than fifty or sixty folks, held in a half-acre field out behind the Big House at Sunrise Hill. The year before this, there'd been well over five hundred, overflowing even Louis Amys' stupendous dairy barn, the pride of six counties. (Unlike Max Yasgur—and possibly because North Mountain Hippies as a group still felt collective guilt over that poor Woodstock farmer—Louis swore he'd never had such a good time in his life; he had not so much agreed, as demanded, to host it again this year, and in all future years. No one had any objection. A merry soul, Louis.)

What happened at a Solstice Festival (or Celebration, or Feast, or Party, or Thing—it's indicative that the name was not fixed) was simply that several hundred Aquarian flower children got together and ate immense quantities of each others' organically grown holistically prepared food, and drank immense quantities of each others' organic cider and beer and wine, and smoked immense quantities of each others' organic dope, and talked and sang and talked and danced and talked and laughed and talked and cried and talked and gave each other things. Two things perennially baffled the locals, who observed from a polite distance: that we did not break anything, and that there were never any fights.

Within those general parameters, it was different each year, and always a good time. There was a swimmin' hole just within walking distance, and Amos had hay fields enough to accommodate a hundred couples making love under the stars, or fucking as the case might be, and the acoustics in the barn's top floor were so splendid that even unrehearsed amateurs sounded good. I was particularly looking forward to one of the few things that could have been called a tradition in such a deliberately spontaneous event: to a five-hundred-throat Om. Without Sunrise restraints . . . yum!

I was also looking forward to The Jam, of course. To be sure, there would be at least forty musicians who would drive me out of my mind—nice people, doubtless from good families, who through no fault of their own had trouble with Bob Dylan and Leonard Cohen songs. Or who insisted on playing nothing else *but* Dylan and Cohen songs. But I could also expect anywhere from five to twenty real musicians, singly and in bunches.

Hey, listen, I don't care where you are, the woods of Nova Scotia, New York, L.A., Minneapolis even—you get a chance to play with twenty real musicians in a year, you're rich.

So the day before this Grand Pantechnicon I was sitting in my kitchen, dawdling over the remains of lunch. I was so eager for an excuse not to go back out into the sunshine and split more wood that I decided, quite unnecessarily, to Make Some Plans for the affair. If I had only properly grasped the Hippie ethos of "just let it unfold, man," it could have saved my life.

There would be at least two fiddles, a banjo or so, a few harmonicas, congas and bongos and a handful of people who could tease music out of Louis's beat-up upright piano. I knew for sure of a bass, a clarinet and—most delicious prospect of all—"Fast" Layne Francis from Halifax, the best sax player I ever heard. There was no telling what else would show; I wouldn't have been surprised by an alp horn or a solar-powered Moog.

But one thing was sure. There would be a surfeit of guitars.

I intended to play mine nevertheless. It was my main instrument, the one I was most at home on, the one I could jam best with. But it occurred to me that it would be nice to be able to switch off, from time to time, to some less clichéd, more exotic instruments. Add a little texture to the sound. Challenge myself. Impress folks with my eclecticism.

Flies buzzed around my kitchen, looking for the egress. I got up and scraped the leftovers into the compost bucket. Thank God the water line had finally unfrozen and the pump was working again. It made cleanup so much less painful. Not to mention morning coffee.

Let's see, I thought, I could bring along the autoharp, and the mandolin . . . say, I could finish up that dulcimer, there was just enough time left before the feast for the glue to—

Jesus Christ on a Snowmobile.

Mucus the Moose.

Abandoned—worse, *forgotten*—on a frozen hillside. For weeks. Weeks of the usual crazy climate extremes, at that. Temperature change might have already cracked the noble moose. He might be spilling his guts right now—

Pausing only to grab a shirt, I took off up the hill. I was heartsick at my stupidity. How could I have forgotten Mucus? For so long?

It was like tugging at the one thread that's sticking out of your sock. More questions kept getting teased out as I hiked up the trail.

How can something be important enough to you to bring you out into a blizzard . . . and so insignificant that you forget it for weeks? Leaving it lying forgotten in the Place of—

—Maples—

Jesus in gym shoes! I had completely forgotten the fucking maples!

The season had been almost over, that night when Rachel had arrived. But only almost. Damn it, I knew what I was going to find when I got up there. Plastic buckets brimful of rain and spoiled sap, dead insects of all kinds floating on top. Reproachful maple trees, their blood wasted, spilling on the ground.

Oh, the trees wouldn't really care; nature has no objection to waste, and trees don't much mind anything. But I would. A waste is a terrible thing to mind.

The trail leveled out at the garden and I paused to catch my breath. How in the hell could I have spaced out on my maple trees? Why, I had been right up here in the garden dozens of times, rototilling and seeding and weeding and deer-proofing; the Place of Maples was the next place-of-consequence uphill from here. You'd think it would have popped into my head before now.

Hypothesis: the psychological impact of Rachel's explosive appearance, that night, had been sufficient to drive anything associated with it out of my awareness and keep it out. The hypothesis covered both the maples and Mucus the Moose.

But it didn't *feel* right. I replayed my memories of that night. It was unquestionably the most memorable night of my life so far. I had to admit on reflection that I had not replayed that memory tape very often, not as often as I had replayed other memorable events in the past. But I couldn't find anything exactly *traumatic* in the memory, nothing I shuddered to recall. Oh, the trek back down to the Palace carrying Rachel had been pretty grim: not the sort of memory one kept handy for repeat playing. But it wasn't the sort of thing you walled away from awareness either. I had enough of those to know the difference.

Alternate hypothesis: years of occasional drug abuse were finally taking their toll on my brain; I had simply spaced out on moose and pancake-paint. A familiar hypothesis for many Sixties Survivors. It accounts for absolutely any weirdness in your life, and can neither be proved nor disproved.

But you never play with it for very long. No point. Assuming it leaves you with nothing to do. Except maybe regret.

Maybe you're a city person, and think that this was like forgetting to water the houseplants; no big deal. City people can afford to space out on things. The technical term for a country person who is absent-minded and lives alone is "corpse." If I could space out on my maples, I could space out on my fires.

Okay, the first step to solving any problem was defining the problem and its extent. Were there any other inconsistencies in my behaviour that might shed light on this pair of lapses?

How the hell would I know? How would I go about testing for them? How do you debug your head?

Forgetting Mucus, now, that was irresponsible. But forgetting the maple sap, that was *dumb*. All that flapjack juice gone to waste—not to mention how hard it was going to be to extract taps that had been so long in the living wood.

What did the two screw-ups have in common?

Only location—and Rachel.

My stomach started to tighten up. I left the garden, turned left and headed up the trail.

How was it that I had taken so long to remember my unfinished dulcimer? I'd been looking forward to finishing it, that night I had gone out into the blizzard . . . and then I hadn't given it another thought until the Solstice Jam wedged it into my head again. Or had I? I couldn't be sure.

It was much cooler up here in the trees than it had been down by the chopping block; I was glad I had fetched the shirt. Cold sweat glued it to me. If you are like most people, the scariest, most starkly horrifying thing you can imagine is probably some exotic kind of harm to your body. My ultimate nightmare is damage to the integrity of my mind. As Buckley said, "The frame doesn't matter, if the *brain* is bent." I stopped suddenly and urinated to one side of the trail, copiously and with great force. My hands shook as I rezipped my jeans. I noticed that I was breathing high in my chest; tried to force it lower, breathe deeper; failed.

I remembered the mood of inexplicable optimism that had accompanied me up this trail the last time. This was the backwards of it. I knew perfectly well that I was going to my doom. I know now why I kept going—but I didn't, then, and it was killing me. Feeling foolish, I picked up two stones, one softball-size, one tennis ball. I knew they would not help me. I needed garlic. A cross. Wolfbane. Automatic weapons and a ninja sidekick. But I did not throw the stones away.

Why, I asked myself, didn't you think all this through when you were within arm's reach of a perfectly good shotgun?

I think, I answered, because someone has been stirring my brains. Someone I trusted . . .

The sense of foreboding increased as I climbed. Twice I stopped to try and control my breath and pulse. Each time nervous energy forced me on again before I could. I was going to see something I didn't like. Might as well get it over with.

But still I stopped when the Place of Maples was just around the last bend ahead. It wasn't too late to reconsider. I wasn't committed yet. I could turn around and go home. If Mucus had survived this long, he'd live through Summer. Perhaps the deer had drunk the sap. . . .

I actually turned and took two steps downhill. But it didn't help any; nothing eased. Sometimes the only way to avoid pain is to get past it. I spun on my heel and continued uphill.

There was a tool on my belt that I used half a dozen times a day, that hung there so permanently I was not truly aware of it anymore; just about every adult male on the Mountain wore one at his hip. Five inches of Sheffield steel with a handle on one end, it was technically known as a "knife," and it dawned on me at this last possible instant that the tool could be adapted for use as a weapon. Why, between it and my two rocks, I was a walking arsenal. . . .

Please, I said to whoever it is I'm talking to when I say

things like that, let there be nothing to see around that bend. Let me find only Mucus the Moose and plastic pails of sour sap and a squashed looking place where a birch tree used to stand until it was pulverized by a blue Egg.

I rounded the last bend.

Things certainly had changed. It took a few seconds to sort things out.

The first thing that impressed itself on my attention, of course, was the new Egg.

Double bubble, toil and trouble . . .

Just like the one that Rachel had arrived in, huge and blue, except that it wasn't glowing and emitting loud noise and threatening to disintegrate—fair enough; it wasn't trying to digest the total energy of the total conversion of the total mass of a large tree—and it was translucent, almost transparent. It didn't have a beautiful naked woman inside it. Rather a disappointment all told. What it did have inside it was a bunch of things I did not recognize even vaguely but which I took to be machines or tools of some kind, though I could not have said why. I cannot describe them even roughly, nor name the material of which they were fashioned, nor the method of their fashioning; they certainly weren't machined or cast or carved. They filled the person-sized Egg over two thirds full. I disliked them on sight, whatever they were.

The shape of the landscape around the Egg was wrong. How?

There were trees missing. A dozen or more. But they had not been completely pulverized like the one Rachel had destroyed. I could see stumps and trimmings, and shortly I spotted where the trunks had been stacked, a ways off in the woods. With them was a damned big old-fashioned bow saw. Like a tall capital D, the straight line being the sawblade—the kind of saw that takes either a man on both ends or a hero on one. Someone had deliberately, and at great expense of effort, cleared the area.

Why use such a backbreaking tool? Oh, of course. A chainsaw or an axe might have been heard, downhill, by the chump whose land this nominally was. I might have come to investigate.

So what if I had? It was becoming increasingly apparent that Rachel had the ability to erase specific memories at will, without leaving a detectable gap. To do so could not be more difficult than felling several mature trees with a two-man handsaw, could it? So why not borrow my Stihl chainsaw, mow down as many trees as needed in a matter of minutes, and edit the memory from my personal tape?

For that matter, why had the saw blade not rusted out here?

What else was wrong with this picture?

No sap pails hanging forgotten from taps, after all. Pails and taps collected and stacked over by the fireplace. Big boiling bucket lidded. Probably full of salvaged sap, waiting to be reduced.

Huh. Shape of land wrong over there. A pile of turned earth. Jesus, a large excavation! A fucking hole in the ground. Easily distinguished from my ass, in this light.

Steady, boy, don't get giddy. Get a grip on—

What the fuck is that?

I dropped flat to the ground and covered my head with my arms. I waited. Wind ruffled my hair. In the distance a crow did a Joan Rivers impression. A blackfly tried to bite my ear. I thought about what I thought I had seen, and lifted my head and peeked. It still looked a lot like a weapon—but a dopey one, so it probably wasn't.

What it looked like was a mortar, or a starter's cannon, as modified by the prop department of a typical sci fi movie. It was not pointing at me or even especially near the trail, and it had not, as I'd hallucinated, swiveled instantly to track me, and now that I calmed down enough to look I saw that it *could not*, that its odd armature did not allow it enough traverse.

A satellite-tracking antenna—

I got up, feeling stupid. Crows laughed at me. I looked at the transparent blue spheroid full of high-tech artifacts, and down at the rocks in my hands, and suddenly I was angry. I tossed the rocks blindly back over my shoulders, hard; one hit a tree with a gratifying home-run *thunk* and the other started a small avalanche in a pile of alder slash. I walked slowly toward the blue Egg, feeling the anger build. If I couldn't find an access hatch or a zipper or a seam, I'd chew my way into the damned thing. . . .

It was my own damned fault, I knew. I had done exactly what all my favorite science fiction writers preached against. I had made unwarranted assumptions.

Because Rachel had arrived naked, and said that she must come naked or not at all through the membrane of time, I had assumed that whatever method of time travel her people had developed would work only on organic matter, would only transmit a living thing or something which, like the crown, was part of a living thing's bioelectrical field—

—whereas it was just as reasonable to suppose that the system could handle either organic or inorganic matter equally well, *as long as they weren't both in the same load.*

There was no telling whether this Egg was the second, or the twenty-second, no way to be sure just how advanced and dug-in the alien invasion of my ficton presently was, how big a beachhead my colossal stupidity had let them establish. Was Rachel still the only time traveler around these parts?

Or had I met dozens of her friends and colleagues . . . *and forgotten?*

Angry makes you bigger, and heartsick makes you smaller, and both at once was as bad as I'd ever felt. Yet I knew it would be even worse if they went away and left me with scared shitless. I wanted to kill a lion with my teeth, and then beat myself to death with the bones.

The Egg had no hatch or seam I could discern. Up close, the things inside were still just . . . things inside, quite unidentifiable. Parts seemed fixed, others seemed to *wave* in a way that made me wonder if the Egg could be full of some viscous liquid. I touched its surface with both my hands. Though the day was quite warm, the big spheroid was distinctly, strikingly cold to the touch. Yet there was no condensation, no exhaust heat.

I was beyond surprise or curiosity. I was going to bust this fucking egg open. Should have held onto the rocks; maybe my knife would—

I started to remove my hands from the surface of the Egg, felt something happen, clutched instinctively . . . and found that I was holding a gold headband. It had apparently been synthesized by the chilly surface of the Egg and gently pressed into my hands. It was warm.

I whistled an intricate little scrap of melody from Chick Corea's *My Spanish Heart*, and examined the thing carefully.

It was not exactly like Rachel's headband. It lacked the three retractable locking-pins that anchored hers into her skull, although there were knurled discontinuities like knotholes in their places. It was thinner in two dimensions, and the microengraving on it was an order of magnitude less complex. The gold seemed less pure. It looked like the Taiwanese knockoff copy.

I decided that nothing could possibly hurt me more than I hurt already, and that nothing could happen to me that I didn't deserve, and that I didn't even care if I was wrong. Strike three. I put the headband on my head and was Ruby—

—am Ruby fucking Sam feeling the unfamiliar dick up inside me and liking it (always thought I would) but feeling the touch of Snaker's nearby eyes more vividly than the touch of Sam's hands here on my tits (fingertips on right tit heavily callused) seeing Snaker's unseen staring face more clearly than Sam's wide-eyed here before me (Sam's mouth is beautiful) hearing the catch in Snaker's breathing beside me more clearly than Sam's happy growl (God, Sam's a

good fuck) what joy to help my lover make love to his friend, I hope this isn't a big mistake but I'll worry about it later, unnnnh-yes, *like that, like that, like that, I* like *that,* just *like that,* ***YEAH-YEAH-YEAH-YEAH-YEAH!—***

I ripped the headband from my head; clumps of hair came away with it. I was on my side, in fetal position. My whole body trembled, my calves threatened to cramp, my vagina pulsed rhythmically, my teeth were novocaine-numb—

Oh . . . my . . . *God* . . .

I looked down at the gold oval in my hands. I wanted to throw it as far from me as I could. Farther than I could. I wanted it in the heart of the sun, or passing the orbit of Neptune at System escape velocity—

Did anyone ever leave the theater during the rape scene? Did anyone ever voluntarily stop fucking in the middle of an orgasm? Even if they wanted to?

I watched my hands come close, put the headband back on—

No sense trying to reproduce more of it. I reentered Ruby's head at the exact instant I had left it, between the fifth and sixth *yeahs* of her orgasm. It was like teleporting into the heart of an explosion. I hung on for dear life, trying to keep from being destroyed utterly by the primal fire of Shiva, and all the while the little sliver of myself that is never asleep or drunk or stoned or unconscious was taking notes.

—Tiresias was right. It is *better for them—*

—Bizarre: you can't "come in in the middle"—there is *no middle. In the instant of jacking in, anywhere in the sequence, you know who you are and where you are and what's going on—just the way the originator of those memories did, at the time. What-Has-Gone-Before is implicit in the Now—*

—This is not right; I shouldn't be here in my friend's head, certainly not during such a private—

—Damn, she's right: I am a pretty good fuck. Wow, I can feel me coming; I always wondered if they could—

—oh, really?

(This last because Ruby had just thought, *but my Snaker's better . . .*)

—So many layers to this; I expected maybe a top layer of consciousness and then a layer of subconscious murmuring. But this is like a dozen-layer cake with consciousness icing, like a crowd gathered round a computer programmer all shouting instructions at once—

—God damn, it goes on so long *for them! So long, and all over . . .*

—I've Got To Stop This—

She is hyperaware of Snaker and she isn't a bit jealous, his ecstasy is prolonging her orgasm, how can that be? It's like he's here in her head; he isn't really, but there's a little mental model of him that's very close to the real thing, and there's a third eye she never takes off of it. She constantly checks it (I Really Ought To Stop This Now) against the real Snaker and uses prediction errors as feedback to refine the model; one day she'll have a little Snaker in her head indistinguishable from the real one. Is that telepathy?—

—No! This *is telepathy. What she is doing with Snaker is an inadequate substitute for telepathy, is what people do because they* cannot *be telepathic. In solitary confinement, you make up stories about those whose shouts and moans come distantly from neighboring cells. . . .*

Jesus Christ, isn't she ever going to stop coming?—

—!I AM GOING TO STOP THIS RIGHT NOW!—

I was still lying on my side. There was dirt in my beard, and pine needles. An ant was portaging a piece of maple leaf a few millimeters from my eyes, in the pale shadow of the big Egg. The gold crown was clenched in my left fist. It was quite warm.

I was in shock. The little monitor sliver of me that took notes decided maybe humour would help.

Cushlamachree. Congratulations, Meade. You may just be the first living man in the history of the world to actually fuck himself.

I began to laugh, and in moments was laughing so hard I genuinely thought I might choke.

But you sure as hell aren't going to be the last—

No, humour wasn't all that helpful. The laughter trailed off. I got wearily to my feet. I realized that I now badly needed to kill at least two people and maybe dozens . . . and that an invulnerable invincible enemy was, exactly as surely as Hell, going to prevent me. I began to cry, like an infant, in frustration and outrage. With bleak logic I computed that the very best I could hope for was to be permitted to kill *one* of my targets.

Myself.

Might as well find out. The suspense was killing me. I put the gold headband down most carefully on the forest floor, and dried my sweaty palms on my pants, and took my woods knife from its sheath, and the Nazz took it away from me.

I screamed.

"I'm sorry, Sam," he said. "I thought I could stop you in time."

There was a terrific bruise coming up in the middle of his forehead, a small cut in the center of it trickling blood; soon there would be a whacking great lump. I remembered tossing a rock over my shoulder and hearing it strike a tree. *Now* it came to me that there had been no tree close behind me at that time. Tunnel vision.

Okay, open it out. How many are we? ("You don't want to count the elevator boy?") Just the two of us. Okay, iris back in on Nazz. He's different. How? Start thinking, Sam!

A forehead wound was a major alteration in a man as hairy as Nazz, his forehead being the majority of his visible face, and for once, he wasn't grinning. But there was something else. Something subtler, but more profound.

This was Nazz, all right—but Nazz was a different man now. How, and how did I know?

Jesus—his eyes! *His eyes!*

For as long as I had known him, for as long as any of us had known him, Nazz had been mad. His behaviour was manic and his thoughts were like tumbling kittens: one minute he'd come up with some genuine insight, like that visual-interface notion for computers, and the next minute he'd be apologizing to a chair for farting on it. But mostly it was the eyes that were the tip-off. No one meeting him ever had to wait the five seconds it would take for him to say something totally off the wall to realize that they were dealing with an acid casualty. Equally important, a benign one. Just one look at those sparkling gray eyes and you knew two things: this man was stone crazy, and he was perfectly harmless.

Neither was true anymore. Somehow, *the Nazz had gone sane*. And in so doing had reverted to what he had been before he went insane. Maybe I shouldn't have been surprised by what that was.

He was a soldier.

A good one. I recognized it in the eyes first. The alert, balanced stance, the absence of his usual goofy grin, and the way he had effortlessly taken my knife away before I even knew he was there, all were only confirmation. I knew the look; my father was an admiral. Nazz was wearing his Army camouflage jacket—hell, *all* Hippies wore those, but now it wasn't a costume anymore, now I could see that he had *not* bought it at an Army-Navy store to make mockery of it, now it was his uniform again. He wore a web belt that held a GI canteen, ammo pouches, a coil of rope, a commando knife, and a woods knife like mine. Every few seconds he glanced quickly from side to side, like a cop, or a fugitive.

A lot of guys who came back from the Viet Namese jungle—the ones who survived—got heavily into acid. And some of them moved north, to a country where nobody called them "babykillers . . ."

When two men meet they often—I'm tempted to say, nearly always—make an instant assessment. Even if they don't expect the question to arise in a million years, they can't help quietly wondering: if it came to it, could I take him? (Interesting that the same word, "take," means to beat a man or fuck a woman or steal property . . .) Their two opinions as to the answer will subtly affect all their future dealings.

Nazz was one of the few men concerning whom it had never occurred to me to ask that question before. I did now—

I was candy.

"Holy shit," I greeted him.

"Yeah," he agreed, "I guess that's what it is."

I was full of many things, especially questions. Too many to sort. I let them pick their own order. "That head hurt much?"

"Yah. I never saw you move that fast before, Sam."

"Something about an alien invasion that pumps you up, I guess."

He let that pass. "How'd you know I was behind you?"

"Then you aren't reading my mind now?"

He shook his head. "It doesn't work that way." He grimaced. "Unless you were reading mine. I'd swear I never made a sound."

"You didn't. I just figured rocks weren't going to help me any, so I just threw 'em away."

He couldn't completely suppress a flash of Nazz-like smile. "No shit?" He shook his head. "That's a relief. Between you dropping flat all of a sudden, and then getting up and surprising me again, I thought maybe I'd lost it."

"Junglecraft? No, you haven't. How'd she get to you, Nazz?"

"Get to *me?* I got to her."

"Why?"

"Well, once I figured out what Rachel was—"

"How?"

"It was self-evident, Sam. All you had to do was look at her to know she was a stranger in a strange land, and that exchange student story of yours didn't make it. So I looked closer—and it was pretty easy to see that the body she was wearing wasn't the one she was born in."

I hadn't guessed that. "How do you figure?" Jesus, even his diction had changed.

"Sam, Sam. Not a wrinkle on her from head to foot, not smile-lines or frown-lines or stretch-marks or scars or vaccinations or *anything*. Nobody is that featureless except babies. Well, that made it obvious. Where do they grow brand-new, adult bodies, and change them like clothes? The future. How could people that smart miss such a glaring giveaway? Because they're telepaths—*they don't use facial expressions*."

Hell. I should have figured that out. I even had clues Nazz hadn't had. If Rachel could take a golden crown through time with her, why not head- or body-hair? Because she hadn't grown any yet . . .

A trained jungle-fighter with a mind like this was about unbeatable.

No. Very difficult to beat. Rachel was unbeatable. I had managed to surprise Nazz. I was convinced that Rachel would have known I was going to throw those rocks before I did.

Well, maybe I could find some way to surprise him again. There's no telling what dumb luck can do for you.

I nodded. "Smart, man. Mind if I sit down?"

He sat, without using his hands. I joined him more slowly and stiffly. Jesus, he was in shape.

It seemed appropriate to quote Dick Buckley. "Straighten me, Nazz . . . 'cause I'm ready."

"What do you want to know, Sam?"

Which questions to ask first. "Who is Rachel, and what is she doing here?"

"'They.'"

"Huh?"

"You mean, 'who *are* Rachel, and what are *they* doing here?'"

"Repeat: you faded."

"Rachel is four people. You didn't know?"

"Can they all carry a tune?"

"Beg pardon?"

"Sorry, I'm getting giddy. I was just thinking how nice it would be to sing Mamas and Papas songs by myself. Or Buffalo Bills stuff. You were saying, Rachel is four people—"

"Yah. Uh, technically they're personality-fragments, I guess you'd say. Abridged clones, not originals."

I let that go by. "Who's the leader?" Of the club that's made for you and me—

"Jacques. The others call him the Fader. It's like an inside joke. What he really is, is—" He broke off, hesitated for several seconds. "I guess you'd have to say he's . . . the Saviour. The Founder. The one who brought the New Age."

Oh really?

"His born name is Jacques LeBlanc. A Swiss neuro-anatomist—his original incarnation was, I mean. He started *everything*. A couple of klicks from here, as a matter of fact, a decade from now."

"Run that by me again."

"He's going to be a neighbour of yours. The first Jacques LeBlanc, the forerunner of the one that's one-fourth of Rachel, is going to move into the old DeMarco Place, just up the road from here, in a few years. That's where it's going to happen, Sam—isn't that far out? Right here in Nova Scotia, your neighbour-to-be is going to have the conceptual breakthroughs that let him discover mindwipe, and then mindwrite, and finally true telepathy. That's why

Rachel picked this area for an LZ: this is where the conquest of the world will begin. Amazing, huh?"

And I'd helped.

"Gee, Nazz, that's just keen. Who are the other three Rachels?"

"The other three parts of her, you mean. Well, there's Madeleine, the Co-Founder, she's Jacques' lady—"

"There had to be a woman in there somewhere—or a gay man."

"Because of how good she is in bed, you mean? Not really. Original gender-of-birth hasn't got much to do with it. Then there's Joe—he's sort of Maddy's brother, but not quite—and Joe's lady Karyn. If any one of them is responsible for Rachel being such a good lay, it's Karyn. She used to be a high-ticket hooker."

"Joe is Madeleine's brother, but not quite." If I kept on playing straight man, sooner or later this had to start making sense.

Or maybe not.

"Well, actually it's *Norman* who was Maddy's brother—but then he thought Jacques had killed Maddy, so he took off after Jacques and tried to kill him. Jacques had to screw up his head so drastically that there *wasn't* a Norman anymore, and the personality in that skull became Joe. By the time they got that all straightened out, and he got his memories back, he was happier being Joe than he ever had been being Norman, so he stayed Joe."

"Jacques hadn't killed his sister after all?"

"No. Just kidnapped her. It might have been smart to kill her, she was on the verge of blowing the whistle on the whole conspiracy. But he loved her. So he took a big chance. He made her his first confidante, his partner, the first person to be invited into the conspiracy. Uh, 'first' sequentially, of course, not chronologically."

"Of course. Who is the first, chronologically? You?"

"Why, I really don't know for sure, Sam. For all I know, my namesake from Bethlehem could have been in it."

I was absorbing about one word in ten of this. Mostly I just wanted to keep him talking while I tried to think of some foolproof way to kill him without weapons, skills, or the advantage of surprise. Or failing that, a way to suicide—since he apparently wasn't going to let me.

"I mean, they must be into the Bible," he went on. "That's where Rachel got her name from. '. . . Rachel, who mourned for her lost children, and would not be comforted, for they were no more.' Typical Joe sense of humour. *This* Rachel hurts for her lost *ancestors*, not her children. Does a lot more about it than mourns, too."

This was getting us nowhere. "What are you doing here, Nazz?"

"The Egg here—" He reached out and touched it gently, caressingly, "—arrived a week ago. Ever since, I've been trying to get it safely into the ground, and guarding it in the meantime."

"Guarding it? Here? Against what, the deer?"

"You know how it is with woods trails. Deerjackers, hikers, lovers, berry-pickers, kids playing, horse people out riding, you never know who's gonna come by when. They all tend to follow existing trails. But mostly I've been keeping watch for you, Sam."

"For me?"

"Râchel told me to expect you. Uh . . . this is the second time you've been up here in the last few days."

Aw, *shit*. Really?

I had no recollection of having been here since the night Rachel arrived.

"How did Rachel know I'd be coming?"

"That moose gadget of yours. You thought of coming back up here for it last week, for the dozenth time—and Rachel stopped you, took the memory of that thought out of your head. But she knew it'd recur, and she had pressing business elsewhere. She couldn't erase the moose altogether, the memory was rooted pretty deep and there would've been holes big enough for you to notice. Besides, your most recent memories of it were integral to your memory of Rachel's own arrival here. She didn't want to leave any suspicious holes in that sequence.

"But she knew that the Solstice Thing coming up would keep putting the moose back in your mind. So she told me to keep an eye and ear out for you."

"Wouldn't it have been simpler to ferry Mucus down to the house and plant a false memory that I'd retrieved him myself?"

He shook his head. "Doesn't work that way. I don't think anyone could put a convincing false memory into a man's head except himself. The mind knows its own handwriting."

So I had to be allowed to keep climbing up the damned Mountain, loop and replay—like Sisyphus. Like a robot with a faulty action program. Like a bird blindly banging its head against the window, trying to escape. . . .

My voice sounded odd to me. "What happened the last time I got this far, Nazz? We fought, didn't we?"

"Yes, Sam."

"And I lost, and you cut out some of my memory. Jesus, you did a good job. There isn't the slightest sense of déjà vu."

"Not me, Sam. I'm not even really a novice at this stuff. Hell, I'm just barely a postulant. All I could do was put you on hold and call in Rachel—she did the surgery."

"'Put me on hold'?"

"Yeah, it's not hard. The crown generates a phased induction field that hyperstimulates your septum. Your pleasure center, just over your hypothalamus. You sort of supersaturate with pleasure, and your mind goes away. Like, samadhi. Nirvana."

"Mother of God." I was trembling. No, shivering. "'Death by Ecstasy'—"

He nodded. "That Niven story, yeah, it's a lot like that."

"Oh Christ." That story had figured prominently in some

of my worst nightmares. A man's brain is wired up to a wall socket. Enslaved by ecstasy, he starves to death with a broad grin—because the cord isn't long enough to reach the kitchen without pulling out the plug. . . .

"It could be worse, Sam."

It echoed through the forest, stilled wildlife. *"HOW?"*

He waited until the echoes had faded. Then he said softly, "You could get the identical effect by supersaturating the pain center."

I sat and thought for a while. He seemed willing to let me. Nothing productive came to me. Just bitterness and regret and fury and profound terror.

"I'm really surprised that *you* joined the Pod People, Nazz. I'd have sworn that you'd be the last person on Earth vulnerable to a mental assault. Why haven't you tried to convert *me?*"

"I gave it my best shot last time. Didn't work."

I held up the golden crown I still had in my hand. "Not after what this thing showed me. Is this what you're going to . . . 'put me on hold' with?"

"Not that one, no. The Egg made it for *you*, for one thing, it wouldn't interface with my mind properly. Calibrated all wrong. And that'll be a Read-Only crown you've got there, a passive playback-module. It hasn't got tasp circuits. But the Egg knows I'm authorized for a Command Crown—"

He was wearing an ordinary cloth headband; he took it off and set it down on the ground, shaking his head to tousle his hair. He turned away from me, reached both hands palm first toward the Egg, closed his eyes momentarily—

I jammed my crown down over his hairy head.

It was worth a try—hell, I had no other move—and the results were gratifying. He screamed.

Maybe it was that my crown was "calibrated wrong" to "interface with his mind properly." Maybe it was being unexpectedly dropped into the midst of a woman's orgasm. Perhaps he misinterpreted that first surging rush, thought I had somehow acquired a Command Crown by mistake, and panicked.

Most likely it was a combination of all of those. For whatever reasons, there were two or three entire seconds there during which he was no longer a highly skilled killer commando who could wipe up the forest with me without working up a sweat, but a grinning, gaping space-case rather like the Nazz I had always known and liked—

—and before those two or three seconds had elapsed, I hit him with the heel of my fist, like pounding on a table, impacting solidly below his ear, whanging his head off the Egg so hard that the thing rang like a gong.

FIFTEEN

WHETHER THAT BLOW knocked him unconscious or merely stunned him I could not say for sure. I sprang to my feet and kicked him twice in the head. The second kick caught him on the jaw shelf and snapped his head around, and the crown flew from his head as he went down. By then he was definitely unconscious. I stood over him breathing in great gulps and trying to decide whether or not to kill him. There was some urgency in the question. If I did not do so now, while I was pumped up, I never would.

In those days I believed in the insanity defense. I did not believe that a man should be killed for something that was "not his fault." It was "not fair." Laugh if you will; I was young. The Nazz I knew would not have been held responsible for anything by an reasonable person. This new, sane Nazz was an enigma with an unknown half-life. Perhaps one day with luck this man could be made insane again. I decided I did not have the right to kill him. Then and only then did I let myself consider how inconvenient it was going to be keeping him alive.

First things first. I removed his web belt of tools. The braided rope belt under it that he used to hold up his pants turned out to be long enough to secure both wrists and both ankles behind him in a classic hogtie. His own bandanna headband, which he had taken off in favour of the golden one, made a serviceable gag. I checked him carefully for holdout weapons without finding any. Once he was secured I looked around carefully.

The excavation in which he planned to bury the Egg was only partly a dug hole. The Mountain is a glacier's footprint: there's so much bedrock to it that there might not have been soil deep enough to cover the Egg anywhere within a couple of klicks. So he'd dug what he could, and was now apparently in the process of *dissolving* an adequate hole in the bedrock with some kind of chemical reaction I didn't understand. There were reagents of harmless-looking clear liquids, carefully kept far apart from each other, and lab gloves, and goggles. At the bottom of the trench, a circular film of cloudy liquid was *seething*. There was a faint odour that reminded me of an overheated engine. I guesstimated that in another couple of days he'd be able to get the bubble down in there and kick dirt over it.

Why use such a clumsy, dangerous and slow method when dynamite was so cheap? Because I would have heard the blast and come to investigate. If I "forgot," other neighbours would have heard, and would ask about it the next time they saw me.

I returned to Nazz. My impression was correct: he had not had time to retrieve his "command crown" from the bubble before I put his lights out. So I could not simply . . . "put him on hold," even if his crown would accept my orders and I could learn to use it. Part of me thought that a damn shame. Briefly I thought of trying to press his unconscious hands against the bubble, see if I could fool it. But I didn't think I could. And what if I succeeded—and won the ability to make Nazz a zombie?

Most of me, I think, was awash with gratitude at being spared the moral choice. I would much rather have killed my friend than done *that* to him.

I began to regret that I had not killed him. I couldn't leave him here overnight—he could catch pneumonia. But it was a long way back downhill to the Palace. He weighed more than Rachel had. All that hair. It's very hard to carry a hogtied man without dislocating both his shoulders. I dared not even leave him alone long enough to go borrow a wheelbarrow or a horse. Even trussed up, there might be some way he could use the Egg to free himself, or worse, call Rachel.

In the end I got a bunch of fresh alder boughs from the recent clearing activities, and built a makeshift travois. Probably a Micmac could have done a much better job. I laid Nazz on it on his left side, head end uphill. It was not necessary to lash him aboard.

And I towed the son of a bitch down the Mountain.

To my mild astonishment it worked just fine. I only got stuck five or ten times. The grooves that travois handle put in my shoulders didn't quite break the skin or my collarbone. My cursing would probably not have killed anything outside a thirty-meter radius. Three fourths of the way down the trail, Nazz came to. He grunted behind his gag. I didn't feel like talking to him. I tried turning him over on his right side and maybe that solved his problem; in any case he stopped grunting. Lot of rocks in that trail; couldn't have been a comfortable ride.

After only a thousand years of pain the trail leveled off at the garden. I didn't hesitate. Couldn't afford to lose the momentum. Smashed the gate flat and went right up the middle, destroying seedlings of squash and corn and radishes and carrots, dill and chives and broccoli. What survived was mostly onions and peppers and tomatoes and basil. Italian food all next winter, if I lived that long. Flattened the gate at the other end, bringing down that whole end of the fence, and was heading downhill again.

When I got to the chicken coop I stopped, and thought. I rolled Nazz off the travois and into the coop. It was very difficult to get him through the low doorway without untying him, but I managed. He would not freeze at night here. Chickens are actually dumb enough to mistake a hogtied man for another chicken. They would snuggle up to him. And the henhouse was far enough from the house and road that he could yell all he wanted. (He would rub off that makeshift gag shortly after I left him alone—a good thing, too, as an effectively gagged man can die of the sniffles.)

Of course, Foghorn Leghorn my rooster was going to hate it. And Nazz wasn't going to enjoy the smell much. GIs have a proverbial hatred of chicken shit.

When he understood I meant to leave him there he began to grunt furiously and emphatically, and thrashed around as much as was possible to him. I couldn't blame him. His arms and legs must already have been cramping severely. Twenty-four hours in that position and he'd need expert physiotherapy, maybe surgery. Tough shit.

I knelt by the doorway and waited in silence until he stopped grunting.

"If I get Rachel, I'll come back for you. If she gets me, she'll come looking for you."

He grunted *uh huh*.

"If we take each other out, I guess you're fucked."

He grunted *uh huh* again. His unblinking eyes met mine, trying hard to speak volumes. They were, as Lord Buckley has noted, pretty eyes.

I looked away and prayed the oldest prayer in human history—*make it didn't happen*—and got to my feet. "So long, brother."

He grunted *Sam, wait!* and I left him.

As the house came into view I suddenly swore and

punched myself viciously on the thigh. I had forgotten the God damned moose *again*.

It was good to see my little home. By now I knew it might be my last day there. I was *busy*—but I kept sneaking glances around me as I worked, cherishing what I was about to lose.

The golden crown that had broken my heart and blown Nazz's mind hung from my belt. The first thing I did was put it on the chopping block and whack it a few times with the splitting maul; that deformed it some but not enough to suit me, so I took it to my shop and clamped it in the vise and worked it over with heavy-duty pliers and a rat-tail file and the head-demagnetizer from my reel-to-reel; then I cut it into small pieces with boltcutters and softened each piece with a blowtorch and hammered them flat with a mallet and went outside and threw each piece in a different direction as far as I could. Then I gathered up all the tools I'd used and threw them away too. I started up the Kemac jet, boiled water, scrubbed my hands. As an afterthought I got a facecloth and scrubbed my forehead where the gold headband had rested.

Then I made a pot of coffee.

Halfway through the pot, I heard the Blue Meanie approaching from the east. The pitch of its scream did not change; it was just passing through, on the way west somewhere. I sprang to the window. Snaker was driving, alone. I ran outside and flagged him down.

"Hey, bro," he called when the engine finally quit. "Just heading for Annapolis, guess what? There's gonna be some honest-to-God MDA at the party!" He wore only jeans, a denim vest and boots. I've seen pictures of concentration camp survivors with more meat on them. His hair was tied back in a ponytail.

I was experiencing inner turmoil. Flagging down Snaker had been instinctive. Now I faced a difficult choice. I planned to fight Rachel, and more than half expected to lose. Did I get my best friend involved, and probably get him killed too? Or leave him in an ignorance that would, whenever Rachel took the notion, be too blissful by half?

He misinterpreted my expression. "Haven't you done MDA before? You'll really like it, honest: all the good features of acid, psilocybin and organic mesc, with none of the dis—wow, man, you look like hell."

It occurred to me that I had already *made* this choice—back when Rachel first arrived. The only difference was, now I *knew* the danger was real. "Come on inside."

"Are you all right?"

"Come on inside."

I could feel him studying me as we walked up the driveway and around behind the house. He was silent while I got him coffee. The interval was not enough for me to find the words I needed, so we just looked at each other for a few moments.

"What do you need?" he said at last.

"Shithouse luck."

He nodded slightly. "That can come to any man."

My hands hurt. I looked down. They both clutched my cup, and they were shaking so badly that hot coffee was slopping on them. I tried to set the cup down and bounced it on the table three times. At once Snaker's hand shot out, came down over the top of the cup, forced it firmly down onto the table and held it there until I could let go. It must have scalded the hell out of his palm.

Something broke in me and I was weeping without sound, panting like a dog or a woman in LaMaze labour.

God bless him, Snaker did not flinch or look embarrassed. He looked at me, now that I think of it, exactly as though I were *talking to him*, as if he were listening attentively to me and thinking about what I was saying. Or as though so many people had burst into tears in conversation with him that he had learned to understand weeping as well as words.

Maybe he had. When I finally ran down and got my breath control back, he said softly, "That's hard."

I blew my nose and wiped my face. "You don't know the half of it."

"Talk to me."

"Snake . . . you know how I feel about Rachel?"

"Sure. Same way I do."

"Pretty much, yeah." Deep breath. "I have to kill her, Snake."

His face turned to stone.

"And I am not at all sure I'm up to it. I nearly got greased once already today—by the Nazz, if you can believe that. Did you know he did time in Nam? And she's much more dangerous. We blew it, Snake, you and me, that first day. *She* is *a telepath.*"

Very slowly and deliberately, as if handling a delicate explosive, he removed his makings and a Riz-La machine from the pocket of his denim vest, and rolled a cigarette with the same care. "Tell me all, omitting no detail, however slight."

So I did.

It took us halfway into the next pot of coffee. Or in his terms, eight cigarettes.

"—so as near as I can see it, it comes down to a classic science fiction question: *how do you kill a telepath?* Ought to be right up your alley, Snake."

"There are two ways I know, actually. I started a story about it once. You have to assume that there's some limit on the telepath's range—"

"I'm still alive. I still have my memories—I think. In any case, I have memories damaging to her. And she could have gotten here from Parsons' cove by now. If I had to guess, I'd say her maximum range is on the order of, oh, say earshot."

"Check. So—carefully remaining out of range, you give one of the telepath's socks to an attack-trained Doberman and say 'Kill.' Plan B: you build a killer robot and give it the same instruction. A nonsentient animal or a sentient machine, either will turn the trick."

"Terrific. I doubt there's an attack dog anywhere in the Valley. And the only guy around here who could probably build a robot is up the hill a ways, wondering how hungry you have to be to eat a raw egg with its mother watching. Have you any *practical* thoughts?"

"Abort the mission."

"Snaker, come on! We haven't got time to fuck around—"

"I'm serious."

"I haven't got a chance, you mean? Dammit, don't you think I know that? *I'm asking you to help me pick the best way to die trying.*"

"Sam, Sam, why does it have to be life and death?"

I stared at him.

"Really, man. You have no coherent idea of what the hell Rachel is up to. The one thing you know for sure is that *she* won't kill *you*, for fear of destroying the future she comes from—"

"Wrong! Rachel would *prefer* not to kill my *body*. My mind is fair game. I am my memories, Snake. My 'self' *is* those memories. They are me. Rachel is the Mindkiller. I have to bring her down."

"But what exactly has she *done* to your memories?"

Why was he being so obtuse? "That's the fucking point: *I don't know!* How can I know what things I don't remember? How do I know what transpired while I was 'on hold,' smiling beatifically, my naked brain open to thief or voyeur? I have been raped so intimately that I will never *know* just how badly unless and until my rapist chooses to tell me. Intolerable. Unforgivable. You disagree?"

"No. I share your horror of mind-tampering. As I sit here I keep probing my own head for memory gaps, badly glued seams, the way you poke at a toothache with your tongue. It's a creepy feeling, knowing she's been in my head, your head, Ruby's head. I'm angry at her for it. I want to know what made her do it. I give her enough credit to believe she thought she had a good—"

"Of *course* she thinks she has a good reason. I am not remotely interested in what it is! There *is no good reason* for what she did to you and me and Ruby. She dies. End of story. If I thought I could safely immobilize her, I might ask her what her motives were before I killed her—and then again I might not."

He was shaking his head. "You're not *indifferent* to her motives. You actively refuse to learn them. I can only think of one reason why: you're afraid you might agree with them if you knew them."

"You're wrong, Snake. I really don't care one way or the other."

"Bullshit. It would be tactically sound to know! It would aid you in attacking her. And you're too smart not to realize that. Yet you have left your only source of military intelligence, the man who could tell all and is eager for the chance—our pal Nazz—lying in a chickencoop."

"I think I understand her motives."

"Then you're way ahead of me."

"Think about a telepathic society, Snaker. Everybody knows everything about everybody. There's no more voyeurism. No more mystery. No such thing as a candid camera, an unposed picture, an unexamined life. Everyone's always 'on-camera,' wearing their 'company face,' even fantasies are constructed in the awareness that they will be public property. In effect, everyone is naked, and if you've ever spent any time in a nudist camp you know how bland and *boring* that becomes. A whole planet becomes jaded.

"So a market develops for memory-tapes with a 'candid camera' feel, the experiences of people who *didn't know anyone was looking*. There's only one place to get them, though. From the past, from people who lived in the day before all this brain-robbing technology was developed. From people so primitive they don't even have copy-protection on their brains. We're like the native women in *National Geographic*, too dumb and ignorant to know better than to go around naked. No wonder Rachel's been in and out of every hippie bed in Nova Scotia, and for all I know half the local beds too: better value for the entertainment dollar."

He swung around in his chair, used the wrought-iron lifter to remove the front access plate from the stovetop, dropped a cigarette butt into the firebox, and replaced the plate with more crash-bang than was necessary. "Stipulate that such memory dubs would be desirable, even marketable. Would they be worth exiling yourself to a strange and primitive world, for life? Would they be worth giving up immortality? For the golden privilege of burying them in the woods, for your contemporaries to dig up and enjoy after you're dust?" At the mention of mortality, he began to roll another cigarette.

"On what authority do we know that Rachel has given up immortaility to come here?"

He winced. "Touché. For all we can prove, she has two-way time travel."

"No, that story I believe. If it were that easy to slide back home, she wouldn't be reduced to using local talent like Nazz. Snaker, all of this is totally irrelevant. I told you already: her motives don't matter. Whatever they are, she's ashamed to tell her best friends, but even that is unimportant. A dozen times since I found out what a Command Crown was I have wished that I had one available to me . . . God help me. There is no material problem one of those could not solve. Rachel has brought absolute power into my world. I don't care whether she can be trusted with it. It shouldn't exist."

"But what can you do about it?"

"Snaker, I'm surprised at you. For a writer you aren't very inventive. I've thought of three ways to kill a telepath, in less than an hour." I got up and poured the last of the coffee. "Point of order. We keep calling Rachel a 'telepath.' Is that strictly accurate? She can dub my memory-record, stipulated. Apparently she has to switch off my consciousness to do so. Can she *perceive* memories *as they are forming?* Can she really 'read my mind,' or does she have to *stop* my mind, take a wax impression of it, and read *that?*"

"What the hell's the difference?"

"Earth to Snaker: if she isn't a true telepath, in the sf sense, if she's just a memory-thief who can 'put me on hold' when she wants to, I can walk up to her, smiling pleasantly, and cut her throat."

"Huh. I wouldn't try it. She may not have any facial expressions of her own—but she has gotten very very good at reading other peoples' in the last two months. I'm beginning to understand why. But I see another implication. You audited a dub of an experience with four people present—but you didn't play it through to the end. It might have been recorded later, at a time when she and Ruby were alone. It would be useful to know *how many* minds she can bliss-out at a time."

I saluted him. "You anticipate me. Method number one for killing a telepath: go uphill, palm that Egg about fifty times, bring fifty crowns to the Solstice Thing tomorrow and pass them out. You wouldn't even have to say a word. Rachel could never run far enough fast enough. But you've put your finger on the flaw: suppose she can handle fifty at once? Nobody at that party is going to be surprised if they wake up the next day with memory gaps. A lot of them are counting on it."

"So what's method number two?"

"Number two I wouldn't use myself, but it's a beaut. Pick a chump. Boobytrap him without his knowledge. Send him to see the telepath. Apologize profusely to the corpse."

"Nasty."

"I'm pinning my hopes on method number three. Boobytrap someplace you know the telepath is going to be. Retire well out of her range and stay there until you hear a loud noise."

He said nothing, played with his cigarette. I turned away

and busied myself with washing the coffee pot. Wisely does Niven say the secret of good coffee is fanatic cleanliness.

"She'll be here tomorrow before the Solstice, to help me ferry stuff to the dance. I was thinking of going up the road and borrowing some dynamite from Lester anyway. Make me some scrambled Egg. I could borrow enough for two jobs." I thought a moment. "Actually, what I'd like to do is kick that damned blue bubble all the way downhill, roll it right inside here and do both jobs with the same blast. But it'd hang up somewhere on the way downtrail, sure as hell—or worse, start sending out SOS signals. Pity."

He didn't answer right away. I turned around and caught him staring out the window, looking off uphill toward the Place of Maples.

"I know what you're thinking," I said. "Knock it the fuck off."

He whirled to face me. "Eh?"

"Don't try to look innocent. You're thinking about how much you want to wander up that Mountain and put that sonofabitching crown on your stupid fucking head and find out what it's really like for Ruby when she comes. You transparent asshole, you're salivating thinking about it." I went to him, grabbed his vest with both fists, yanked his face to a position an inch from mine, spoke loudly and firmly. "By your love for your lady, I charge you to forget it. For the honour of your immortal soul, give it up. Love does not give you the right to do that. You don't have the right to that information. No one does. I shouldn't have that information. The second most horrid moment in my whole life was when I knew that I could not help myself, that I was going to put that crown back on again." I shook him gently. "You and Ruby have something special going. *Don't fuck it up.*"

He did not try to pull away or avoid my gaze. "I'll try, Sam."

"You'd better, you—oh, mother of Christ! Look at that—"

Peripheral vision had alerted me. Through my back window I could see Rachel approaching my back door from the direction of the chickencoop, Nazz walking stiffly and awkwardly behind her.

I sprang for the woodbox behind the stove, snatched up the big double-bit axe. "Battle stations! Grab down that shotgun, Snake, it's full of double-ought; dammit, is there no fucking peace anywhere in the jurisdiction of Jesus? She must have come right up over the Mountain through forest, for God's sake! duck around the corner into the next room, man; I'll draw her attention, you pop out and try to skrag her—"

I stopped talking then. Snaker had the shotgun.

Pointed at my belly—

"No, she didn't," he said quietly. "Come through forest. She was lying flat in the truckbed. You didn't look close enough."

He hadn't been thinking of Ruby's memory-dub when I caught him looking out the window. He'd been wondering what the hell was keeping Rachel and Nazz.

"Sam," he said, "cut loose. Give it up, man, and Rachel'll *tell* you why she's doing all this."

"Sure," I snarled, "and any parts that don't make sense, I forget, right?"

"Sam, my brother—"

"When Rachel's head comes through that door, *my brother*, I am going to try to bisect it with this here axe. You do what you have to do." I shouldered the axe.

He cried out: "Sam, *please—*"

The door squeaked open. Rachel entered. The axe left my shoulders, began to swing. "Ah, *shit*," Snaker said, and shot me in the chest with both barrels.

SIXTEEN

DO YOU HATE clichés as much as I do? Then perhaps you can imagine how exasperating it was for me to have, as the load of buckshot was traversing the distance from gun to my torso, my whole life pass before my eyes.

In detail, just like everybody said, the works, *z-z-z-ip!* The duration and rate of speed of the experience cannot be described in any meaningful way. I can say only that it seemed to go by very quickly, like speeded up Mack Sennett footage, yet not so quickly that I lost a single nuance of emotion or irony. Objectively, of course, it had to be over in considerably less than a second of realtime.

I did sort of appreciate the second look, although it went by too fast to enjoy. But it was a cliché I had never for a moment believed in—like time travel—and I was vastly irritated by its turning out to be true. For Chrissake, thought the part of me that watched the show, next I'll find myself floating over my own corpse—

I caught up to where I had come in.

WHACK!

There was no pain; the buckshot killed me, and then I was floating in the air, a few feet above my corpse. I looked like hell. Snaker was having weeping hysterics. Nazz kept saying oh wow man. Rachel was expressionless, saying something preposterous to Snaker. I tried to speak to Snaker myself, but it didn't work. I didn't seem to have vocal cords with me.

Oh, for God's *sake*, I thought. Now I rise up through the ceiling, right? And after a while I'll find myself floating down a tunnel toward a green light?

I began to rise slowly, passed through the ceiling as though it were made of cobwebs, things began to spin and twist sideways and down, I was rocketing through the air just above the forest like a low-flying missile or a hedge-hopping pilot, my God, I was heading for the Place of Maples, the bubble came up fast and WHACK there was a sense of impact, a wrenching, a stutter in time, then a terrible rising acceleration like the ending of *2001: A Space Odyssey* like the ending of "A Day in the Life" like both of those there was a crescendo, a peaking, a cataclysmic explosion, then a long slow diminuendo, a gradual return to awareness of my surroundings—

—and there I was in a damned tunnel, big as the Grand Canyon, drifting with infinite slowness toward a green light at the far end of it. . . .

It was visually staggering, exhilarating in the way that *vastness* always exhilarates. It was also infuriating. I had long since settled to my satisfaction that all those Near Death Experiences, the Out-Of-Body reports by those who had briefly been clinically dead, were merely fading consciousness's last hallucination, the Final Dream, the hindbrain's last attempt to replay the birth trauma and have it come out all right. I was disgusted to find out that my own subconscious mind didn't seem to have a better imagination than anybody else's.

I thought of a Harlan Ellison collection I had liked once. DEATHBIRD STORIES. Death was giving me the bird, all right.

Can you hear me, Death? This is *boring*. I'm Death-bored. Show a little originality, for God's sake. Is He around, by the way?

I say I was infuriated, exhilarated, disgusted, staggered, but all these sensations were only pale shadows of themselves, memories of emotions. I no longer had a limbic system to produce emotions; I continued to "feel" them from force of habit. Already a great sense of detachment was beginning to come upon me. I was no longer worried that my world was being invaded by brain-raping, zombie-making puppet mistresses. It wasn't my problem anymore. In time, I could tell, the echoes of all passion would fade. I mourned them, while I still could.

All my trials, Lord, soon be over . . .

Fat chance.

I had a lot of time to think, drifting lazily down that most Freudian of tunnels. And a lot to work out.

I *seemed* to have a body. It was there if I looked for it; if I concentrated I could make myself turn slowly end over end by flapping my arms. But I could also pass my hands through my trunk if I tried, and when I clapped them together there was no sound. . . .

I was afraid. I could not have said of what. I certainly did not fear the pains of Hell, nor for that matter anticipate anything like Heaven. The Christian Heaven had always struck me as remarkably like an early Christian martyr's last fantasy of turning the tables on his Roman torturers. I go to a place where *I* shall be one of the elect and wear white robes and live in a great white city with big gates and do no work while listening to the screams of sinners being burned for my amusement.

(I know that harps and haloes are no longer the official position of any modern Christian church, at least not if you work your way up to the top rank of intellectual theologians. But just try and pin one of them down on just exactly what Heaven *is* like. These people claimed that they had once hung out with God; they'd seen him nailed up, watched him die, three days later the cat showed up for lunch so they *knew* he was God—or if he wasn't, anyway he'd *been there*, he knew all the answers to all the great mysteries—and they'd had him around for thirty days, and nobody thought to ask him *what was it like being dead?*, or if they did the answer wasn't worth writing down. How does a story like that last two millennia?)

Indeed, the only reason I was not intellectually offended to the point of stupefaction by the whole concept of an afterlife was a conversation I'd had with my father once when I was seventeen.

My father was emphatically not a superstitious man. Unusual, perhaps, for an admiral. He held to his marriage contract and allowed my mother to raise me as a Catholic, but he always tried to see to it that Reason got its innings, too. At seventeen I told him that I had decided I was an atheist, like him. He told me to sit down.

Three times in his life, he said, he had lain near death, in deep coma. Each time he heard a voice in his head, a deep, warm, compassionate voice as he described it. Each time it asked him, "Are you ready now?"

Each time, he told me, he had thought about it, and concluded that he was *not* ready yet. The first time there was too much of the world he had not yet seen, and there were men under his command. The second time there was my mother. The third time I was still too young to do without a father. There may have been other factors he did not name.

Each time, he said, the voice accepted his decision. And

each time he awoke, and a doctor said, "Jesus, you know, for a minute there we thought we were going to lose you."

"An atheist," he told me, "would say I had three dreams. And might be perfectly correct. I have no way to refute the theory. If that voice was a god, it was no god I've ever heard of—because it evinced no desire whatever to be worshipped. But son, I am no longer an atheist. I am an agnostic. By all means hate dogma—but I advise you not to be dogmatic about it."

Two years after that they diagnosed his cancer—lung cancer, which usually takes so many merciless months of agony before it kills—and in less than a month he was gone. He was retired from active duty. I was grown. Perhaps he calculated that Mother would have a better chance of surviving and remarrying if she did not have to watch him die by slow degrees; in any case, she did both.

So I was able to tolerate the concept of an afterlife—here it was, big as life. I just didn't have the slightest idea what it would be like, nor any guesses.

Nor any way to guess. Insufficient data. With cold rigour I admitted to myself the possibility that in a little while I would come to a vast pair of Hollywood gates and have to account for myself to an old gentleman named Pete, who fronted for a particularly vicious and infantile paranoid-schizophrenic. (I hoped not. The one thing all Christian theologians seemed to agree on was that, *whatever* Heaven was like, there was no sinning there. It would make for a long eternity.)

Phooey. It was equally likely that the Buddha waited at the end of the tunnel to show me the Eightfold Path. It was, in fact, precisely as likely that at the end of the tunnel I would find a stupendous, universe-spanning Porky Pig, and he would say "Th-th-th-th-that's all, folks!", and I would cease to be. Until you know what the postulates are, all hypotheses are equally unlikely.

But my father had persuaded me to hedge my bets. Just in

case I *was* going to have to account for myself to Someone or Something. . . .

Sitting in judgment upon oneself may be a uniquely human pastime; some feel we invented deities at least in part to take the job off our shoulders. (Whereas we always seem to have enough spare time to sit in judgment on others.) Lacking that assistance, I felt that I had, in my life, done a little more self-judgment than most, if less than some. I had tried, at least, to judge myself by my own rules—and accepted the responsibility of constantly judging those rules themselves in the light of experience, and changing them if it seemed necessary.

But I had never before had so much uninterrupted time in which to consider these questions, or so little emotional attachment to their answers. I had never managed to sustain, for more than the duration of an acid trip, the detached point of reference from which such judgments must be undertaken. And I had certainly never before had such a spectacular and useful visual aid as having my entire life pass before my eyes in a single gestalt, in such detail that I could, for instance, see at once both what my childhood had really been like, and the edited version of it I had allowed myself to carry into adulthood. The lies I had sold myself over my lifetime were made manifest to me, my very best rationalizations crumbled like ice sculpture in boiling water; I looked squarely at my life now past, and judged it. Coldly, dispassionately. Honestly, by my own lights, as they were written in my heart of hearts.

And if, as some maintain, a life must be judged on a pass-fail basis, then I failed.

I had loved no one; few had loved me. I had pissed away my talent. I had, in general and with rare exceptions, hated my neighbour. I had left the music business when the folk music market collapsed—not because I didn't like other kinds of music; I did—but because folk music was the only kind you could play alone. I had never truly learned to stand other people. They seemed to break down into two groups.

The overwhelming majority were determinedly stupid, vulgar, cruel, tasteless, superstitious, dull, insensitive and invincibly ignorant. And then there were the neurotic artists and intellectuals. I was just plain too smart and sensitive for anybody, when I came down to it.

So I had fled my world for the woods of the north country, and there, out of two billion people I had managed to find a bare handful I could tolerate at arm's length. And I had let them down, failed to protect them from a menace I should have been best equipped to stop, had bungled things so badly that my best friend had killed me and the rest were being mind-raped.

If Philip José Farmer was right, and I "owed for the flesh," then I was going to duck out without paying. I had taken nothing with me from life. In no sense and at no time and no place in my life had I ever pulled my weight.

As that judgment coalesced in my mind, I learned that not all emotions require flesh to support them, for I was suffused with an overwhelming sense of—not shame, not guilt, I was beyond them now, but sorrow. Sorrow insupportable, grief implacable. I had failed, and it was too late to do anything about it. I had wasted my birthright, and now it was gone.

No wonder I had feared a telepath. This much honesty, back when I was still alive, would have killed me.

All intervals of time were now measureless; I lacked even heartbeats as a referent. After a measureless interval, I had marinated in my failure for as long as I could bear. I turned my attention to the immense tunnel in which I drifted.

It seemed, to whatever I was using for senses (probably the same memories I was using for emotions), to be composed of dark billowing smoke shot through with highlights of purple and silver. I thought of a thundercloud somehow constrained into a cylinder. I was equidistant from all sides. My body-image was wearing off; I could see through my hands. The cool green light in the distance was getting closer, but since I did not know its true size I could not tell how quickly. I could not even be sure if it was the end of the tunnel, or a light source suspended in the center.

It is said that the pessimist sees mostly the overwhelming darkness of the tunnel, and the optimist sees mostly the tiny point of light that promises the end of it . . . whereas the realist understands that the light is probably an oncoming train.

All three are shortsighted. The *real* realist knows the ultimate truth: that if you dodge the train, and reach the end of the tunnel . . . beyond it lies another tunnel.

I reviewed what I had read of Near Death Experiences. If this one continued to follow the basic *National Enquirer* script, shortly I would closely approach the green light, and there be met by my dead loved ones.

The problem with that was that I didn't *have* any loved ones. Dead or otherwise.

(Did dead friends and intimate acquaintances count? And if so, what would we have to say to each other, in these circumstances?)

Oh, it was possible I had loved my parents in childhood, though I doubted it strongly. I was sure that from the time I had the intellectual capacity to understand what the word 'love' meant, I no longer felt that for them if I ever had. As far as I knew I had *always* been selfish; my parents' welfare and happiness had meant nothing to me except insofar as, and precisely to the extent that, they affected my own. I'd had no siblings to practice loving on. My mother's love for me had generally struck me as a cloying annoyance whose sole virtue was that it could sometimes be exploited to advantage. As for my father, once my storms of adolescence were past I had come gradually to respect and admire him—but I had never loved him. Whether he had loved me or not, I honestly did not know.

I had to admit, though, that he was the most likely candidate to greet me if anyone would. Of all those I cared about who had died before me, he was the one who (I thought) most visited my dreams and most evaded my waking thoughts. I wondered if dead admirals wore their uniforms. Would he steam up to me in a floating aircraft carrier—or, more likely, his first command, the USS *Smartt?* Or would he manifest as I best remembered him, sitting bolt upright at his desk, chainsmoking Pall Malls and coughing like a snowmobile and doing incomprehensible things with paper that changed the lives of people halfway around the globe?

Let's get this show on the road, I thought, and as though in response, my universe began to change.

I'm not sure how to describe it. I'm certain I won't convey it. It was as though my senses of light, hearing, taste, smell and touch all coalesced into a single sense, with the special virtues of each and the limits of none. It seemed to me then that there had really only been one sense all along—the sense of touch—and that all the other senses had only been other ways of touching. This too was a new way of touching, as wide-ranging as sight and as intimate as taste. Nothing could block this vision, nor distort this hearing. It was similar to the LSD experience in several ways, not least of which is that I cannot describe it to you and you will not know what I mean until you have been there. As with acid, most of the metaphors that spring to mind are visual. The scales have fallen from my eyes. I once was blind and now I see. I can see clearly now. Oh, *there's* the forest—

With this new sense, I probed ahead of me, as one reaches out an exploratory hand in a dark cave. And found that I was come nigh the end of the tunnel. The "green light" was "blinding," but between it and me I dimly made out a number of . . . *somethings,* hovering on the edge of tangibility. One of them came to me, and without body or limbs or features somehow became an entity, a self, a person. Recognition was a massive jolt, even in that detached frame of mind. I should have expected to meet her. I had not. I was wrong about my father being the one who most visited my dreams. He was only the one who most visited the dreams I remembered on waking.

"Hello, Pooh Bear."

"Barbara!"

I tried frantically to back-pedal somehow, to flap my arms and escape, kick my legs and swim away back upstream like a salmon. I no longer had even phantom arms and legs, and the force that drew me was as inexorable as gravity.

We were touching.

So there was retribution in the afterlife after all. . . .

The others could "hear" us, but for a time they left us alone. I knew them not. Music was playing somewhere, and I paid no attention.

There was no hurry here. I tasted her, and all the memories flooded back with aching clarity, their emotional colorations faded almost to invisibility but none the less powerful for that. A black and white two dimensional photograph of Rodin's *The Lovers* can yet stir heart and loins.

She was no longer the Barbara I had known, of course, except in the sense that the flower is still the seed, but her aspect was familiar. I understood that she had put on that aspect to welcome me, as one might nostalgically put on an old garment to greet an old love—and that she had had to rummage a while in a musty trunk to find it.

To convey what happened then I must pretend that we used words.

"Hello, Barbara."

"Hello, Sam."

"I'm sorry."

"For what?"

"I'm sorry that I didn't love you."

Her response will not really go into words. She was like one who tries not to laugh at a child, but cannot help smiling, because his fear is imaginary. None the less real for that, nor less painful—but imaginary and thus comical too. "But you *did*."

I could make no response. Many times I had fantasized this conversation, in the days before the wound had finally scabbed over . . . but this statement I had never imagined Barbara making. Could a ghost be mistaken?

"Truly you did."

"I never."

"You taught me to stand up straight. To be strong. To accept no authority above my own reason. You stood up for me, even when it cost."

"I cheated on you. And let you find out."

"You knew we were not meant to be permanent life-partners. I didn't. You knew how badly you would hurt me if I stayed with you, and tried to deal me the lesser hurt—at greater cost to yourself."

"Bullshit. I wanted to get laid and I just didn't care if it hurt you."

"Then why let me find out?"

I made no reply. Pressure of some kind built. Finally: "Barbara, you *know* I did not love you. Or were you too busy there at the end?"

"What do you mean, Sam?"

"Barbara . . . I killed you. And our child."

"You did not."

It boiled out of me so fast she recoiled, it spewed out like projectile vomit or a burst boil or a slashed artery: "I let you both die! I saw the truck coming, and there was time for me to run and slam into you and knock you out of its path, just like in the movies, plenty of time. *And I didn't*. It's what a man would have done. What even a worm would have done . . . for a woman he loved. There was time. I was not willing to die in your place. I stood there and watched the truck crush you. Your belly burst and our baby came out. He lay there in your giblets and kicked a little and died while I watched and tried to think what to do. Just as you had a moment before. I already thought I was a monster, I guessed when my grandparents died and I didn't give a damn, and I felt it again and stronger when Frank died and the first thought in my head was 'Thank God it was him and not me,' but that day as I watched you both die I knew for certain that I was not capable of love, and that *I must never again pretend to myself or anyone else that I was!*"

She waited until I had regained control. Then.

"First things first. Only one person died in that accident."

"I saw him, I tell you—"

"You saw 'it.' You *know* better, Sam. You've always understood the anthropomorphic fallacy. *I was four months gone*. What came out of my belly looked like a little tiny person . . . and was not, any more than a four-celled blastula is a person, or an ovum, or a fingernail clipping. It did not have *any* neural cells. No brain, no spinal column, nothing that could be called a central nervous system. Not an axon or a dendrite or a ganglion. Nothing that could support sensation, self, let alone self-awareness. It could have *become* a person in time, if chance had so ruled—but it did not, *or it would be here now.*"

I knew somehow that she was correct, and a part of my pain began slowly to recede. I clutched after it. "It was alive, and it was *going* to be our baby, and I let it die. I let you die."

"You had a split second in which to make a complex decision. You have just tasted your life as a single piece, grokked its fullness. Don't you see that if you and I had let pregnancy force a bad decision on us and talked ourselves into staying together, our marriage and our life would have been a misshapen, stunted thing, crippling both of us, *and* the child caught between us?"

"What has that got to do with it? It was my duty to save you. The crunch came and my true colours showed. I'd told myself I loved you, I had myself half convinced. But when the nitty gritty comes, when the chips are down, you can't lie anymore. Bullshit walks. And I stood still, and watched you die."

She did something that was even more like touching than what we had been doing, that was a caress and a hug and an embrace and a massage and a kiss, a thing that was infinitely soothing and comforting. Lacking a bloodstream to keep reinforcing it, my pain began to lessen, like a fist relaxing. I was baffled by her forgiveness.

"Sam," she said when I had relaxed enough, "I'd like you to think about two things. First, think about how much you've suffered, over all the years between, for what you think you did to someone you did not love.

"Second, replay that accident just one more time. I heard the air horn the same moment you did. I had precisely as long to jump out of the way as you had to knock me out of the way. And better motivation. *And I didn't move a muscle either.*"

And then she was gone and the next greeter came forward.

"Hello, Dad."

"Hello, son. It's good to see you."

"Guess you didn't hallucinate that voice after all, did you?"

"No."

"What's the procedure now?"

"The usual procedure is being modified."

"Really? How?"

"Barbara greeted you first because we all agreed that it was necessary for you to make your peace with her before anything else. You and I have our fish to fry, too, but it is not necessary that we do it now.

"There are things we will talk about, things unsaid between us, things I never gave you and things you never forgave me. There will be a time when I will make my apology to you, for letting my selfish motivations call you up out of nothingness to be born and suffer and die, and demanding that you be grateful. That time is not now. There are others here who would talk to you, and what they have to say is not urgent either. There is no time here, and so there is no hurry.

"Nonetheless, we are—all of us—under enormous time pressure."

"I don't understand."

"Son, you are a clever, self-serving son of a bitch. You managed to maneuver yourself into a position where you could die honourably and painlessly, commit suicide without getting busted for it. You had been wanting to for a long time, ever since Barbara died. It is not going to work."

"Huh?"

"You are going to have to go back."

"*What?*"

"But first you need a history lesson. You have to understand What Has Gone Before . . . and What Will Have Gone After."

What I got from him then was just what he said it would be. A lesson, a long monologue, which I did not interrupt even once, so I am going to abandon the quotation marks and dialogue format. (I *know* you're not supposed to drop a long lecture in near the end of your story. It's like that dark and stormy night business; this is the way it happened and there's nothing I can do about it.)

Mankind (my father told me) studied the brain for centuries, seeking the key to the mind/body problem. It began to achieve glimmerings of real understanding in the Nineteen-Forties and Fifties, as sophisticated brain surgery became technologically possible and ethically permissible. Newer and better approaches were found; newer and better tools made; newer and better models were built and studied and correlated: the brain is like a switchboard, the brain is like a computer, the brain is like a hologram, the brain is an incredibly complex ongoing chemical reaction, the brain is a reptile brain draped with a mammal brain with humanity a mere cherry on top. By the Sixties, it was obvious that many of the brain's deepest secrets were close to being solved. By the mid-Seventies, a few years after Snaker killed me, a respected scientist was willing to predict before the American Association for the Advancement of Science that the "information storage code" of the human brain could be cracked within a decade or two, that neuropsychology was on the verge of grasping how the brain wrote and stored memories, that science stood at the doorstep of Self.

In the audience, a lonely widower named Jacques LeBlanc frowned. He was one of the half dozen neuroanatomists on Earth, and easily the best. He completely agreed with the prediction, and it terrified him. Alone in the room, he grasped the awful power implicit in understanding the brain, and he knew how power tends to be used. He had been alive when the atom bombs went off; a protégé of Dr. Albert Hoffman, he had seen LSD used by the CIA for mind-control experiments.

He saw that if you understood how memories were written and stored, why, then you could make direct copies of a memory, rich and vivid and multilayered copies, and give them to others, and that would be a wonderful thing. If the trick could eventually be extended to *short-term* memory, you would have something approaching telepathy, and if you could actually extend it to consciousness itself—

He saw just as clearly that those refinements might never come to pass.

All information is a code, and entropy says that it will always be easier to destroy information than to encode it in the first place. A library that took thousands of years to produce can be destroyed in an hour. A lifetime's memories can be ended by a stroke in an instant. A tape-recorder's "erase" head is a *much* simpler and cheaper device than its "record" and "playback" heads. First they invent a weapon; then they look for ways to use it as a tool.

So the first result of understanding memory would be mindwipe. LeBlanc knew that if that power were loosed on the world unchecked, then what may as well be called The Forces of Evil might win for centuries to come. Tyranny never had a greater ally than the ability to make your slave forget he opposes you. The other side of the coin—the aspect of memory that permits it to be *shared*—would be studied haltingly if at all, implemented slowly if ever. A preacher named Gaskin once said, "Between ego and entropy, there is no need for a Devil."

LeBlanc looked around him at his world, seeking some institution or individual who could be trusted with such power. He saw no one whom he trusted more than himself. He was one of those rare people who are not capable of evading responsibility once perceived. With trepidation, with great humility, he set about conquering the world.

He used his superior knowledge and prominence in his field to misdirect and confound all others, using disinformation, falsifying data, throwing out red herrings and sending trustful friends and colleagues down blind alleys. Meanwhile, he raced ahead alone down the true paths, learning in secret and keeping his knowledge to himself.

By 1989 he had a crude, cumbersome form of mindwipe. The conquest of the world began to pick up speed.

In the next decade surgery—including brain surgery—suddenly got drastically simpler, and computer power got drastically cheaper. By 1995 LeBlanc had married his second wife Madeleine, and thanks to insights she provided he made the breakthrough that brought him true mindwipe. He could now walk up to any person and, without surgery or drugs, using only an induction gun and a microcomputer the size of a wallet, turn off their mind and take from it what he wished. He could open the vault of long-term memory storage, rifle any memory more than a few hours old, Xerox it or erase it forever as suited him. He strongly preferred to kill his enemies, given a choice, but did not allow his scruples to keep him from raping minds by the dozens when he deemed it necessary. He did his level best to minimize the necessity.

From that point on, he effectively owned Terra. He moved through human society at will, yet apart from it, unseen, or at least unremembered, by all save those he chose. He had access to *anything* under the control of any human being. He built his conspiracy slowly, carefully, putting full trust in no one except Madeleine. She had come underground with him—and that was nearly his undoing, for when she vanished, her brother Norman Kent thought that LeBlanc had killed her. It became necessary for LeBlanc to do mindsurgery on Norman, creating a new, amnesiac personality named Joe. Four years later, Joe and a friend named Karyn Shaw put enough of the pieces together to come after LeBlanc a second time.

LeBlanc told them everything. He showed Joe and Karyn his own secret inner heart and asked them to judge him. They joined his conspiracy, and that very night killed a policeman to protect it.*

Two years later, twelve years after he had achieved the first clumsy form of mindwipe, in the ironically apt year of A.D. 2001, Jacques LeBlanc, neuroanatomist and amateur tyrant, and Joe No Last Name, gifted programmer and professional burglar, together developed mindwrite, co-wrote the computer language called Mindtalk, and perfected the brain-computer interface. They had true telepathy.

They no longer lived alone in the dark in meat-wrapped bone boxes. They no longer needed meat or bone to exist, could survive if need be the destruction of the brains from which they had sprung, could grow if need be new brains with bone and meat to haul them around, could if they chose replicate themselves perfectly and indefinitely. Barring catastrophe, they could live forever; no enemy could

*Publisher's note—for a more detailed account of these events, see MINDKILLER (Berkley/Ace 1985).

threaten them. At long last, human beings had taken a significant step toward immortality. Four of them finally held that previously abstract and hypothetical commodity, absolute power—more of it than had ever existed to be grasped before now.

They spent another eleven years manufacturing terminals—golden headbands—in large numbers, and warehousing them all over the planet without drawing attention, and assembling an army that did not know it existed. And the moment that task was completed, with a sigh of relief that came to be audible all over the globe, the secret masters of the world abdicated.

For this was their secret, self-evident strength: those whose power is genuinely absolute are incorruptible.

There came a morning in 2012 when every news medium on the planet that had any connection to the world computer network (virtually all media), print, audio, video, electronic, all opened with the same lead, though not a reporter alive could remember having written it and no editor had approved it for publication.

THOU ART GOD, said the headlines and broadcasters and datafeeds, in a hundred languages and dialects, to people who built spaceships and to people who herded goats, to saints and sinners, generals and monks, geniuses and fools, pros and cons, graybeards and children.

As God does not appear to exist, they said, *it became necessary to invent Him/Her. This is now being done. The Kingdom is at hand, and you are welcome to join. Any living human whatsoever may become a neuron in The Mind, and all are equal therein. Go to the nearest telephone company business office or switching facility. There will be a lot of golden crowns. Put one on. You need never fear anyone or anything again. No money down. Satisfaction guaranteed. Act anytime you like; this offer will* last. *But remember: a smarter God is up to* you.

And then viewers were returned to normal news programming.

Within minutes, curious people were logging on to the new system, and The Mind began to grow.

The CIA and KGB, the Joint Chiefs and the Politburo and their counterparts all around the Earth, the guardians of national security and the balance of terror and business as usual and the unnatural order of things, all went individually and then collectively berserk, for the end of status is the end of status quo. But as fast as their servants developed leads, they seemed to forget them. . . .

For so audacious a mind, Jacques LeBlanc was curiously conservative in his projection of the demand: in that first run he provided only three hundred million of the golden crowns. That is to say, he assumed that no more than one percent of humanity would take his offer within the first week.

Fortunately three hundred million minds in communion and concert can work just about any miracle they choose. What had taken Jacques, Maddy, Karyn and Joe eleven years was duplicated in a week, and again in a day.

And *everything* changed.

To join The Mind you did not have to lose your ego, your identity or free will. You could leave The Mind and restore the walls around your own personal mind as easily as switching off a phone—that being in fact how it was done—and for as long as you chose. There were no constraints whatsoever on freedom except consensus; no one neuron of God's Brain had or could have any more, or less, power than any other. Conformity was finally no longer necessary, for there was no static "state" to be threatened by its lack. The codified and calcified rituals that form a state are what humans must do because they do not have telepathy. The Mind was not static; it flowed. The ancient stubborn human conviction was right; in most disagreements, one side is rightest—and now both could know which, neither could refuse to admit it. Nothing could supersedc the truth, not who you were or who you knew, for everyone knew everyone and everyone knew the truth. Consensus decisions were self-enforcing. All came to learn what computer hackers had always intuited and prayed for: that in a shareware economy, with free flow of information, there can be no hierarchy, and all users are equal.

Not everyone joined The Mind, of course. It is possible to adapt so well to pain and fear that you cannot shift gears and adapt to their lack. Black Americans, knowing more about these things than most, had a colloquial expression for this common response to unremitting pain: *It got good to him*, they said. Those people who had made cruelty or malice or indifference into an essential integral part of their self-identity, a sadly large portion of humanity, found that they were forced to reinvent themselves, or leave The Mind. Cruelty is love twisted by pain, malice is love twisted by fear, and indifference is love twisted by loneliness, and there was no pain or fear or loneliness in The Mind.

Others were so incurably afflicted with intolerant religious doctrines of one sort or another that they could not accept the damnable heresy of human beings daring to make their own God, could not bear to live in any Heaven where they were not a privileged elite by virtue of birth.

Within a single generation, all gnosis was ended; every religion that did not have tolerance built right into the very marrow of its bones (almost all of them) had vanished—at long last!—from the face of the globe, and those who had been afflicted by them were forgiven by their surviving victims. Something like a new religion came into existence almost at once, quite superior to simple "secular humanism" (a fascist code-word for "intellectual liberty").

(The new religion was simple. Clearly the universe is mindless. Equally clearly it was written by a mind. A program of such immense size and self-consistency cannot form by random chance; the idea is ludicrous. The new religion sought The User, the intelligence that had written the program, for no other reason than that it was the most exciting game possible. Some individual minds felt that by the act of collapsing into The Mind, the human race had debugged itself and would thus soon attract the pleased attention of The User ["soon" defined by whatever he/she/it used for "realtime"]; others argued that The Mind was as yet no more than an integrated application, an automatic routine beneath notice, and would have to *deduce* The User from contemplation of the Operating System.)

Many tore crowns from their foreheads in rage or shame, and swore to fight The Mind and all it represented. Of course they never had a chance: by definition they were unable to cooperate enough, even with each other, to seriously threaten minds in perfect harmony. Evil, however clever, is always stupid.

They were not punished for trying. In time, they forgot what they had been angry about, forgot that they had been angry, were allowed to live out their lives and (since they insisted on it) die in the fullness of their years without remembering their bitter defeat. Rugged individualists who could not live without their loneliness became nothing when their bodies died, and there is nothing lonelier than that, so perhaps they too had their Heaven. Within one generation there were no more of them.

But an astonishing number of even humanity's most bitter pessimists chose, freely, to reinvent themselves rather than leave The Mind once they had tasted of it. Most human bitterness had derived from lack of The Mind. All evil derives from fear.

And the majority of human beings had always, in their heart of hearts, at least *wanted* to love all mankind—if only there had been some sane, practical way to do so. The problem with living in total perpetual honesty and openness had always been making sure that no one *else* lied either. People had tended to be untrustworthy because they lacked trust, to be selfish because they needed to be, paranoid because it worked—but for a million years they had never lost the sneaking awareness that *it ought to be other-*

wise, had never ceased dreaming of a society in which it *was* otherwise. People had feared that others might see their secret thoughts—because each and every one was convinced that *his* or *her* secret thoughts and sins were fouler and more shameful than anyone else's (a delusion that could not survive an instant in The Mind)—and yet had never given up the search for a lover or confessor to whom they could unburden themselves. They had always yearned to be telepathic, and yet had suppressed most tendencies toward planetary awareness that they did develop—because the first thing any telepath notices is that most of his brothers are starving to death *and there is nothing he can do about it*.

But once that last clause no longer obtained, once world hunger and the arms race and death and pain themselves were seen to be soluble problems, humanity leaped to embrace telepathy with such ardor that it was as though Jacques LeBlanc's golden crown had been a seed crystal dropped into the heart of a great supersaturated solution, which collapsed at once into a structure, a pattern, of awesome complexity and beauty.

In the instant that Loneliness and the Fear of Death were ended, Evil died for good and for all.

At the point when there were approximately a billion minds in The Mind, there was a quantum change. A switch was thrown and a new kind of awareness came into existence. The pattern became a living, functioning, growing thing, learned how to teach itself, approached at long, long last both intelligence and wisdom.

On an evolutionary scale the change was instantaneous. At the computer rates of thoughtspeed now available to its members, it seemed subjectively to last for hundreds of millennia. In old-style, Homo sapiens terms, the metamorphosis was essentially complete in something under three months from a standing start.

By half a century or so later, The Mind was something utterly unknowable to any old-style human, indescribable in any preexisting language. But it can perhaps be imagined that it was both intelligent and wise. Some of its members had lived thousands of subjective lifetimes of uninterrupted thought, without ever losing a friend or a colleague to death. It can be understood that The Mind spread to fill its solar system, and began to contemplate how best to reach the stars. And it can be reported that it had discovered—and discarded as much too dangerous to have any practical purpose—a way to bend space in such a way as to travel backward (only) through time.

Then one day one of the neurons in The Mind had an astonishing idea—

SEVENTEEN

IT WAS ALMOST irrelevant that this particular neuron had once been known as Karyn Shaw. Having been one of the original Four earned her respect—but not "status" or "authority," since these things no longer existed, and certainly not "worship," for worship is a kind of fear.

It was the idea itself that was so irresistibly appealing. It was suffused with the same sort of dazzling audacity that had led Jacques LeBlanc to conquer the world in order to save it, the same kind of arrogance it took to wipe minds and subvert wills in order to make a world in which no mind would be wiped or will subverted ever again.

We have (Karyn argued) overcome Death but not yet conquered it. We've managed to plug the massive information leak it comprised. Half of the human minds that ever thought are thinking now, and their thoughts are no longer wasted—

—*only half.*

Perhaps (she proposed) humanity was now grown mighty enough, not only to beat Death, but to rob it. To wrest *back* from it the half of the human race it had stolen before we learned how to circumvent it. To recover the trillions of man-hours of human experience that had been stored as painfully-collected memories, and then ruined.

Perhaps (she urged) we could go back and rescue our dead.

It was odd and ironic that this idea should have been conceived by Karyn Shaw, for she had less reason than most to love her dead parents. (Her father had been a sadistic child-molester, her mother a cipher.) Equally ironic that the first to agree with it was Joe, who had no parents . . . but less odd, for he and Karyn were married, both old-style and in the fashion of The Mind. Together they communicated her thought to Madeleine Kent—who saw at once that it was just what her own husband needed.

Though basically at peace with himself, Jacques LeBlanc was still plagued with a lingering echo of something like guilt, a persistent regret for some of the things he had been forced to do in pursuit of his dream, pain which even the vindication of his judgment could not entirely ease. Chief among these was that he had—in order to preserve his secrets, until it was time for all secrets to be ended—been forced to kill quite a few men and women. Not all of them had been evil people.

He seized gladly on the idea that perhaps he could undo this harm.

And so The Four, reassembled once more, studied Karyn's idea, refined it to a plan, polished it, and presented it to the rest of The Mind. . . .

The debate was titanic. Never in the history of The Mind had consensus been so hard to achieve.

The risk was horrible. Careless time travel could change history, shatter reality, destroy The Mind itself and the universe in which it inhered, waste everything that had been gained so far and all possibility of future gain.

(On the other hand, a race which had feared nothing for countless subjective lifetimes was not utterly opposed to some risk in a good cause. It did not seem reasonable that the dissolution of the universe could *hurt*, exactly, and who would be left to mourn?)

The sheer physical task was daunting: to place, somewhere in the spinal fluid of every human being that had ever lived, a tiny and fantastically complex descendant of a microchip which would copy every memory that brain formed—and when triggered by death trauma, would transmit that copy to the nearest buried "bubble" for storage and future recovery—all this without ever getting caught at it by touchy ancestors.

(On the other hand, this was a manageable problem for several billion supergeniuses who could subtract memories at need and had an entire solar system to plunder for parts.)

The cost was also daunting. Any individual mind that volunteered to go back in time would go one way, to a ficton which did not contain The Mind. After a lifetime of solitary confinement in the equivalent of a deaf, dumb, blind and numb hulk, such a one would *die*—not permanently, to be sure, but it would *hurt*. Should its true intentions be suspected, and it be surrounded by more minds than it could control alone, it might very well be burned at the stake. . . .

The potential benefit was irresistible. To undo two million years of tragedy, the aching psychic weight of grief and mourning represented by billions of deaths! The Mind would almost precisely double in size, both in numbers of "neurons" and in man-years of human experience. *The Family would be together again!*

The debate surged through The Mind from one end to the other, provoking more vigorous disagreement than that entity had heretofore known. In objective terms, it must have taken over an hour.

It was decided to perform a careful experiment.

The Four made copies of themselves. Heavily edited copies, extremely abridged copies, versions of themselves so close to the solitary old-style humans they had once been that they believed the copies could live among such without going insane. They grew a body out of germ plasm which, by now, was thoroughly racially mixed, and poured themselves into it, and called themself Rachel. They picked a target ficton close to the historical moment of The Mind's birth, but enough short of it that there would be time for a proper thirty-year test of the plan.

And then they hurled themselves through time and into my birch tree.

Because of that single unfortunate error (my father explained to me now), the secret was compromised from the start. By the time Rachel had recovered from the near-fatal trauma of blowing up that tree, got her crown back, and was once again physically capable of controlling my mind, I had shared what I knew with Snaker—and he and I had lived through too much subjective time. To edit our memories now would leave gaps too large to remain unnoticed for long—and by horrid mischance we were both science fiction readers, perfectly capable of deducing what had been done to us.

A practical solution would have been to kill us both. The part of Rachel that had once been Jacques LeBlanc had had a bellyful of that particular practical solution.

Instead she opened Snaker and me up and examined us—and decided to invite Snaker into the conspiracy, and keep me in the dark. Between them they did their best to cure me of the spiritual illness that made me dangerous, the sickness that feared its cure . . . and when that failed, they committed themselves to keeping me in ignorance of Rachel's true mission.

They had very nearly pulled it off. They were foiled by the preposterous chance involvement of a plastic moose, and by the unexpected savagery with which I defended my poisoned mindset.

And so I had brought the universe to the brink of disaster, by making a change in history too great for it to heal itself around. By changing the date of my death.

Imagine an immense computer program composed of billions of files, quadrillions of megabytes of data, an immense and intricate array of ones and zeroes, of *yes*es and *no*s. A cosmic ray strikes one bit of data, alters it. Does the program crash? Of course not. A program that vast has mighty debugging routines written into it, or it could never have reached that size in the first place. As the altered bit causes tiny errors to accumulate, they are spotted, collated, analyzed, and the bit is "repaired," restored to its correct state. If it cannot be, through media failure, a good debugger will rewrite the program around the damaged sector.

But if a whole file, millions of bits of related data scattered through many discontiguous sectors, suddenly seizes up and dissipates prematurely—before the results of its operations are made available to the other subroutines that depend on it—if the discontinuity is too large to work around—

—then cascading errors ripple outward like shock waves and the system crashes. And all the information—in this case, *all information*—vanishes, lost forever.

It was explained to me that my premature death—first cause, Rachel choosing to use a time machine to monkey with history; final cause, Snaker choosing to pull two triggers—was just such a potentially catastrophic disruption.

It was further, and most humiliatingly, made clear to me that this was not because of any profoundly significant effect or affect upon the universe as a result of my premature absence. By the time of my death I was an ingrown toenail of a man, halfway to hermitage, interacting with my world as little as possible and doing my very best to influence no one's life. Between Death and the remaining life I had planned for myself there was very little difference. There were no children who would now be unborn, no albums that would go unrecorded.

What made my death significant to anyone but myself—what made my own personal folly the rock upon which the universe itself might be broken—was that in my blindness and fear I had forced Snaker to kill me.

For he *did* interact with the world. He was a writer, an artist, and it was written in his kharma that he would one day be a fairly influential one. But some public explanation had to be found for my death, and policemen always bet the odds. History would now record that Snaker O'Malley had been convicted of murdering me because I had slept with his wife Ruby. Killing me would abort some of his greatest works, and distort all the others beyond recognition, with far-reaching effects on people neither of us would ever meet. Similarly, Ruby's paintings could never now be what they would have been, and she was fated to be a greater artist than her husband, though less commercially successful in her lifetime. And Nazz would, in his grief and guilt, fail to pass on to friends an off-the-wall, blue-sky insight that would have so profound an effect on computers in the Eighties as to forestall nuclear war in the Nineties. . . .

So disastrous was the projected outcome that there was only one solution. I must climb back on the Great Wheel of Kharma, return to my own time and undo the damage I had caused.

My father finished speaking. It was time for me to make my reply.

"Dad," I said, "are you telling me you want me to go back to that miserable planet and live out another thirty-odd years of being a hermit and not accomplishing anything and not having children and knowing just when and how I'm going to die (it will be quite painful, I grok, not like the last time) and generally being a waste of space? You're saying that I can alter the basic shape a *little*—perhaps experiment with loving my friends just a little more—but not much, not enough to risk screwing up the shape of the miserable life I had planned out for myself?"

"Son," he said, "I'm saying that I hope it's what *you* want. As a voice said to me, once: *are you ready yet?*"

I thought about it.

I could choose as selfishly as I liked. No sanctions could be applied if I chose not to do this thing. No retribution would come to me—not even disapproval, for there would be no one left to disapprove of anything. Not even regret; no self to do the regretting. If I refused to abet this unimaginable Mind, then it and the universe in which it inhered would cease to exist, fade away like the Boojum. I would have what it seemed I had always wanted—death, nonexistence, the peace that passeth all understanding—as well as my ultimate revenge on a world that had failed to love me enough to soothe my fear.

As I pondered my answer, I contemplated the shimmering green light. Now that I knew it was The Mind, I found that I yearned toward it inexpressibly. Absently, I recognized one of the shadowy forms that floated between me and the light. I knew him by his flickering grin, and knew that I should have been expecting him.

"It serves me right, I guess," I told my father. "All things considered, I think I got off lucky, if you want to know the truth. Moses spent longer than that in the wilderness, just outside the city limits of Promised Land. I can do thirty years of solitary confinement standing on my head."

Can there be many feelings as good as your father's warm approval? "Thank you, son. You make me proud."

Something came out of the green light and approached me. A body. Not a person, like Barbara and Dad and the others, but a physical human body. I recognized it as it came near, even bald.

It was me.

"Sam," my father said, "don't forget to tell Rachel she must take tissue samples from your old ruined body and bury them in her Egg, so that this one can have been cloned without causality paradox."

"Yes, Dad."

"Sam?"

"Yes, Dad?"

"If you ever decide to share any of this with your mother . . . give her my love."

"I will, Pop."

Something else came out of the light. A Time-Egg, bisected open like a clam to receive me . . .

Experimentally I tried on the body. It was familiar, like getting back on your first bicycle. Everything seemed to work right—

With mild dismay I realized that I could not get back out of it again. I was committed. Dad and Barbara and the others, the timeless tunnel and the green light itself began to fade from my ken as I lost the senses with which I had perceived them.

Damn, I thought, it would have been good to talk with Frank again. I'd really missed him. I realized too late that the music which had been playing unheeded somewhere in the distant background of my thoughts had been his attempt to soothe me with wry humour: Dylan's "I Shall Be Released."

Ah well. He would still be there when I returned. And perhaps by then I would have learned more about how to love him back.

The Egg closed around me and sealed. It filled with air, and my new body took its first breath.

Without tears—

I thought I heard my father say, "We'll all be waiting for you—"

And then he was gone and there was a me and a not-me, an up and a down, a sky and an earth, both tinted blue.

I could see the Place of Maples all around me. My Egg was two meters to the west of the one Nazz had been trying to get buried. I touched the inner surface. The Egg opened, and sunlight and colours seared my brand new eyes. I stepped out onto the forest floor, onto the planet Earth, into my life—which was already in progress.

I breathed clean country air, smelled the good smells of the woods, felt the cool breeze on my naked body and the pleasant discomfort of twigs and leaves and pine needles under my bare feet. The day was beautiful.

I checked the sun, decided that I probably could spare the time . . . and after a brief search, found Mucus the Moose. Rachel, or possibly Nazz, had stood him up in a shady spot where he had a good view of everything. We said hello, and I gave him Frank's regards.

When I was halfway down the hill I heard the shotgun go off, and began to hurry. . . .

EIGHTEEN

IT WAS A bright and balmy night.

The huge loft writhed with hundreds of hippies, colorfully costumed and exuberantly high. The air was saturated with sounds and smells and smoke. Sounds of greetings and laughter and music and gossip. Smells of beer and food and the sweat of happy horny hairy people, and, under all, the smells of the cows who customarily lived downstairs (boarded elsewhere for the night). Smoke of grass and hash and tobacco and kerosene. The great hardwood floor shuddered under dancing feet; the ceiling trembled with the roar of chattering throats; the walls quivered from the energy and merriment contained within them.

On a couple of hay bales, at the east end of the second story of Luis Amys' fabulous barn, I sat and played my new dulcimer with a dozen other musicians—three guitars I knew and two I was glad to meet, Skipper Beckwith's standup bass, Norman's flute, Layne on sax, Bill on electric piano, Eric with his bongos, Jarvis making a fiddle talk in three languages, and a lady I didn't know with a handmade lute; all of us jamming around a figure in 4/4 that was alternately folk, country, R&B and three different flavours of jazz—and told myself that if this was, as all reports indicated, the Sunset of the Age of Aquarius, it was in many ways as sweet or sweeter than the Dawning. The music was better, the drugs were better, the people just as goodhearted but less naive—even the damned war seemed to be nearing some kind of an end.

It was looking like a promising year. LBJ had died in January, his hair grown as long as any hippie's; that same day the U.S. Supreme Court had guaranteed a woman's right to an abortion in the first trimester; five days later the United States had abolished the draft. The Watergate pack were savaging Nixon like sharks in a feeding frenzy; a month before a black man had been elected mayor of Los Angeles; Brezhnev had that very day signed an agreement not to provoke a nuclear war; the first Skylab crew had splashed down that morning; and next month they were expecting over half a million people at a rock festival in Watkins Glen, New York. (They got 'em, too.) Telesat Canada had launched the Anik 2 satellite in April; the Montreal Canadiens had whipped the Chicago Blackhawks in six to take the Stanley Cup in May; the Canadian government was in the process of withdrawing its cease-fire observers from Viet Nam.

The ending of the U.S. draft alone would have been sufficient cause for joy in a community of mostly ex-American residents of Canada, and since that had occurred in January this was our first chance to celebrate as a tribe. Between that and Nixon's public humiliation and the splendidness of the weather, it seemed that this was fated to be the most festive Solstice Gathering ever held on the Mountain.

But the joy ran deeper than that. There was more to it than that.

I could see most of the Sunrise Gang from where I sat. Malachi, Tommy, Lucas and two of the summer crew, Roger and Elaine, all were doing an indescribable dance that Sally had made up and taught them, and several dozen others were trying to imitate it with only modest success. You had to have lived with your partners for a year or so; it was that kind of dance. But even those who couldn't quite get it right were having fun.

"Fast" Layne finished a solo, and somebody else yelled, "Let's go home," and we all jumped in on the final chorus, licks flying like fireworks, harmonies meshing like the gears in the wheel that winds the world. We finished with a barroom walkout, held it, held it, held it, grinning like thieves—then let it resolve, and beat that final chord to death with a stick.

The room exploded with applause, and we musicians smiled at each other without words or need for any, and people came and gave us homebrewed beer and apple cider pressed that day and joints and pipes of freshly cured homegrown reefer and handshakes and hugs and offers of sex and invitations to come play in their neck of the woods anytime, by Jesus.

George and Bert began to play the Beatles' "Come Together"; half of the room began to sing along. There was no place for a dulcimer, and the vocal was out of my key; I cased my instrument and decided to circulate a little. I greeted and was greeted by twenty people on the way across the room, three on the ladder, half a dozen at the foot of it and perhaps a dozen more on my way past the dairy stalls to the outdoors. As I passed out through the huge double doors I met my host, Louis, a broad-shouldered heavyset man with a pirate's grin, a philosopher's soul and the constitution of an ox, and congratulated him on throwing the best party since Christ was a cowboy, an assessment with which he heartily agreed. Louis was going to be a rare and special spice in The Mind one day.

I was a few yards into the shadows, finishing a piss, when

I spotted Snaker and Ruby over by Louis's house, sitting on a huge chopping block and nuzzling each other. I ambled over and joined them. "Hi, you two. Sorry: you three. How are you?"

Snaker looked up and smiled. "Growing. Changing. All three of us."

"Well, there's only one way to avoid change."

Ruby shook her head. "Even that doesn't work. We know that now. When you die, you just end up in The Mind—and start going through the biggest changes of all."

I shook my own head. "You're right, but that's not what I meant."

"Oh." Now Snaker shook *his* head, violently, but she ignored him. "All right, how *do* you avoid change?"

"Never break a dollar."

She turned to Snaker. "In the future, my darling, I will place greater reliance on your judgment."

He nodded. "It's in the eyes. When his eyes get big and round and innocent like that, you know he's going to lay one of those."

"I'll remember."

He squinted up at me. Ruby had taken his glasses off. "Jesus, Sam, you look exhausted."

"With my factory-new, wrinkle-free face, how can you tell? People have been telling me all night how *young* I look."

"The way your shoulders slump. How do you feel?"

"Shot," I said, and then seeing his face, "Hey, I'm sorry, brother. Bad joke."

He looked down and to the right, back up, turned red—and shrugged. "It's okay, man. You're entitled. I never thought I could shoot at a guy and still be his friend—nevermind I *hit* the son of a bitch. I grant you the right to break my balls for life. It was just that I thought you were about to ruin *everything*—"

"I was."

"Rachel had already stashed about five hundred people in

the Egg, more than enough to see that The Mind would carry on the task—but you were talking about not just killing Rachel but *blowing up the Egg*. The experiment wouldn't have been repeated if it failed, you know? The Mind would have assumed that history had rejected the attempt to mess with it."

I put my hand on his shoulder and met his eyes squarely. What passed between us was not a true telepathic exchange, perhaps, but when it was over we both knew that we forgave each other. "This is not something I say a lot, but . . . thank you for killing me, my friend."

That took the sober look off his face. "My pleasure," he said, and giggled. "Any time." Ruby smiled approval at me. "Maybe you can do the same for me someday—" We were all laughing now. "—one good turn—" "He's bleeding terrible," Ruby cried, quoting a Carry On movie we all knew, and Snaker and I chorused the antiphon: "Never mind his qualifications, is he all right?" and before long we had laughed ourselves into anoxia.

"Ah God, Sammy," she said after a while, wiping tears, "it must have been so *weird* to bury yourself."

Sprawled on the ground, I giggled again. "I won't say it wasn't. But how many men get to attend their own funeral? Without getting soaked by a mortician for an arm and a leg?"

"Still," she said. "I'd be all sentimental about my first body."

Snaker snorted laughter. "Sentimental? You know what this fucking ghoul did? He robbed his own body!"

Ruby looked at me.

"Well, shit, I was naked. And they were my best Frye boots, I wasn't going to *bury* the—"

I'm not sure just what it was she threw at me; it was dark.

After a while they got up hand in hand. With his other hand Snaker did his magic trick, took a toke, gave one to Ruby, and passed it to me. "Here you go, Sam. Ruby and I are going to go over by Louis's lower forty and engage in a small religious ritual together."

"Really? Which god?"

"Pan," Ruby said demurely.

I accepted the joint. "Pot and Pan, a good combination. Joy, you two. Don't drown the baby."

When they left I took over their seat and contemplated the great barn full of party, blazing against the night, radiating happy sounds and good vibes. People passing in and out of the big doors seemed to move in groups of at least two. I saw no other singletons. Vehicles came and went. Mosquitoes sang, stoned to the eyebrows. The sound of Layne's sax drifted across the clear Summer night. Maybe a distant train whistle in the night is as poignant as a distant sax, and then again maybe it isn't. Ah, there was a singleton—

She looked around, saw me, and came to me. "There you are, Sam. Your hair and beard look good."

I'd been growing them all night. "Thanks, Rachel. What's happening?"

A smile was getting to look more and more natural on her face these days. She didn't have smile wrinkles yet, but maybe she was developing creases. "I'm having a wonderful time. I have met so many people, Sam! I understand people better when I see them in a large group, interacting in harmony."

I sighed. "You must really miss The Mind."

Her smile wavered slightly, then firmed. "I left behind most of my memories of it. Had to. I remember enough to know that it will be very good to rejoin it. Yes, I miss it."

"So do I."

I relit the roach of Snaker's joint. Now that she no longer had to keep track of a complex lie around me, she could afford to toke with me, and did so.

After a little silence I said, "Rachel?"

"Yes?"

"It seems like I've got decades more of this shit to live through. It's going to be real hard, trying to live it just exactly as if I were the same jackass I was the day before yesterday."

"It doesn't have to be 'just exactly,' Sam. History can heal itself around small things, or else I could not be here. You must not—since you did not/have not/will not—marry or have children, and you must not die until your fate kills you. And it would be a good idea not to become famous if you can help it. But I don't think even natural law can command a man to be a fool." She took my hand.

"Huh." I pondered that for a while.

"Sam?"

"Uh?"

"I've been invited to so many communities around the province tonight that you will not be seeing a lot of me in the next year."

"Well, sure. That was the plan. The Task—"

"There's a ride leaving for Cape Breton next week."

"Oh. That soon, eh?"

"I can put it off if you need me. You've been through a lot."

"And you help. But a week should be plenty. Thank you for asking."

"I'm grateful to you, Sam. For everything."

"Well, I hate to think of some guy dying in Cape Breton next week and missing the boat because you were hung up on the North Mountain holding my hand."

She shook her head. "It would just mean that the second team would get him—or the one after that. The next stage of the plan calls for recruiting obstetricians and midwives as we move back through the centuries. We're not going to miss *anyone* if we can help it, Sam!"

"I believe you."

I tilted back my head and looked at the stars. "Rachel . . . do you suppose there are *other* Minds out there?"

"I think there must be. I wonder sometimes: if we could find them, and learn to bond with them as we have with ourselves—if a billion Minds become neurons in a Super-Mind—would we become The User? Would we go *all* the way back and begin and end everything with a Bang?"

"Wow." I watched the stars and thought about that one. A shooting star fell; I made a wish.

"Sam?"

"Yes?"

"Would you like to walk out under the stars with me now and make love?"

"Very much. But there's something else I have to do first before it gets too late. Come with?"

"Of course."

When we got upstairs the crowd was still doing mass sing-along, songs to which everybody knew the words, and most of the musicians had drifted away to readjust their bloodsugar. The Sunrise Gang were still where I'd left them. I brought Rachel over to the hay bale I'd been sitting on earlier, sat on an adjacent one facing her. The group singers were into the final mantra section of "Hey, Jude," and Rachel and I scatted with it until it was dissolved by common consent.

And then I began to Om.

She joined me with her strong smoky alto at once, and others nearby picked it up immediately. The Sunrise Gang came in with the particularly pure tone I had expected of them, and were reinforced by dozens of others. The note hunted, then steadied, tonic and dominant, a drone that grew and swelled and filled the barn, filled my head, filled the world—

—and Malachi caught my eye, and winked, and began to scat around the drone—

I laughed right in the middle of my chant, for sheer joy; it gave the sound a transient vibrato. And then I jumped in after him.

• • •

What we all built together then was—briefly, too briefly—something very like my mental picture of The Mind.

Remarkably so, when you consider that at that point in time, probably not more than twenty or thirty people in the room were actually members of Rachel's conspiracy. . . .

Does that seem like a lot? All I can say is, why not? Membership doesn't require a special, extraordinary, highly educated mind. A mind as simple and unsophisticated as Mona Bent's can encompass our conspiracy and accept telepathy. The mind need not be brilliant or well stocked with information to be one of us, to respond to our call: it need only not be suffused with self-hatred. And our membership committee is a telepath.

I know: hippies can't keep secrets, especially juicy ones.

Well, suppose each of us *had* spilled the beans to some one close friend, and in the end, half the hippies at the Solstice Party had learned the secret? Suppose further they even believed it. What would be the effect?

They would all begin to live their lives as though conscience meant something, as though kharma was real, as though there is a god. Well, *most of them were trying to learn to do that anyway,* even though they knew better. Now they would know better than to know better, is all. They'd tend to leave the woods, over time, scatter over the planet and live as righteously as possible, find or invent all kinds of right livelihood. They'd stop banding together in self-defense, and spread out and go where they were needed, disappear into the mix.

Do you understand now why I'm telling this story to you, and why I don't care much one way or the other whether you believe it? If you choose to do so, all that you can do about it is to stop being so afraid of death, personal and planetary, and to start living as though you are one day going to have to account for your actions to everyone you've ever loved. How can that hurt?

It's now the Nineteen-Eighties, and pessimism and

despair are in fashion. There are almost no hippies left on the Mountain. Fundamentalists rage through the world like hungry beasts. Belief in apocalypse is everywhere, and a numb dumb fatalistic yearning to *get it over with*. Wonderful excuses to abandon responsibility. Every day our news media bring us a billion cries of pain, and there is nothing we can do about any of them—as individuals. Small wonder we feel the growing urge to put ourselves out of our misery.

Hang on. Just for a couple of decades, that's all I ask. The cavalry is coming. It is a pitcher of cream you're drowning in: keep churning. If you don't, you're going to feel really stupid one day soon. Keep living as though it mattered—because it *does*.

If you've ever really wondered where all the Hippies went, and not merely used the question as a way of denying that they ever existed—well, I will tell you where *some* of them went: they diffused throughout the planet like invading viruses. They went underground in plain sight, simply by changing their appearance, and they put their attention on lowering their race's psychic immune system, dismantling its defenses of intolerance of anything new or different, and thus making it ready for the ultimate transplant, the ultimate invasion.

And they all lived happily ever after.

EPILOGUE

I guarantee that every word of this story is the truth.

About the Author

Since he began writing professionally in 1972, Spider Robinson has won three Hugo Awards, a Nebula Award, the John W. Campbell Award for Best New Writer, the E.E. ("Doc") Smith Memorial Award (Skylark), the Pat Terry Memorial Award for Humorous Science Fiction, and Locus Awards for Best Novella and Best Critic. A member of World SF, he has recently been reprinted in **Журнал Изобретатель и Рационализатор** (USSR) and in *Fantastyka* (Poland). TIME PRESSURE is his eleventh book.

He has been married for twelve years to Jeanne Robinson, founder, Artistic Director and resident choreographer of Nova Dance Theatre, a five-year-old professional modern dance company. The Robinsons collaborated on the Hugo-, Nebula-, and Locus-winning classic STARDANCE (Dial Press, 1977), which involves zero-gravity dance.

The Robinsons met and married on the North Mountain of Nova Scotia's Annapolis Valley; presently they live in Vancouver, British Columbia, with their twelve-year-old daughter, Luanna.